THE CODED WORLD

THE FAR HORIZONS
BOOK 3

A.R. KNIGHT

ONE

HUNTING SEASON

The metal mouse scurried, neon violet playing over its rounded body. It traced the small black tile landing, scattering sand grains as its tiny legs ran. Several small stalks poked out from its forehead, each one ending in a fuzzy spike. Back in the Garden's early days, a pollinator wouldn't be out here in a place without plants, searching for . . .

Me?

"Take it," I whispered to the scrap metal hound at my side.

Alvie kept himself quiet, leaping with the slightest scratch from the treaded step and landing on the pollinator. The dog's jagged steel jaws split the target, its wires and circuits sparking as Alvie shook the dead mech back and forth.

"Good dog," I said, joining Alvie on the landing, its blank back wall telling us we'd come to the end.

On my left sat a double-sealed door leading outside. Rivets and shining steel blocked an exit to a ladder leading down, away and eventually to the makeshift home for the last humans alive on Starship.

Well, home for some.

Now Val, Leo, and the fifty or so fighting survivors were holing up far above, where the Garden offered more than sand and cacti to eat. They'd turned our massive vessel's breadbasket into their fortress, where they planned to wait out the journey's end.

A cowardly play, a blind move.

And a confusing one. Humans kept surprising me. One would be filled with wrath, ready to brave all dangers to win. Others would wrap themselves in their places, fear of loss tying them to failure.

Kaydee would say I was being dramatic. Delta would tell me to get on with it.

Alvie just looked up at me with his small yellow eyes.

The desert waiting for us wasn't large. Black-and-purple walls split small dunes into sections, each one laced with plants that'd once been manicured and now grew at nature's intent. Small cacti and brittle flowers dotted the view, interrupted now and then by another pollinator.

My goal sat in the level's center. Alvie and I made our slow way, the dog chomping any pollinator daring to cross our path. In my hands I held a weapon with a rounded top, a barrel extending half a meter from its trigger, and a bright orange line on its stock. I kept my finger ready, tight: power would be scarce, the rifle hard to recharge down here.

Cacti packed the level's middle, a biological reservoir. Their needled stalks made a spiny forest for several wandering mechs. Bigger than the pollinators, bigger than me, their every scalloped step puffed up sand as they stomped. I watched from around a wall, judging their intent and finding it random: the mechs moved around, taking no notice of each other and often retracing their own steps.

Their arms, with clunky claws or grips welded to shrapnel knives or blunt blocks, hung at their sides.

On patrol, most likely. Left to founder by their leader.

Their routes circled the level's middle, a shadowed hole blocked by the dunes. Water clued me into its location, a steady, if small, drip from levels above. The slight shrinking level by level ensured a few sprinkles would be caught by the desert, spread amongst its life. The water drops meshed with Starship's rumble and the mech's shifting sand to create a soft soundscape.

"Two on three," I whispered to Alvie. "You go right, I go left. Aim for the legs."

When I dropped a finger, signaling go, Alvie dashed off. The dog wrapped around my watching wall, his metal paws using the sand to keep stealth. I crouched and made off left, using a cactus cluster for cover to approach a mech from behind. With my gun back in its makeshift strap—borrowed from a Forger who'd never need it again—I had both hands free. Like some jungle cat, I crept up on the mech.

This one had a squat cylinder for a body, one leading to a treaded base. A hose and two grasping arms, each with its grips filed to points, left the cylinder, giving hints to its former life. I'd return the thing to that life if I could, a wish ditched as I executed my ambush.

Coming from behind, I ran up, scooped my hands low, and gripped the mech's underside. The machine's cylinder swiveled, bringing a beady camera and several blinking lights into my face. I heaved, sand flying everywhere as the several hundred kilogram mech went up and over. Its treads spun in the air, the mech's arms swiping towards me. With its belly exposed, I reached into the hot core, gripped the wires funneling the mech's power to its wheels, its arms, and pulled.

A squeal, the wrenching whine of an engine losing its thrust, and the mech died.

"Sorry," I whispered, before Alvie's fight drew my attention.

The dog didn't have my strength, but Alvie beat my agility. The robo-dog darted around the slower, clumsier mech. The boxy thing flailed, even striking a lucky, glancing blow off Alvie's back, but with every snap Alvie tore another chunk from the robot's shell. As more and more insides grew exposed, Alvie returned to his earlier wounds, digging deeper and leaving with coolant, circuits, cables.

My grim viewing ended as my own victim rolled aside. The cause came lumbering in, a taller, thinner massage machine. Knobby ends covered its joints, though something had welded spikes onto each one. It swung, jerked, and jabbed itself towards me as I backpedaled, feet slipping in the sand.

Without an up-close weapon, I had to get clever, and sliding around on my heels while the mech chased me wouldn't cut it. Options splashed across my vision, my programming highlighting possible weapons, escape routes, and openings in the attacking mech's routine. All good stuff, and all things I couldn't use when I misstepped and collapsed back into a dune.

The spiked mech bore down on me, a wordless, soundless adversary lifting its arms for a pounding finale.

After all I'd lived through, no way was this dumb thing taking me out.

I kicked out with my left foot, shifting the sand beneath my enemy's leg. Built for balancing on level ground, the mech wobbled. Its attack veered into the sand beside my head, coating me in grains. As the mech lurched back into position, I used my own right foot, sliding the mech's left away before the machine found its balance.

The thing swiped its left arm out wide, grazing my forehead in the process, to catch itself as it fell forward. A pretty good move, except it put the mech in a push-up position, its vulnerable core half a meter over me.

This time, I didn't say sorry as I punched up, breaking in the mech's chest. Blue-white sparks fizzled out as I crunched the circuits inside. My synthetic skin took the scratches, filling back in almost as fast as the wounds came. With a push, I sent the mech off to the left to join its brother in the sand.

I felt a gentle nudge on my head, glanced to see Alvie waiting there, wire bits dangling from his jagged metal maw. A victory trophy.

"Good dog."

TWO

DEEP DIVE

Purity's blue-black depths lay below us. The tanned light at my back didn't project all that far down the hole, letting dark swallow the passage until the neon cerulean outlined skeletal steel walkways. Any hints at the water were few, a shadow at twilight. Next to me, Alvie commented on the view with a worried whine.

"You get to stay up here," I said. "If I get into trouble, you run back up and get help, all right?"

Alvie tilted his head, gave me some side-eye.

"Don't be like Kaydee," I replied. "I can handle myself."

The dog chuffed twice.

"You know what?" I picked myself up, put the gun down on the ground. I planned for a swim and Leo told me the weapon wouldn't work after a bath. "I could use some more support here."

I must've summoned up enough pity, because Alvie gave me one light headbutt to the shin, about as close as the dog could come to straight-on affection. Those metal claws and jagged edges made the robo-hound a decidedly poor cuddle buddy.

With the goodbye stated and orders established, I double-checked my jump to confirm I wouldn't be leaping headlong onto a walkway, then went for it. A glorious three-step run-up and a leap into open air. Humans in their movies tended to shout at moments like these, battle-cries or delighted whoops.

Kaydee would've wanted one, but I kept my mouth shut: someone might be listening.

Someone, definitely, was watching.

The arms shot out as I plunged into the black gap between levels. I caught a silvery blur, the metal coat mingling with Purity's light. They caught my feet in a vice, my fall suddenly changing from pencil dive to face-first plunge, only I wasn't falling anymore but dangling over Starship's watery garbage disposal.

Biological bones might've snapped, but my hardy exoskeleton withstood the force, giving me a chance to curl up and see what'd decided to interrupt my rescue. Through a walkway's black lattice, I saw the limber frame of Alpha's newer creations: flexi-mechs, as I called 'em.

This version matched the humans limb for limb, trading extra arms for stiffer construction, these flexi-mechs took the bipedal arrangement to sinister lengths. Ten pointed fingers dotted each hand, forming almost a circle, while their arms and legs stretched further than their living inspiration, which is how this one held me over the drink, yet kept me from grappling range: my own arms swung useless in space.

"Let me go," I said to the flexi-mech, whose cubed head, perched neckless on a thin spine, shone its red light at me.

"No," the flexi-mech replied, in a posh woman's voice. "I don't think so."

I froze. Never before had a flexi-mech talked back to us, and we'd already fought a couple dozen of the things.

They'd not had any personality either, just straight up fight-to-kill commands. This one talked. This one might offer a chance at negotiation.

"You have a personality?" I asked.

"I have orders," the flexi-mech replied. "We are to destroy you."

Ah. So much for diplomacy.

"We?" I asked, trying to stall and figure out a plan.

New lights hit my face, although their distance kept it from being blinding. All red, and all scattered about Purity's basement. I counted at least eight in a quick swivel, all flexi-mechs and all watching me. They stood on the other walkways and along the hard platform at Purity's rim, as if I'd crashed some musical mid-number.

"Well then," I said, and the flexi-mech yanked me up, holding my face before its own.

"Goodbye." The flexi-mech cocked its right arm back, seemingly ready to pull some heart-ripping maneuver.

I brought my hands together as the flexi-mech punched, catching the machine's wrist a few centimeters before my chest. The flexi-mech's hand spun, those ten fingers zipping around like a drill, giving a very clear idea of what would've happened if it made contact.

"Now look at us," I said. "All tied up."

"Irregular," the flexi-mech replied.

When the machine pulled back its hand, I came along for the ride, yanking down with my trapped leg. We formed an awkward lever, the flexi-mech and I, with the former bashing into the walkway's railing as my force and weight reversed its retreat. The grinding bang made a fine echo around the area as the mech's poor drilling arm caught its joint on the railing and snapped with the pressure. The sudden release threw our whole thing off balance, and now

I did let out one of Kaydee's shouts as I fell straight down with the mech into Purity's waters.

The icy chill seeped through my synthetic skin, activating my thermal controls and splashing a little meter over my eyes. The high power draw meant I'd turn into a useless hulk when that meter ran to zero, and while I'd have plenty of time before that happened, any clock meant stress when you were dealing with flexi-mechs.

The one who'd fallen with me still held my foot, even as we both sank. More dove into the sea, bubbles and splashing announcing their entry into the arena. And what an arena it was: Purity's sapphire lighting cast rays through the water, highlighting the metal mechs swimming towards me. Spreading up and around us like some sunken forest were the Chancellor's long arms. Already pitted by Purity's feasting recycling system, the towering stalks rose up around us, gray and still.

Beta had been pierced by one before the fall, and Delta knocked down after her, but I saw neither of my vessel friends, my reason for coming down here, right away. Understandable, seeing as I was more preoccupied with freeing myself from the pesky flexi-mech.

The water gave me the fluidity to curl up my clung-to leg, enough so I could reach down and grab the flexi-mech's remaining holding hand. I didn't have as much power beneath the water, but the flexi-mech's wrists weren't made to hold against my strength. I pushed down and, coupled with the water, the flexi-mech's hand slid off my ankle.

Not that the mech cared: as soon as I freed myself, the flexi-mech kicked forward, its remaining hand spinning up into that drill again and coming right for my face.

So I dropped. Kicked and swam deeper into the dark, the red lights trailing after me. Purity's bottom came up quick, a pocked place, almost like an insect's eye. Fine-filtering nets stretched over various pipes to handle waste and weed out water to send back into Starship's closed ecosystem. Their borders twinkled, reflective coating giving me a guideline, letting me find the right path.

Laying amongst those glittering nets were three humanoid shapes. Two I wanted, the third I loathed. Delta drifted off to the right, her shorter hair frizzing out behind her head, a dark line near her marking her blade. To the left and closer together sat Beta and the Chancellor. My friend and fellow vessel had a Chancellor's arm still sloping down and piercing through her chest, a wince-inducing sight. The Chancellor, at least, looked as dead as my friends, and with any luck would stay that way.

A flick back gauged my distance: my flexi-mech friend came closest, but with only a single arm, the mech hadn't kept up with me. Its friends were further back, their swimming strokes random and ungainly: not too surprising they didn't have logic for moving through water.

Thankfully, Leo thought to teach his vessels how to swim.

I pushed towards Delta first, as much going for the blade as for the vessel. My hands found the jagged hilt there on the grim gray base, the weapon's bulk easy, if slow, to move in the deep. As I pointed the edge towards the closest net, I felt the first telltale prick along my synthetic skin: Purity's solid-destroying recyclers.

The little monsters had already dealt damage to Delta's blade, pitting it throughout. Delta herself looked nibbled around her edges, the synthetic skin regenerating enough to keep her core protected while her clothes, her hair, her shoes already were little more than scraps. Eventually those microbes would find a way past the vessel's skin and into more vulnerable wires, chips, memory.

Hopefully I'd be fast enough.

Kicking towards the near net, I led with the blade. The edge poked into the thin fibers, meant to stop rogue debris from entering the pipes, and sliced them apart with a gentle glide. Like shredding a spider's web, built to withstand impact but not a cross-wise cut. With a second slice, the net cleared off altogether, vanishing down the meter-wide pipe.

I whirled, as fast as one could whirl in water, looking to get Delta. Instead I found my flexi-mech foe gurgling down at me, drilling hand spinning up froth. Before, in my dangling moment, I didn't have a weapon.

Circumstances had changed.

I swatted the blade across my body, a sludgy motion in the water, but fast enough to intersect with the mech. The spinning hand hit the blade and went to work on itself, the motor's force enough to slice through the mech's fingers in an instant, the spinning palm shortly thereafter. I figured the mech would keep on coming, hoping to bludgeon me with its stump in single-minded rage, but Purity prevented that: its circuits exposed to water, the mech twitched as its body shorted out.

Dead, the mech's momentum carried the thing past me into a thud against the basin's bottom.

With more mechs lurching my way, I didn't have time to pity the poor machine. Keeping Delta's blade in my left hand, I kicked towards the downed vessel. Like the flexi-mech before me, I went for Delta's ankle, gripped it with my right hand and pulled, kicking my feet hard to get some momentum on my side. Delta shifted, sliding off the bottom and coming with me towards the open pipe.

I didn't have time to carefully drop Delta in, instead

opting for a swinging pull to throw Delta towards the pipe's entrance. For a human, the move might've relied on luck. For me, once I told my systems what to do, my right hand swung Delta with the perfect force, released at the perfect time. The vessel floated towards the pipe and in, flawless placement.

Take that, humans.

Beta wouldn't be quite so simple: four flexi-mechs floundered between me and my vessel friend. Two had the shrapnel knives so often equipped by Alpha's mechs, haphazard weaponry deployed by a haphazard army. The other two had those whirling hands, though every time they spun those ten fingers up, the whirls acted like motors, pushing the mechs around in wild loops.

Nonetheless, with the pinpricks growing as more Purity protectors found my soft skin, a single bad blow down here would be fatal. Even if Alvie went up to get Leo and Val and they bothered to send help down, all they'd likely find would be half-eaten remnants. If that.

Faced with little time and poor odds, I decided to pull a Delta.

Kicking hard right towards Beta, I hugged the basin's bottom. With Delta's blade still in hand, sticking close to the ground let my feet move me along at speed. The flexi-mechs tried to intercept, scrambling down at me, limbs akimbo. Their red eyes lingered in the dark, reflecting off their knives, their metal bodies. Like being pursued by shimmering phantoms.

Mortal ones.

The first flexi-mech hit me two meters out from Beta. The mech lunged in with a stabbing point, angling towards my back. The thing's eye-glow gave it away and I rolled, facing up and bringing Delta's blade back across my body for the intercept. Underwater, the collision lacked impact, a flimsy clang. My blade's bigger body swept the knife out wide, the force spinning the mech so its side faced me. Pulling the sword back, I jabbed it forward, aiming for a skewer. My own momentum, drifting me towards Beta, meant I didn't achieve the devastating blow I'd hoped for, but only nicked the mech's mid-section.

Again, the water made the small slice enough. A white crackle blew from the cut, followed by a sharp spasm across the flexi-mech's lanky limbs. Like its brother, the machine stopped flailing and sank, dead, to the floor.

Two down, three to go.

The remainder weren't total morons either. Despite their crappy swimming the three moved to encircle me, the drill-handers coming to good grips with their makeshift motors to scoot towards Beta and beat me to her, while the other knife-wielder swept in at my feet.

Surrounded and alone amid the Chancellor's looming arms, I steadied the grip on Delta's sword and kicked off again, going the last distance towards Beta. I could've run, could've taken Delta as my prize and left.

A coward's play, Kaydee would've said, and I was no coward.

Not anymore.

THREE

DOWN THE HOLE

I swam towards shadows and the shadows chased me. My target didn't move: Beta lay against the basin's floor, a blurred blue-black block with a dark line running through her back and up towards the surface. The claw that'd speared her. Less than a meter away lay the Chancellor's own bulk, a dead spider nestled in her own arms.

Swimming through those arms, coming from behind, alongside, and before me came three more flexi-mechs, their red eyes tracking me like the Devil's own cameras. I held Delta's blade in my right hand as I kicked. When I crossed over the Chancellor's body, I stopped, brought my left hand over into a dual grip. The Chancellor's arms rose around me like a cage. Sapphire light laced in from above.

The flexi-mechs hit within a second of each other, the trio's sloppy swimming nonetheless giving them a synchronized strike. I tried a wide swing, bringing the blade across to try and catch them all together.

Turned out I was dealing with martyrs.

The flexi-mech coming from Beta's way took the hit, grappling the blade with both hands and wrapping itself around my weapon. The added weight slowed my swing, dragged the angle down so I missed the next one, the middle flexi-mech diving from above. Its hands struck my head, pushing me towards the basin's bottom, and I dropped the blade to deal with the immediate threat.

While I'd turned off my pain sensors long ago, that didn't stop my head from telling me the flexi-mech's fingers were going to pop me like a balloon if I didn't relieve the pressure. Worse, the third flexi-mech swept in to take my legs, shredding at my synthetic skin with its claws. The water made the swipes less effective, but I felt the ends peel away my clothes, leave long gashes in my skin that Purity's recycling robots could exploit.

But my head. That came first.

My hands found the flexi-mech's wrists and pulled as we crashed down on the Chancellor's body, my back hitting the rust-colored mech's battered casing. I dialed up enough strength to peel back the flexi-mech's grasp, the flickering alarms vanishing from my eyes as the pressure eased. The flexi-mech itself kicked its feet, angling for a head-butt.

Bold move, robot.

I swung my hips to the right—another clawed swing ripped a chunk from my thighs—and pulled on the flexi-mech's wrists, throwing the machine past me and into the Chancellor. With a dull thud, the mech dented its dead ally and bounced away. No major damage done, but I'd bought myself a second as the machine flailed, trying to right itself.

Kicking my damaged legs, I drifted with my back towards Beta. Her dark form glittered up close, unspent knives cluttering bandoleers and belts. Her long pink hair rose up, a wavy beacon.

Froth flew as the mech harassing my legs went for a drilling stab at my gut. An all-in attack compared to sniping my toes. I kicked again, stretching out my arm behind me towards Beta. The drilling hand, ten finger-claws whirling, helped me some: its force meant the mech had to kick harder to overcome the motoring push away, bought me a second.

Finding a hilt, holding the wrapped cloth at the knife's base, felt like jubilation. I tore the weapon free and, in a single over-hand toss, launched the blade at the flexi-mech's death hand. Charging at me like some superhero going for a punch, the flexi-mech's head, its hand, and me were all just centimeters apart when the knife struck home.

A bulls-eye, right into the spinning palm's center.

The knife nailed the engine in the flexi-mech's hand, stopping gears running too hot to slow down. The hand broke apart, the knife splintered, and piping hot shards blasted out around us. I felt three blaze into my stomach, one into where a human's lungs might be. The flexi-mech caught its own shots too: a spark flared from its skull, and its right arm jerked as a knife fragment severed some wire in its elbow.

Still reaching, I found a second knife and repeated the stroke before the flexi-mech could come to grips with its blown reality. This time I didn't release the knife but curled over, jabbing the blade with more control into the flexi-mech's chest, right where the thing's processor would be. The cut did the trick, a little frizzy heat puffing bubbles around us before the flexi-mech joined the Chancellor on the basin's floor.

My vision flashed. Static for a millisecond.

Those recyclers. They'd sneak into my cuts, devour me from the inside out. My synthetic skin, repairing rapidly, would keep the monsters to a minimum, but even one or two left alone would turn me into an expensive statue before long.

But I couldn't leave Beta. Not now, not here.

A glance at the Chancellor's impaling arm showed my pilfered knife wouldn't be able to cut my friend free. Lifting her up along the arm's length and back over the claw seemed an impossibility with my looming death. So I went back to the basics.

Kicking once, I closed on Delta's falling blade, the skewered mech clinging to it. The flexi-mech still ran, but the razor hooks on Delta's blade, an imperfect scrap-metal sword, made it hard for the robot to free itself.

Easy work for my knife.

A few slashes cleaned off the mech and let me re-arm again, the black blade in my right hand as I returned to Beta. As I readied an arm-severing cut, my right ankle went numb. The wires carrying information severed. Devoured, more like. No matter. I swung.

The blade bit deep into the Chancellor's arm just above Beta. Not quite through. I wiggled the blade, working it free from the arm, and swung again. This time, a clean cut. The big arm wobbled, then began a slow fall away even as I dropped Delta's blade to reach for Beta.

My body spasmed, circuits flaring as my every part of me screamed something was wrong. I tried to twist around, my sensors telling me my back was under attack, only to find I couldn't. Something jammed in my upper back, sharp and solid, and its grip kept me facing the basin's bottom. The source answered my question an instant later as its other hand raked across my left shoulder.

The mech I'd bounced back at Delta's body, coming back for more.

I stopped moving, sank towards Beta and Delta's

dropped blade. The black sword touched the bottom, settling with its edge up. This time I didn't twist, but kicked my right leg as the mech dug its stabbing hand in deeper. Warnings blazed over my eyes, ones I didn't have time to read. With my kick, my body rotated even as we continued to sink.

Straight up, through those red-glazed warnings, Purity's blue light glowed soft. The water's surface rippled as several more mechs dove in, apparently concerned with their colleague's performance. Even so, the water held a certain beauty to it.

Not the worst thing to see in one's last moments.

I kicked both feet, flailed my arms to push myself down. The flexi-mech dug deeper, and I felt a cool rush as water leaked in through the cuts. Our spin continued, the flexi-mech beneath me now. I half expected to die then and there, but Leo had me built well, my circuits secured against some small leak.

We hit Delta's blade at speed, the sword biting into the flexi-mech fast enough to keep from bending. I felt the vibration, the sudden cease as the mech's hands went loose. The claws jabbing into my back fell away as I pumped my hands up. A quick glance confirmed the kill: Delta's black sword had cleaved the mech in two, leaving me free to reach for Beta.

I balanced my feet on the basin to get enough leverage to pull the vessel off, a move made harder as Purity's little monsters devoured my extremities. Warnings blinked off as my sensors died, as wires lost cohesion. I wondered if this was what it felt like to be eaten.

If this is what all those mechs felt as Delta carved them up, limb from limb.

The pursuit wasn't over. Another flexi-mech trio came

down at Beta and I as we lurched towards the open tube. These mechs weren't any better at water navigation than their peers, and the sloppy scrambling bought me time as I kicked, bounced, and pulled Beta along the bottom.

With one heavy thrust, I shoved Beta the last bit through the murk to the tube's entrance. The pressure found her then, sucking my friend in after Delta. The closest flexi-mech made it within two meters, but fell to its own flaw: activating its drilling hands and shooting itself backward. I would've laughed if I hadn't lost control of my own mouth seconds earlier.

Instead, I dove after Beta, hands pointing before my head as I crossed the tube's lip and vanished down its tight depths.

FOUR

SEWER SPARK

No lights lit the way, but choices weren't offered in this particular maze. Instead I pressed forward, hands pulling me along the cramped confines. Grates appeared here and there, routing me this way and that. Winding up with Delta and Beta would be luck, but I had to hope we were fast enough after each other to avoid random cycling diverting us.

How stupid it would be to get through all this only for my friends to wind up in an oven, baked to ash while I floundered in a pipe?

Kaydee would find it grimly hilarious.

All my flailing dumped me, at last, into a tank. Several meters wide and long, the space nonetheless felt tight. Water here was more sludge, leftover matter congealing together. As I flowed in, I heard, or rather felt, clicks behind me. Gates shutting, rerouting the next batch elsewhere.

Which meant this one would be cooking.

Thankfully, I'd been almost baked before. Not an experience I figured would be useful, but here, again, I punched up, pressing against the oven's lid. The thing relented, opening into a cavern I recognized. Little bulbs stretched along the sides, a colorful display illuminating wreckage that'd once been a neat little study, if one run by a monster.

Hello again.

My arms, twitching from busted wires, managed to get me free from the oven and, clambering over the edge, I sat for a second on the soggy floor. My boots, coat, clothes weren't just soaked, they were destroyed. Ribbons only, scraps clinging to my ragged self. Synthetic skin raced to coat me in biological armor, but the stuff couldn't do anything about the worse damage beneath the surface. That would take time, skill, and tools I wasn't sure I could find here.

But!

I lurched up, turned around, and peered into a mouldering swamp. At first I saw nothing, only a desolate paste. A twinkle, then, a slip caught by the lights at my back: pink hair bleeding through, covered in muck. I leaned over, shoved a numb hand beneath the gunk, found something solid, and pulled.

Beta's lifeless body came out, dripping and ruined. Her leftover knives, like loyal soldiers, still hung in their holsters, and they clanked as I dragged her away from the oven up and onto the encircling platform where Purity's mech had assembled its random collection. Torn up books, battered shelves laden with toys, busted gadgets, and moldy garments loomed.

"*Be right back,*" I mouthed at my friend, speech still a non-starter. Whenever I tried to use my voice, it felt like talking into a muffling pillow: suffocating and impossible.

Back at the oven I saw no telltale sign of Delta. She didn't have Beta's longer hair, for one. With a wince at my own circumstances, I climbed back over the edge and scrounged. My hands swept from side to side, clearing sludge away and holding it back for a slurping second as I searched. My numbed feet scuffled along the oven's bottom, feeling nothing until a vibration climbed up to my working wires.

Delta had sunk to the front corner, buried deep. Would've been forever, except I kept at it, whipping away the crud until I hefted her free too. Together, our vessel trio soon sat on the platform, bearing both a sight and a smell so awful I refused to let my sensors process it.

Well, I'd done what I said I'd do: I'd recovered the two vessels. Delta and Beta. Right here next to me.

And they were nothing more than bodies.

I blinked away banners, the flashing alerts from my vision. My own systems weren't far off from joining my friends, and the degrading hadn't stopped just because I'd left the water. Some of those recyclers seemed to still be inside my guts, nibbling away. Flushing them out would take time, tools, surgery of a mechanical sort.

In other words, not something I could do myself.

Beta, on my right, had a bad hole in her chest. No doubt, like me, it'd been infested with recyclers too. Even if I could start her up, if her central circuitry hadn't been toasted by the damage, who knew what wouldn't work? Who knew whether she could feel anything at all?

"*Which means you.*" I gave Delta a closer look.

She'd been snared by the Chancellor, knocked and battered down to Purity, but I didn't see any grievous wounds. Certainly no big cuts or busted limbs. I glanced at my right hand, pressed my thumb and forefinger together. The pressure performed its purpose, turning my fingertips into a port. I scooted up next to Delta's head, lifted her right ear lobe aside, and plugged into the tiny opening.

And went nowhere. I'd restarted Delta once before, and that at least gave me a place to go. Here, my fingers plugged in and nothing changed. The port had no power. I quickly searched my own schematics, the reams Leo stored within my drives explaining how I worked. Possibilities splayed out before my eyes: a damaged power supply, a blown line transmitting said power from the supply to Delta's processor, a whole host of other busted parts that could be the culprit.

"This sucks," I muttered to Delta, who didn't react.

If Kaydee were here, she'd offer up some ideas. Something crazy, most likely, but with logic at the core. Like, say, we can't focus on the broken parts because we can't fix that, so let's roll with the other ideas.

I'd dealt with reviving a dead machine once. Alvie, my plucky puppy, hadn't been as dead as Delta, but he'd been close. I'd had to deliver a shock to his system to get him back online, effectively forcing a reset. If I could hit Delta with a similar bolt, it might force her into a restart. A blunt force attempt, but with little else to go on, what was the harm?

Then again, where could I get a power surge? My own batteries, battered, wouldn't serve.

I started taking an inventory of the space, my eyes going first to the obvious: the strung-up lights. They'd be tapping into Starship's power, but their draw would be too low for the kind of energy I needed. What else?

More minutes ticked by as I crossed off options until a hissing gurgle drew my attention back to the muck oven. The thing would be roasting its contents, burning it to nothing. I'd left the lid off, so smoke rose out into the space. Fire would follow, contained by the stove's curving pale sides. A thorough elimination, a process that would require—

"Hah!" I tried to stand fast and toppled over onto my stomach, not used to unfeeling feet.

The next time I went slower, then dragged Delta—sorry, buddy—along the floor down past the burning oven. At the big burner's back sat the power line, a coated cord vanishing somewhere behind metal tiles. Where it connected to the oven, though, sat possibility. Stumbling back to Beta, I pried a knife loose and used its point to break the seal where the fat black cord went into the smoldering stove.

Okay. This was where things would get tricky. I needed to shock Delta awake without giving her so much juice that she'd fry.

I took the knife, set Delta's fingers around the blade. It cut into the synthetic skin far enough to make contact with the metal bones in her hand. Holding the cloth hilt to keep myself safe, I mentally told Delta I was sorry for what I was about to do and jabbed the blade right into the cord.

And found myself banging off another oven several meters away, sparks fading from the air. The knife quivered above me, embedded in the ceiling. Smoke rose from Delta's still form. No sign of movement.

Okay, perhaps not my best experiment.

A new sound, clamps and clacks, rebounded through the space, seeming to come from all 'round. At first I wondered if my shock'n'awe play had damaged something, but my sensors did their job and isolated the source, filtering out the echoes and placing the origin as the one door into our makeshift hideout.

Something was coming.

I lurched up, unsteady on numb feet, and made my slow way forward. The door sat wide open, a barrier I probably should've closed first thing. I could hear Kaydee now, castigating my poor choices, but hey, I'd been distracted. Been half-eaten, gone swimming in sludge, and carried the bodies of my friends to safety. I wasn't gonna knock myself for not catching every little thing.

So I grabbed a busted desk leg, a thin metal stick that'd serve as a bat. With my right arm using shelves, piled garbage, and the wall for support, I made my way past Beta towards the open door. Like all the ones outside Starship's apartments, the round portal offered up a gemmed lock that'd be awful nice to employ. Awful nice, except I didn't have any time left.

The noise's culprits came pounding into view. Flexi-mechs, two leading the pack. And more behind them. Worse, without the energy sapping water, the pair came armed. The snub-nosed guns sat in their hands, raised and ready as they stomped through the doorway.

Outnumbered, outgunned, I did what I could and threw my table leg like a javelin.

The bar lanced into the leading mech as it clomped through the door, striking its chest and driving it back into the second one. The table leg lacked a certain lethality, leaving the mech with a dent and little else. But I bought myself a second, and with that second I lurched forward, dragging my right hand along a shelf to pick up another missile. My fingers found it, curled into its soft contours, and I didn't even look before launching it.

A spindly doll, with patches decayed due to time, flew and bounced off the recovering flexi-mechs. The damn robots didn't even blink.

Instead they shot and I dove.

One beam blazed the air where I'd been. The second hit where I was going to be, a strike that would've killed me if I'd been competent. As it was, my dive was more a forward fall, slow enough to miss the strike, yet land on the hot metal. My skin burned. I looked towards the two mechs, flipped them Kaydee's classic gesture.

Their metal faces gave me no satisfaction.

The sudden trash sure did.

Scum, wet and disgusting, flew in from my back and left, splattering onto the guns. The gunk sank into the barrels, preventing the weapon's gas and light from interacting when the mechs pulled their triggers, both at me and my rescuer. They tried twice more, then dropped the weapons as my hero stepped over me, pilfered knives in her hands.

"Let's play," Delta said, and while I couldn't see her grim smile, I knew it was there.

The vessel leapt at the mech pair, both of which started up their drilling hands. Delta met their swipes with ducks and dances, getting in her own cuts on every reach. The mechs, showing more ingenuity than their older counterparts, adapted: one jumped up and over Delta, pincering her between the two bots.

Unfortunately, it also put the mech in my reach.

As the flexi-mech landed, with Delta weaving a knife storm at the one still back at the doorway, I reached out and grabbed the thing's ankle. Sweeping my hand right, I pulled the mech off its feet into a clattering fall. Those spinning hands gouged the floor, throwing up a hot metal rain. The embers glowed against the yellow light, showering us as I climbed up the fallen mech, pinning the machine with my weight.

A good strategy, until the flexi-mech proved true to its name and rotated on its spine to face me. Those two drilling arms flipped in their sockets, diving towards my skull. I caught the attack, my hands on its wrists, a temporary fix: I might be stronger than the flexi-mech, but the machine had leverage, and hadn't been just soundly rocked for the last hour.

I wanted to yell for help, but my stupid mouth didn't work, so I settled for looking Delta's way and trying to put on the most frantic expression I could. My ears filled with the gnashing motor sound as those spinning hands came close.

But Delta wasn't looking my way. A third mech had joined the fray, and while Delta had her first foe in pieces, the second kept its distance, lacing laser fire her way. No time for me.

Guess I'd have to save myself for once.

FIVE

FIXING FRIENDS

Sometimes the best way to win was to let the enemy beat themselves.

With the drilling hands pressing in on either side, I let go of the flexi-mech's wrists and rose my head. Whirling death passed beneath my neck, snarling a bit in my shredded coat's collar, and found itself. Both hands gnarled into one another, fingers slicing and breaking and spitting their shards everywhere. Pinpricks littered my skull, my neck: new decor for my synthetic skin.

Meanwhile, my own hands went to work, slugging the flexi-mech's chest and knocking the machine off me. The robot lurched back, its processes no doubt trying to figure out what to do with its mauled hands, now just hanging wires spitting sparks onto the ground.

I couldn't wait for it to figure something out.

Rolling forward, I dove towards the mech, a sloppy maneuver with the numb bricks I had for feet. Nonetheless, my outstretched arms snared the mech's metal-boned waist, letting me drag the machine to the floor. Down on my level, the handless mech flailed, banging on me while I pulled on and out every wire, cord, tube I could find.

The flexi-mechs had, well, flexibility, but their sparse shells left little defense. Like opening a stiff present, I unwrapped the machine and shut it down. Dead, the mech collapsed on me, the two of us tangled in Purity's sudden silence. A break in the fighting, one I could use.

My cheek pressed on the hard floor as I skipped through my systems, figuring what could work, what could be repaired. I'd almost completed the list when someone lifted the flexi-mech skeleton off me, launching the robot to the side as I might've tossed a ball for Alvie.

"Get up," Delta said when I looked at her, "or is your new plan to lie there and let Alpha win?"

I pointed to my mouth. Delta narrowed her eyes, gave me a more thorough once-over.

"You look like trash," she said.

I couldn't argue.

THE ROAD to recovery began with used bits. Purity's former owner had knickknacks aplenty, but random toys and debris weren't going to return me—much less Beta—to functional status. We needed working parts, or at least solid substitutes if we were going to get back to the action. And getting back to that action was an ever present goal as I helped Delta dive into what options we did have.

Kaydee, my former mind and my best—only?—friend waited for me, a prisoner on Starship's Bridge and a potential bargaining chip I had to take off the table. Delta seemed to sense my urgency so she scrambled to dissect our best resource: The flexi-mechs.

Those limber machines had working arms, legs, hands and mechanical hearts. Their circuit boards were, somewhat, undamaged. The battery packs on a couple hadn't been cut. Wires and bars could be torn up, pared to the right length, and spooled together. With Delta as engineer and surgeon, and me playing manager, we severed and swapped pieces of me.

Using Beta's knives, Delta would slice into my synthetic skin at the right point, cutting a narrow channel that could be peeled back to reveal the damage beneath. We'd unscrew a plate or lift off a sealing patch to get at hidden pocked pieces. Delta's murderous precision came in healing handy here, as she could pull out busted bits with a knife's point, then re-tie a wire's copper cabling with her fingers alone.

When my feet came back online, it wasn't so much like waking from a numbing dream as gaining a new feature. One moment I felt nothing, and the next there they were: ten toes, two feet, ready to walk and wander. With those in place, I started helping Delta and our four hands made swift patchwork, returning me to working order.

Though, as Volt had warned above, my overall integrity continued to degrade. Core parts of me, my spine, my motherboard, my memory, were growing nicked, fuzzy. Already some pockets were slower to respond, some files simply gone as a wayward blow had damaged the hardware. So far, the casualties had been contained to the Librarian's archives, to extra space, like where I'd dumped the Voices during our space walk not too long ago. All the same, I felt tight there, like my head didn't have room for much more.

Which, strictly speaking, it didn't.

"What about Beta?" Delta asked as I stood up, flexed my limbs and tested their range.

"Same deal," I replied. "We're not leaving without her."

Sure, I might've said that, but turning words into reality proved difficult. Even with the flexi-mech scrap, Beta's damage looked grim. Her synthetic skin had been blown back, unable because of the wound or Purity's nibbling monsters to heal over the hole in Beta's chest. Wires were broken, along with critical processing circuits. Her power supply had lost a third of its bulk, rendering it inoperative. After our diagnosis, both Delta and I frowned at our former ally.

"It's not going to work," we said at the same time.

"Leave her, then?" Delta said, looking at Beta without a hint of pity.

"Leave her? Pretty heartless, Delta. Even for you."

"She's dead. What do you want?"

"Just because you and I can't fix her, doesn't mean it can't be done."

Delta picked up her blade, settled it on her shoulder. "We're wasting time, Gamma. You said Starship's going to land soon. Alpha has control. We can't let that stand."

"You were just as dead as she was a few minutes ago." I bent down, gripped Beta's shoulders and sat her up. "All we need is a better mechanic." I brought Beta up the rest of the way, shifting her weight to carry her cross-wise. "And we need her, Delta, if we're going to have a chance."

Delta sniffed, "We killed Alpha's toy. He's not that dangerous."

Like arguing with a wall, this one.

"Look. We have to go up anyway to get out of here. I'll carry her, you keep me alive, and then we figure out what's next. Okay?"

"Every time I make these deals with you we wind up in trouble."

"You'll be in trouble anyway."

Even Delta couldn't argue with that logic.

We climbed. Step by step out from the cozy basement into the Garden. We passed by Purity's dark catwalks, Delta freeing several more flexi-mechs of their souls in the process. There were lifts we could've taken, but I avoided those even with Beta in my arms. Alpha controlled Starship's systems now, and even the chance he could paralyze a lift with us inside kept my feet moving towards the steps.

Seeing Delta return to her efficient death-dealing prompted a niggling question I thought might never be answered. Though it seemed so long ago now, when we'd escaped Alpha's mechs and journeyed along Starship's outer hull, Delta had taken up a stargazing hobby, frequently delivering long stares out to the nebulae surrounding our vessel's journey. Several times Alvie had nudged her from the reverie, but I'd never had a chance to dig into why.

So, unprompted, as we left behind the sandy landing of the Garden's deepest level, I asked her why a killing machine would take an interest in the stars.

"Do I need to explain myself to you?" Delta asked.

"You don't."

"Good."

Delta stayed quiet until we reached the next landing, Beta laying across my arms like some old-style princess in need of a rescue. She would've hated that comparison and would kill me if I spoke it aloud to anyone, but in my lonesome silence I chuckled anyway.

"We are what our programming allows, right?" Delta said as we started up again, footprints left in the sand.

"Sure, I'll give you that."

Delta patted her blade against her shoulder, "Then

everything I do is because of some function Leo wrote into me, right?"

"Not quite," I said, thinking of Kaydee. "Leo, I think, gave us a base. A foundation that we're building from. We can learn, Delta. Obviously."

"A foundation," Delta muttered, mused on that for another few steps. "Then my foundation is pursuit."

"What?"

"A chase. An assault. Call it what you want, but I was made for action."

"Think you've proved that more than a few times now."

Delta didn't throw me a glare at my crack, which made me shut up. I watched the back of her head, but even so, she looked like someone in focus. A steady cadence, her mind elsewhere.

"After Alpha, I'll find something else to pursue," Delta said. "I hadn't thought about that until I saw outside Starship. There's so much out there, an infinity. I'll never be done."

I mulled the words.

"Does that scare you?" I asked.

"I . . . don't know. I should be relieved," Delta said, "because I'll never be without purpose. If Starship lands and the humans survive, then there will be tasks to carry me on forever."

"A mech's dream."

Delta didn't reply. Didn't say anymore on it, even when I prompted her to continue. The open door to her thoughts closed shut again, in part because we were hearing noises. Vague chatter, stomps and shuffles from feet in motion.

The sounds gave me my own relief: Alpha hadn't attacked and destroyed the humans while I'd been away.

Leo, Val, Chalo and the rest still held their camp. We'd have a chance to find Beta help. The mission to Purity wouldn't have cost more than it gained.

It'd been a long time since I'd had a big win.

A real long time.

SIX

KEEPING IT SIMPLE

At first I thought it was Starship's noises making the sound, but as Delta and I drew closer to the human center—less sand, more soil—the steady beats and brighter flourishes resolved themselves into something entirely unlike the mechanical grinds, whines, and rumbles. No, this here was honest-to-goodness music, creative stuff tapped out by hands, pushed through several small flutes, and bonked out on an overturned bucket.

We came upon the band as we neared the temperate forest's center. Pine needles formed a soft cushion for the musical foursome, sitting off to the side and with weapons in arm's reach. The military chaos that I'd ditched to go digging for Beta and Delta had been molded over the hours to resemble something saner: the band, yes, but also spots carved out for food, planning, messages and medicine.

The people here crossed a short spectrum: all were fighters first, but some were also part of Leo's post-apocalyptic band of survivors. These weren't hard to pick out: their metal makeovers put them at hard contrast to the battered, dirty folks sharing their space, people who'd either been raised via technology from a vial in Starship's Nursery, or who were the last descendants of Starship's original populace. Meshed now, the groups busied themselves working on salvaged or stolen weapons, reviewing defensive alignments, and, shocking enough to see, playing a small game with carved steel chits.

Val, the only leader I saw monitoring the enterprise, staked herself out beneath a sprawling pine. She sat on a shot-up log, reviewing etchings on a flimsy plastic sheet. As we approached, Beta in my arms, we drew everyone's attention save hers. Not until we stopped at her feet did Val tap her finger idly on a small folding table in beat with the band —who hadn't broken their performance at our arrival—and look up.

A bearer of burdens, Val wore her mantle with sharp severity. She regarded us with analytical eyes, reviewing my shambled state, Beta's lying in my arms, and Delta's re-armed danger. A slow review, one I tolerated without comment: Val had shown time and time again that to work with her was to accept her dominion. Anything else would mean casting out, dismissals, refusals.

"And?" Val said, her eyes returning to the scratched sheet.

Not exactly the response I wanted, but better than a banning or a chastisement.

"Where's Leo?" I replied. "I need his help to fix Beta."

"Leo's not here."

Before I could handle Val's short temper and shorter sentences, Delta slammed a hand on Val's table. The sound rang through the room, overwhelming the quartet and throwing off their notes for a discordant moment till their jumble sorted itself. Nobody else dared interfere or let their eyes linger too long.

"Help us and we'll save you," Delta said.

Val glared, but few could match my vessel friend in a heated stare. Delta didn't need to blink, didn't need to breathe. She could bend her entire will on outlasting Val's efforts and she did so, forcing Val into a sigh, a forehead rub with dry, scarred hands.

"He's gone back," Val said. "He's taken it on himself to fix the Nursery with that other robot, the one you've shown up with a couple times now."

"Volt," I said.

The black mech, a machine of many arms, kept a close eye on Starship's power supply. Battery racks and watts uncounted burned through Volt's domain in a careful dance according to his tune. A single misstep, to hear Volt tell it, and our great big ark would disintegrate in a spectacular display, one our vaporized selves wouldn't be witnessing.

"That one," Val nodded. "So, like I said, they're gone. There's some Forgers here, though. They might be able to help." For once, Val seemed to thaw, iciness replaced with exhaustion. "There's scrap to spare and we could use her, if you're able."

"I'm sure you could," I replied, "but I didn't save her for you."

"No?"

Even Delta gave me a questioning look there. Fair, I hadn't told her the why on our climb up, only the story leading to this very moment.

"I have a friend that needs helping," I said. "When that's over, if Beta wants to help you, that's up to her. So I'd suggest you be a bit nicer to us."

"You want nice, go read a book," Val shot back. "All we have here is war."

. . .

VAL'S DEPRESSING pronouncement turned out to be false: the humans had quite a bit more than war in their enclave. For one, they'd piled and sorted the leftovers from Alpha's motley mech army. Most bits and pieces, slashed apart by blades or burned away by laser fire offered little more than garbage, but nestled in the piles were pieces that could fit Beta, or so Clara said.

The saucy Forger had, through skill or force of personality, taken a certain role in Leo's absence: scrap master. She presided over the jumbled parts, directing fellow forgers and what humans were interested in how to find useful pieces. As we approached, Clara, clothes not quite covering shimmering metal patches on her skin, pointed here and there to send her charges scurrying.

Much like Val, her mood did not improve upon seeing me and what I carried.

"I have parts, not people," Clara said. "You donating her, great. Break her down first."

Ruthless, this one.

"I'm trying to repair her," I replied, "but I need help."

Clara studied Beta, seemed to see the wounds for the first time. "What is it with you vessels and always bringing problems into my life?"

"Sorry?"

"Don't apologize. What makes her worth repairing?"

"She can destroy more mechs than everyone here," Delta cut in, "except me."

Clara, probably recalling Delta taking her hostage not long ago, accepted the claim, barked out some orders, and in seconds we had a makeshift workbench—constructed by cutting together mech parts—cleared off and Beta slapped on it. I pulled up the vessel's schematics and we started work.

Doing full-on team surgery felt, in a word, amazing. I would ask for this or that and Clara would do it, would get someone else to do it, or Delta would make the cuts where needed. Forger tools for molding metals soldered on new circuits, old wires were pressed into new service. I fell into a trance, following my functions to identify the best order to patch Beta up. One line led to the next, each success a check mark off the long list.

Until, several hours later, we had Beta's eyes blinking up at us. While the pink hair streaming down half her head held knots, while her synthetic skin wouldn't heal as before and a Forger-style metal patch covered her chest, Beta lived.

"Bring me back and the first thing I see is your ugly mug?" Beta said to me.

I grinned.

"That doesn't help."

Alvie, my metal dog, reunited with us too in the forest. My wheeze-barking puppy showered me with nudges and nuzzles while we worked on Beta, at least until I told him to sit. Alvie then simply sat, staring at me with yellow eyes, unceasing until I gave him permission to move. When I asked Val, after Beta's surgery, whether the dog had delivered my message, she once again looked up from her strategizing and told me he did.

"We had neither the people nor the knowledge to go after you," Val said. "Don't take it personally."

"I've learned not to do that with you."

"Good."

Val reached up, stroked a pine needle branch hanging over her head. "I'm glad Beta's awake."

"Me too," I said, wanting to get back to the vessels. All the same, Val didn't continue conversations lightly, so I waited. "She's not going to be like she was, but close."

"Everyone gets scars in this life."

Okay. I waited a long breath.

"Gamma," Val said, glancing back down to her scratched sheet. "I've been staring at this thing for a long time now."

"I noticed."

"So has everyone else," Val replied. "It's a hard decision."

"Are you looking for advice?"

Val laughed, full-throated. "Advice? No. You said you were going to take Delta and Beta and go after a friend of yours? One held by Alpha?"

"Yes."

Kaydee had already been left far too long.

"I don't know if I should tell you this, but because you've helped us, I feel you should know," Val began, "Starship is getting close to landing, or so Volt is saying." A breath, a scratch at her cheek tracing an old white-rimmed scar. "Leo isn't at the Nursery to defend it. He's getting it ready for transport. The embryos."

"Why?"

"After Starship lands, we're leaving," Val said. "We humans, anyway." She held up a hand as if to stop me from speaking, not that I would. "Alpha simply has too much power. His mechs are too many and we are too few. I won't have our first moments in our new home stained with death."

I followed what I'd seen so many humans do and tilted my head, "Alpha won't let you leave. He'll chase. He sees humans as a threat."

"He won't get the chance," Val said. "This is what I'm warning you about, Gamma. When Starship lands, we'll leave the ship fast. Hopefully too fast for Alpha to figure out. Then Volt's going to blow this place apart."

"Destroy Starship?"

"And Alpha and every other mech in this damn place," Val said. "It's the only way to be sure."

I went into overdrive, ran the plan through and it came up possible. Volt could overcharge any and all of Starship's batteries. He could spark fires, blow up substations throughout the ship. A cascading failure that'd turn this hulk into ash and rubble.

"You're telling me this because you want us to come with you?" I guessed.

Val shook her head, "No. I'm telling you this so you and your friends can live, if you want. But not with us, Gamma. When we leave Starship, the humans are leaving it alone."

"IT'S A WASTE," Delta said as we climbed up the levels.

I'd sealed the Garden's doors towards the Bridge side, creating a wall to keep the humans safe for a while from Alpha's attacks. That act meant we needed to climb up to get out, get to a point where I could open a door.

"Humans don't think like you, but they're not stupid," Beta replied, lurching up last in line. She was getting better with every flight, her processor coming to grips with her changed insides. "Not all the time."

"I'm doubting that."

I had to side with the sword-wielder here. Starship had material by the ton packed into its bulk. Resources, tools, energy to help get a new human colony started. Simply blowing it all to pieces would be a terrible plan.

"I don't know why Volt would agree," I said. "He just rebuilt his wife."

"I do," Beta replied. "If you think Alpha's going to win, then what future do you have?"

A corrupted one. Alpha had a rotten tendency to rewrite mech code to follow his own instructions. He'd nearly rewritten my own once, sending me spiraling down a terrifying tunnel where my every action had to comply with his orders. I could, maybe, see Volt deciding such a future wasn't worth risking.

"So it comes down to the same thing it's always been," I said, boots padding on mossy ground as we hit the humid, overgrown upper levels.

New clothes decked us out, taken from humans and Forgers who didn't need them anymore. Stable, workman-like gear not so much suited to battle as welding plates or fixing pipes. If we chanced on it, I'd vote for going into an old store, doing some scrounging. The lighter the better for dancing with flexi-mechs.

"Stop Alpha, save Starship," Delta replied. "Keeps it simple, doesn't it?"

SEVEN

CINEMATIC

We emerged from the Garden high up in the Conduit. A wealthier place, where the air glowed with a brighter blue. The vast corridor cutting through Starship had large walkways on either side, all passing by cut-in homes and stores, their entrances marked by spiraling doors. Red and green inset gems, each as large as my head, showed closed and open options as we put feet to metal, leaving the Garden's plants behind us.

After the door we used shut, Beta turned and jammed a knife beneath the red gem. She wiggled the blade, throwing off sparks while Delta and I watched.

"No mech's going to hack their way in now," Beta said, once her mangling had ended.

"Still on their side," Delta muttered.

"Some of us don't drop their purpose so fast."

"Hey," I tried.

"Some of us aren't blind," Delta shot back, talking right on over me. "Who came after us? It wasn't the humans. Gamma here's the only one who cared, and he's a mech."

"A vessel," I said.

Beta, knife bandoleers glittering in the Garden's leftover humidity, shrugged, "I don't need their love to do what needs doing."

"And when they throw you out? Shoot you in the back?"

"I'd like to see them try," Beta replied.

Stares simmered. Alvie stood between the two, yellow eyes flicking back and forth. I leaned on the walkway railing, trying to figure out what magic combination of words would cease the fighting, when I found it.

"Chandler's Kitchen and Home," I said into the breach. At the incredulous looks I pointed a few spots down the walkway where a hot white neon sign fitfully lit the storefront. "Let's go."

My two friends suppressed their stingers and joined my walk, coming with me into the ruined store to see what could be salvaged. Most places in Starship had been ransacked by desperate humans in their dwindling days. Others had been torn apart by mechs as their code broke down or, possibly, Alpha twisted them to a sadder state.

However, this high up on the Conduit, fewer humans and fancier mechs meant the damage wasn't so extensive. Kaydee might've said this was some commentary on humanity as a whole, but I was more concerned with the cutlery.

Gamma and Beta shared my passion, and we skipped by ovens, boxy squat refrigerators, and dishwashers no taller than our knees. The appliances glimmered in wild colors, from crimson reds to a starburst yellow. For all Starship's gray, it seemed the trend in hipper circles was to go anything but.

True, well-crafted knives, cleavers, and other implements of bodily ruin sat in cases or hung from various racks towards the store's back. Beta and Gamma yanked them out one by one, comparing them with the forged shrapnel they'd made back in Starship's aft. Some new blades earned places in their armories, most were left alone. Too thin, too small.

Me, I slipped a couple knives into thigh holsters Beta made up for me, but my main prize came from the pots and pans: a heavy, nigh-immortal cast-iron one. A laser gun stolen from the flexi-mechs hung behind my back, and I didn't have Gamma and Delta's speed, their dexterity. A big ol' blunt object that could work as well as a shield played better for me than the pointy things. Bonus, I'd used one before.

"Nice choice," Delta said when we all met up at the store's entrance. "You can fry the humans some eggs when it's all over."

"All about utility," I agreed.

Where we would get the eggs, not to mention the oil to fry them in, went un-asked and un-looked for.

Harder to disregard was the Conduit's color when we returned to the shop's entrance. A trade: sky-blue for burnt orange, as if, going by the Librarian's archive in my memory banks, a gorgeous Earth dawn had arrived. Along with the light came a message repeating several times over:

Starship will be landing soon. Please prepare for arrival.

Sybil, Starship's architect spoke the words. Recorded who knew how many years ago. After three repetitions, the Conduit's blue glow returned.

"Change anything?" Delta said.

"No," I replied. "When the ship starts to shake, we can sit down. Until then, we're going after Alpha."

After Kaydee.

"Good," Delta said.

Together we stepped off down the walkway and

continued on. Sybil's arrival announcement caused little flurry: whatever official mechs were designated landing duties, they'd been long since destroyed or absorbed by Alpha's swarm. Speaking of, we saw mech clusters roaming the walkways, bands of five or ten flexi-mechs accompanied by couriers, those floating bee-like bots turned from trans-porters to laser-throwers.

The mechs didn't seem to have an objective in mind, and the ones we watched from above tended to walk straight along, stopping at every house or shop to go inside and search.

"Alpha's getting paranoid," I said.

"He's getting smarter," Beta said. "How many times have you walked right up there?"

"A few."

"And every time, you failed to destroy Alpha." Beta made a clicking noise. "C'mon, Gamma."

"I had other objectives that seemed more important."

"He's not a fighter," Delta added. "That's not his mode."

Not exactly the defense I needed, but sure. Beta shrugged away the comment and we kept moving, conver-sation over. I understood Beta's point, though: the next time I found myself near Alpha, only one of us would be leaving.

Twelve mechs stomped towards us, steady and slow. The University sat below to our left, its level-spanning bulk not quite making it this high. Halfway to the Bridge and Delta, Beta wanted to fight.

"I vote discretion," I said, ushering us into an open, large door to our right. Open might be the wrong word: its spiraled ends were bent in, the opening smashed through. "Any mech might be able to tell Alpha where we are, and I don't want to fight through an ocean to get to him."

"I do," Delta replied, but she stayed inside with Beta and I.

And what an inside. I'd been in shops, ruined restaurants, and homes before, but the wide space here confounded me. Ragged carpet covered the ground, leading to a single long desk from entry to back. The desk had a broken glass section in the center, sprinkling the lipstick red stands inside it with shards. Behind the desk sat another long shelf, one decked out with glass tanks, each one with little metal bowls towards the top and openings on the right. Stacked, flat containers lay next to each tank, with pump-toting jugs nearby labeled with Butter and Salt stickers.

"Where'd you bring us?" Beta said, staring up at the ceiling.

A few recessed lights still worked, illuminating a wild mural. A character, scene, setting mishmash lay above our heads, pitting action heroes and their guns alongside gnarled tree creatures, racing cars, a flying white ball getting swung at by some guy with a large bat, and several things that looked like rudimentary spaceships flying around a big gray blob.

"No idea," I said. "Kaydee would know."

Our reverie didn't last long: the mechs neared, their clanks giving them away. Though Delta pushed for an ambush, I angled for a deeper retreat. The lobby gave way to a hallway at the back, with four options to choose from. At random, Beta picked the second, so that's where we went.

At first I didn't understand: the room, large but not massive, because few things were on Starship, held nothing more than chairs lined up row by row. They all faced the same thing, what looked like a blank black wall. Delta solved the riddle, finding a control panel just inside the door and pressing several buttons while Beta and I wandered ahead.

A grinding sound filled the hall, making me freeze as a screen, silver-white plastic, lowered itself from the ceiling to cover the wall. The lights along the room's sides dimmed to darkness, putting us in absolute black for precisely two seconds until bright light crashed my sensors. A scene splashed along the screen, a rolling film splashing through discordant scenes quickly. Sound poured out too: voices, effects, music.

I'd never heard all those things together, never put in place purposefully, and it threw me. The Librarian's deposited files had those things, sure, but replaying them—as if I'd had the time—in my own memory wasn't like this, wasn't like being surrounded by the experience.

"Turn it off!" Beta called over the noise. "They'll hear, dammit."

"I can't," Delta replied, and I looked to see the control panel had receded into the wall, locked away by an access code. She hefted her blade. "I'll cut it."

"No!" I said, surprising myself. Something exploded on the screen, and a deep voice read what sounded like the title. "Don't. We don't know if the other rooms work."

"So?" Delta gave me one of her patented Gamma-you're-insane looks, made even more so against the movie's reflection.

"This might be the last one. The only place like this left." I pointed behind me. "There's magic here. We don't need to destroy it."

Delta continued to give me a blank stare, but at least she lowered her blade. A momentary victory, one I planned to follow-up with a hopeful quip about the mechs walking right on past.

You'd think I'd have learned by now.

The flexi-mechs didn't obey theater etiquette. They did not step softly through the door, but bashed on in, weapons up and at the ready. Delta, Beta, and I dove for cover.

Or, I did.

Beta's knives whistled over my head as I flew towards the seats. Landing on the hard old floor, I heard the seat backs squeak as Delta loped on them, dancing her way towards the mechs while making a good shot hard to find. Alvie wheeze-barked, picked a row to wait in for an ambush. Overhead and around us, stirring violins and pounding drums blotted out any other noise.

I curled back on the ground, scraping my big pan along the floor between the seats to get a peak. Orange laser lights flashed. Occasional shredded metal shrieks broke in between the music. When I peered around the edge, mech bodies lay smoking near the theater entrance, but my friends' initial salvo hadn't ruined the entire force.

Delta, back near the projector, tangled with three flexi-mechs. They used their weapons less to shoot Delta and more to force her back, catch her in a combined fire net. On my left, Beta had ducked behind the first row, taking cover as five mechs ran down the aisle firing. Alvie found his moment, springing out on the five and slashing into their crowd.

I could go after either group, but which one?

The easier win trumped the harder fight.

I rose, dropping my pan and flipping my laser around my shoulder and into my palms. Nowhere near the best shot, even I could get a good hit or two on an oblivious target. My gun thrummed as gas and light mixed, spitting out hot blue energy at the mech trio. My first shot missed behind their advance, my second torched a torso.

"Gotcha!" I shouted.

And received the intended response: not just the mech I'd torched, but the other two with it jerked my way.

Delta took care of the rest, springing forward with a wide slash. All three mechs, standing in two separate seat rows, lost their heads. I gave Delta a patented Kaydee thumbs-up, but the vessel ignored me, landing her slash and sprinting past towards the theater's front.

Right. Two friends and a dog.

Wheeling after Delta, I tried to angle for a pot shot and saw orange coming my way. I ducked, saw the seats behind me burst aflame as errant bolts superheated old and dry fabric. The whole time, some dramatic speech played out onscreen, a general or some other commanding their forces to battle. Appropriate.

I leaned out from my aisle, keeping behind the seats. Delta had been pressed into cover, layering fire from the flexi-mechs proving difficult to pierce. I couldn't see Beta, but curses launched from the theater's opposite side seemed a good guess. Alvie flew through the air, launched by a flexi-mech, and crashed into the seats behind me. For the moment, I seemed to be the least threatening target.

Much as I preferred it.

Without going for precision, I held down the trigger and drained my poor gun to send a steady scorching stream. The azure bolts went wide of the screen—somehow, the canvas hadn't been hit yet and I felt it needed to stay pristine—and well wide of the mechs, but they drew attention. Those red flexi-mech eyes, like floating dots in the dark, shone my way.

"Go get'em," I whispered.

Delta heard.

The dismantling came fast, hard. I threw out a couple more bolts in solidarity while my vessel friends pincered and processed the mechs in their fashion, one cut, stab, or slice at a time. Behind me, the theater's fire continued to burn, consuming several seats as I watched, unsure.

Unsure, at least, until the ceiling decided to rain on us.

Starship's fire defense came down as Beta and Delta cleaned up the last mech, soaking the theater. The fire dwindled in the damp. My weapon shorted, as did the others, leaving me with only the pan. I held it up as Delta and Beta returned, all of us no worse for wear. Well, not quite true: Beta and Delta had both taken hits, ones soaked up by their synthetic skin. No internal damage. Alvie, too, shook himself free from the rubble, looking around for more mechs to bite.

"Nice work," I said to the pair. "We're a good team."

"We?" Beta asked.

"Gamma did what Gamma does," Delta said. "At least we didn't have to save him."

Time was, I'd get miffed by the characterization. Now, I nodded.

"Exactly," I said. "And look, the theater's still working."

The movie kept on playing, the aftermath of some violent battle playing out on screen. Characters walked past corpses, their faces marred with dirt and blood. Altogether a more disgusting affair than the cords and coolant dripping around our battlefield.

"I know this one," Beta mused. "Not great."

"Whatever," Delta said. "Let's go."

So we left, my frying pan in hand, a slight smile on my face, clothes soaked. Somehow, I felt the Librarian would be happy we'd left the theater working. I owed the old man for taking him in only long enough for Kaydee to obliterate the dude's digital soul.

If I had to pay that debt one cinema at a time, I would.

EIGHT

DANCE PARTY

For all the work we did in the cinema, it would've been nice to get a reward. Instead, Alpha's mechs must've been chatting because we only made it a few dozen meters more along the walkway, with the Bridge still far off ahead, before couriers floated right on up at us. The bee-like mechs, designed to ferry packages from one place to another, had been outfitted with lasers instead of cargo. They weren't especially accurate, and their mini-jet engines tended to puff them around at random, but volume counted for something.

"Five," Delta said as the quintet, glowing orange against the Conduit blue, bobbed over the railing ahead. "Run or fight?"

"No question which one you'd prefer," I replied.

Beta didn't even wait. A knife flashed passed Delta's ear, streaking straight ahead for a lightning hit on the closest courier. The sharpened metal bit into the courier's thin skin, showering sparks. Doubling down, the knife's momentum knocked the courier into a spin, turning its engine up so the machine's panicked burst sent it careening down into the walkway.

It died with a satisfying crackle and pop.

"Off we go," I muttered, following Delta and Beta.

The four remaining couriers didn't get a shot off. The fight ended in seconds as Beta's arms pumped knives while her feet crossed meters. Each shot was dead on, spinning couriers around, blowing their weapons or engines. The one left aloft, struggling to find its aim, found Delta's blade carving it in two.

I, pan totally ready, caught up to find a slaughter awaiting my assault.

"Good work team," I said as my friends confirmed their kills.

"Oughta keep going," Beta replied, restocking her knives. "The big guy knows we're here."

"Alpha's not really that big," I said, putting a hand on my head. "He's like my—"

"Not important," Delta cut me off. "Let's go."

Beta dashed off with Delta, the two taking the clear walkway and using it as their personal sprint track. I jogged after them, built up damage reducing my running speed. Kaydee mentioned, and the Librarian's resources confirmed, that humans degraded as they aged. Muscles and memories didn't work as well as they used to, making humans and other biological creatures slower with time. I figured that couldn't be far off from what I felt now, every step pinging little alerts in my eyes about structural weakness, joints slipping, wires fraying.

The last few days had seen a half-dozen hack-job repairs on my body, all done by people and mechs who weren't experts. After all this, I'd need someone like Leo, or maybe Volt, to do a full tear down. Rip out my guts, my nerves, and replace them with brand new, better versions.

That, of course, would only be possible if Starship landed safe. If Alpha didn't win.

Then again, if Alpha did win, maybe he'd fix me right up after corrupting my programming. A perfect lieutenant, standing shining with Delta and Beta beneath Alpha's throne on his new mech-run world. What a nightmare that would be.

The worst part? I wouldn't know it. Not like some human who found themselves enslaved or captured. My memories would be literally erased, literally altered. I would be a happy servant in every way, forever operating by Alpha's whim without a hint of discontent.

I couldn't let that happen. Couldn't. If things went that far south, I'd push the button. Erase everything that made me function and become truly a blank vessel. Sure, Alpha could install some other program, but it wouldn't be me.

Wouldn't be me.

Delta and Beta eventually realized I wasn't as fast and slowed up their race, letting me catch up. Alvie, at least, stayed at my pace the whole time. We passed by fancier houses, more restaurants and high end stores. If time allowed, I would've gone inside, curious about human society up here. Instead, I repeated Kaydee's name to myself and kept on going.

Mechs interrupted as we went, flash squads leaping off a rising lift or more couriers flying in. Every time Delta and Beta dispatched the arrivals without ceremony, knife and blade-work flawless, fast. I counted one solid frying pan whack on a flexi-mech not quite annihilated by a Beta knife-strike. After, Beta would scoop up her spent blades and we'd be dashing on again, keeping ahead of any trap.

"He's got to know where we're going," I said as we stood among another downed courier collective. "Why isn't Alpha just sending his mechs there?"

"Hoping to get lucky?" Beta offered, picking up her last spent knife and slotting it back into its thigh holster.

"Delay," Delta said. "Every second gives him more time to prepare."

Splitting his forces. Spending a few to buy the rest precious time. The idea made some sense. Especially if Alpha had some other monster mech like the revived Chancellor. Give that beast a few more minutes to get perfected, and—

"Not yet," I said as we kicked off running again. The blue ahead darkened as we neared Starship's bow, the Bridge and the Conduit's end. "We damaged the Lines enough. Alpha wouldn't be able to build a new army so fast."

"Then what've we been fighting?" Delta replied.

"All he has," I said.

"Then he's a dead vessel."

"Very," Beta added.

Approaching the Bridge from near Starship's top meant we had to descend, a task made harder by the lifts not working for us. Alpha controlled Starship's network, meaning those convenient elevators played to his tune and nobody else's. Our walkway met its end against a painted-over spiral door, one busted open and leading into a massive apartment with glassy views to outer space. A stairway, all treaded steps and handrails, sat just before the end on our right.

"Down?" Delta asked.

"There's no other way to the Bridge, is there?" Beta asked, looking at me.

A central platform, laser-guarded entry, then a long pathway to the Bridge itself and its terminals. No other way, save crawling down Starship's outside and trying to break in, something I bet even Delta wouldn't be able to manage.

"For once, I think our only tactic is smashing in the front door," I said.

"Simple. Good," Delta nodded. "Let's go."

Alvie wheeze-barked his approval, and off we went. Jumping down the steps wasn't much better than running on the flat walkway, and again Beta and Delta proved their physical bonuses by leaping one flight after the next. I preferred to skip down the steps, keeping one hand on the railing and the other holding my frying pan. Slower, sure, but less likely to spill myself across a landing.

I couldn't handle the mockery I'd get for that.

Alpha, though, let us make the descent without pestering. We saw the reason soon enough in peering looks down: flexi-mechs, couriers, and an older mech medley congealed on the Bridge's entry platform. Alpha, apparently, had decided to condense his forces into one last wall. Unlike a wall, though, the mechs moved.

"Why?" Delta asked as we paused on one landing near our destination to take a last look.

The machines shifted around the platform, some walking in long circles while others hopped from spot to spot, back and forth without end. Couriers flitted up and down, as if bobbing to some silent beat. Unceasing motion without apparent purpose.

"Dance party?" Beta offered.

"We'll ask Alpha when they're all gone," I said.

Whatever pity I had for the mechs didn't extend much to Alpha's new variants. Particularly after the assault in

Purity, I couldn't find much common ground with the flexi-mechs and laser-burning couriers. Those few trash and cutlery mechs, so far beyond their designed scope, earned my remaining regret. Everyone else was a machine made for war and deserved its end.

Like a spider's core, the Bridge began with a swooping platform in the Conduit's center. From the sides, walkways curled to meet at its edge. Stairs and lifts brought visitors to those paths, and we were no different, coming down to a familiar nexus.

"What happened here?" Beta asked as our stair ended in a wreckage strewn walkway.

"Long story," I said.

"Big fight," Delta added. "I would've won."

"You would've died without me," I shot back.

Delta glared, Beta flicked her eyes between us both, then chuckled.

"You two are special, know that?" Beta said, picking knives from her holsters and spinning them around her fingers. "How about we set a new high score?"

Delta seemed eager to do just that, and I was done arguing, but our presumed charge into the mechs wasn't met with a scrambling defense. Instead, even though we couldn't hide on the open walkway beneath the Conduit's blue light, the mechs didn't stop their hopping around. Even the couriers, who should've swarmed us, ignored our approach. The machines bopped and bounced and cared not in the slightest that three vessels neared.

"Do we destroy them anyway?" Beta asked when we were a few meters away from the closest flexi-mechs. "They could encircle us. Ambush us from behind."

"The old me might've argued the other way," I said,

"but these are Alpha's mechs, one hundred percent. If they're doing this, it's because he wants them to."

"Agreed." Delta punctuated the word with a single long leap, an overhead cut at the end.

The dancing flexi-mech found itself separated into halves, the mech falling to the floor and sputtering out. I crouched, ready with the pan to defend myself. Alvie growled. Beta had her knives ready to throw. A counterattack seemed inevitable.

Nothing.

No change. Just Starship's rumble and dancing machines.

Delta shook her head, glanced at me, "Don't hold me back."

"Not planning on it."

She went to work.

While Delta crunched through the mechs, her blade delivering perhaps unjust desserts to the dancing machines, Beta, Alvie and I looked on from the walkway. Every second we expected the mechs to turn, to fight back. Every second they kept on with their jerking, random movements.

"I can't figure it out," I said finally, as Delta took to jump-slashes and devoured the floating couriers. "What's Alpha gaining here?"

Beta, knives dangling from her hands, looked on with me, "He's not the most stable dude."

"You think this is just a mistake?"

"Possible."

"Lucky break for us then."

"Makes you suspicious, huh?" Beta eyed me. "Gamma, you ever see a good thing in your life and not get suspicious?"

I took a sideways step, raised my eyebrows at her. To my

left, Delta sent her blade spinning through a half-dozen flexi-mechs.

"Of course I have," I said. "I mean, uh . . . "

I searched my memory, sure that such a moment existed, but 'suspicious' was too vague a term. Just about anything could be considered suspicion, and, wow, I'd had surprisingly few good moments since waking up.

"Point being," Beta said into my silence, "is that Leo left us open to grin a little bit, my guy. You can embrace a good turn, so do it. Watch Delta and be happy all those things aren't going to carve us up."

"Is that what you're doing?"

"Sure."

"Because you're such an expert on being happy?"

Beta laughed. Delta pierced a trash mech on her sword's end and threw both into several other robots, the bunch going up in a small explosion.

"I didn't know a damn thing about being happy for a long time," Beta said. "Then I found Val, that mean mugger Chalo. All the humans." Beta flipped a knife, caught it with the same hand, repeated it with the other and soon had a knife juggle going on. "See, they did pointless things. They sang songs, they danced, the kids played this game tag among the Junker's crap piles. When I asked why, they said it made them happy."

"And?"

Beta caught the knives, spun them into their holsters.

"They invited me to give it a try, and you know what? They were right." Beta nodded towards the platform. "She's done. Time to go."

Delta's efforts left the flat Bridge entry a shrapnel display, with sharp ends glinting everywhere. Sparks and cooling fluid pooled around, with glittery white puffs kicking up whenever a component failed and kissed its energy goodbye. Delta herself acknowledged her work, standing near the Bridge laser gates and looking back at the ruin with folded arms and a set, straight face.

"Looks like she could learn about being happy too," I said to Beta as we joined our third vessel.

"Nah, Delta gets it," Beta replied. "Delta, you know how to be happy, right?"

"See that?" Delta pointed her blade at the mess. "Happiness."

Beta put her hand on my shoulder, "You'll find yours someday, kid."

The last leg to the Bridge meant going through laser gates. Thin stands rising up as the platform narrowed to a hallway going straight to Starship's bow. The red-glowing bands were three meters high, stretching between the poles. Earlier, I'd thrown Alvie's toy into the glow to see its effects and watched as the ball disintegrated. When Alpha came this way, I'd helped him hack through Starship's computers and disabled the fields.

Now they were up again.

"Shiny," Beta said.

"I might be able to hack it again," I offered.

"No need," Delta said, and Beta dealt a quick nod in agreement.

Before I could ask why, Delta bent down, picked up Alvie, and flung my poor dog up. Way up. Up enough for the metal pooch to soar over the glowing barrier and land with a hard bang on the other side. Alvie dismissed any concerns quick: the dog popped on his claws, issued his wheeze-bark, and gave us his best yellow-eyed grin.

"You're not throwing me," I said.

"Sure are," Beta replied, moving to my right side while

Delta neared my left. Beta pulled my frying pan away. "I know you've always wanted to fly, Gamma."

"How could you know that?" I said, wanting to edge backwards but finding Delta's hand firm against my back.

"Because I've always wanted to, and we're made of the same stuff."

Before I could argue, the two vessels dropped their hands, grabbed my legs, and heaved. One moment I stood flat and stable on the ground, in another I flew, flailing, on the same trajectory as my dog. A swooping flight, my nose coming way too close to the red, before my systems caught up with my direction.

I landed on my feet, a perfect ten.

"Catch!" Beta threw my pan, I snagged it as it fell over.

Behind me, the hallway to the Bridge stood empty. Waiting for us, really. But I didn't hear footfalls landing. Turning back, I found Delta and Beta chatting soft and fast to one another. I tried to catch what they were saying, but failed before they ended the sequence with a synchronized nod to one another.

Before I could come up with something witty to say, Beta moved behind Delta, picked her up and lifted her in a perfect balance on her hands. Both squatted, then shot up, Delta leaping off the momentum to flip over the glowing barriers. She landed beside me and Beta, like with my pan, tossed Delta's blade over after. Another clean catch.

"What about you?" I asked Beta through the red.

"I get to watch your backs," Beta said, grinning. "Now go in there and get him."

"I could've hacked the things?" I suggested.

"If Beta gets unlucky, that barrier helps us as much as Alpha." Delta said. "The decision's made. Let's go."

Her tone left no room for disagreement, and with

Kaydee being so close, I didn't have much will to contest it anyway. I offered Beta a wish for good luck and our trio took to the hallway.

Almost to Alpha, and this time he wouldn't be getting away.

NINE

ALPHA AMBUSH

One more hallway, a serene corridor built with respect in mind. Starship's standard gray walls gave way to silver slates with names etched into the gleam. Engineers, architects, and Alpha's endless scrawls. The first time I saw his name burrowed into the sides over and over again, it'd filled me with a programmed dread, a caution that the person I would be dealing with had left sanity behind a long time ago.

Now, the words brought a different feel: an angry edge.

Alpha, this monster, had Kaydee. Had nearly destroyed my friends and myself several times over. The vessel had planned to ruin Starship's mission, the sole goal all these years had been spent to achieve, by landing on a desolate rock without an atmosphere. All the humans onboard, including every one waiting for a chance to live, would be erased.

My most basic drive, programmed by Leo years upon years ago, pushed me to save humanity at any cost. That meant Val, yes. The Nursery. With a bit of tweaking, some fuzziness at the edges, it meant Kaydee too.

Delta kept quiet the whole time. Alvie's metal paws

serenaded our walk with clacks. Starship's rumble continued. The air stank, a noxious smell from all the coolant and
other chemicals released by Delta's massacre. Not that I
needed to sniff it: a simple flick and my sensors filtered out
the ugly.

At the hallway's end we came to the Bridge proper, a T
entry forcing us to go either right or left. Delta nodded left,
so I went right, Alvie following me. I had the pan up and
ready. No noise, no mech dancing came from the Bridge
itself. A concerning quiet: Alpha could send silent signals to
his mechs whenever he chose.

Tiers climbed the Bridge, each one coated in long desks
with workstations embedded into the surface, sticking out
like odd triangles. Chairs, old but left so alone as to be in
great condition, clogged the aisles between those tiers.
Nested lights made the ceiling resemble, if you stretched,
the same starry field outside the giant glass front.

At least, that's how I remembered it.

Now I saw a ruin. Overturned desks lay atop one
another, some dangling over tier edges. Busted chairs spread
their parts around the floor, though on the Bridge's right
side, nestled against the wall, the chair cushions had been
stacked into a box-like shape. If we were dealing with kids,
I'd have called it a fort. Workstations had their screens
smashed.

Across the huge viewport, in what looked like brown-
black coolant, someone—I could guess who—had written
HOME. The word would've covered black space, but now
stained an altogether different view: a yellow ball, sandy
and streaky and shifting even as I stared at it from my entry.

The planet the Voices had mentioned before Alpha
obliterated them. The direction I'd put us on at their
request. There it was, Starship's future home, its completed

mission. In the moment, it reminded me of the Garden's desert, and I hoped we weren't doomed to land on some sand-covered morass.

For mechs, a world like that would be dangerous: a few grains in the wrong place and circuits could fry.

"Gamma!" Alpha's voice, as ever exploring tonal ranges with every syllable, called my name. "Welcome, welcome, welcome!"

The vessel stood at the Bridge's base, near the glass. Around him danced more flexi-mechs, bobbing to some hidden beat. Alpha looked much as I'd last left him, long red hair and scarred over body cloaked in a dirty robe. The vessel had no weapons visible and I'd never seen him use one.

He did, though, have that same bug-eyed, wild grin, like some cult preacher reaching his zenith.

Next to him, tied to a backless chair seat, sat a mech I recognized. Kaydee. Or rather, the body she'd stolen to save me. Its arms and legs had been popped off, leaving only a torso and a head. A processor and its memory bank.

She'd been mutilated, but, unlike Val, Leo, or another human, she wouldn't be feeling any pain. Those missing limbs were like rooms with their lights turned out: no longer options, and that's all.

And lights could be turned back on with the right equipment.

On the run over, the vessels and I had put together a plan. A flexible one, and I put it into action with the slightest twitch of my right fingers. Alvie, taking care to walk on his claw points to keep quiet, slunk off to the right. He followed the wall while I strode into the Bridge's center, sucking up the attention.

Delta had disappeared. Good.

"You know why I'm here," I said.

"To witness history?" Alpha replied, mimicking my stride to match me in the center, at the bottom of the thin stair crawling down the Bridge's tiers. Hard black tile interlaid with silver starbursts. "To embrace with me a millennia's journey?"

"I'm here for her." I pointed to Kaydee. "You can have your history."

Alpha's face twitched, the grin he'd been sporting flashing to a deep frown before settling to something straighter in the middle.

"Her? This thing?" Alpha turned, made a gesture. The flexi-mech dancing nearest to Kaydee stopped its jaunt and put its ten fingers around Kaydee's mechanical throat. "What do you want with her?"

My sensors went into overdrive for a hot moment, taking what I recalled of Kaydee's robot body and trying to determine if destroying the head would obliterate the memory. That was most important, those tiny sticks where all that made us would be stored. Some mechs had heads simply for show, to make humans find them more normal. Others used them just like their biological counterparts.

My sensors had no idea. Kaydee could be dead. She could be fine.

I couldn't risk it.

"The only thing that matters is what you want," I said, "and whether you'll give me her for it."

"Oh, Gamma. You've already given me so much," Alpha replied, sweeping up several steps towards me. On the far right, I caught, but didn't look towards, my dog making his advance. "This Bridge, all thanks to you. The Voices? You put them back on the network for me to destroy. That fiend running the Nursery and corrupting all those mechs before me? You again. Tell yourself whatever you like, my friend, but you've done more to advance my cause than anyone on this ship."

Some barbs I could let go unanswered. Others, well, others demanded a response.

"Then why are we landing here?" I said, bringing my frying pan up to my chest. "You wanted a rock."

"One is as good as another," Alpha replied. "I've made my peace with it, my friend. If the humans survive the landing—unlikely—then I'll simply have more entertainment. I've even begun designing a zoo already. We can keep them, Gamma. Show them to future mechs as a lesson, that even creators can fall to their creations."

"Sure," I said, nodding past Alpha towards Kaydee. "If you've got what you wanted, can I have her?"

At the Bridge's middle now, Alpha stopped. He sighed.

"Her idea, you know," Alpha said. "All the dancing. I wanted you all shot dead. Burned to ash. Bent into scrap. She said I'd lose too many mechs that way. She said you were peaceful Gamma, that you wouldn't dare harm the harmless."

He let the words lie there. I gave him nothing.

Alpha strode up several more steps against my stare. We stood less than two meters apart now. This close, with the yellow planet's glowing bulk in the viewport, I saw Alpha had been adding to his accents. Glass tangled in his hair, bits likely taken from the smashed workstations. They didn't have a pattern, just thrown into the red. I couldn't imagine what coding error would've prompted that: perhaps what Alpha had been doing from the beginning, bending the expected just to do it.

"At first I didn't think you'd changed," Alpha said,

quieter now. "Here you are, in your human clothes, trying to look just like them. Still following Leo's orders."

Behind him, Alvie scooted past several oblivious dancing mechs. The dog reached Kaydee's hampered form on the chair. The plan hadn't accounted for an immobilized Kaydee but the dog could improvise.

I hoped.

Alpha kept on, going over me like an artist looking over a painting, spotting all the points where I should've realized by now that the humans had no interest in my survival, my success. They would use me until I died. Whatever.

"Why?" I interrupted, finally.

"Why?" Alpha replied, for once not making a connection.

"Why aren't you trying to destroy me. I'm standing here, opposing you, and you're giving me some speech," I hefted the frying pan, feeling a tad ridiculous as I did so. "Are your functions falling so far apart?"

Alpha stood there. His face twitched. Frown. Smile. Laugh. Growl.

Alvie cut through the tape. Off to my left I saw a glint. Delta, getting into position.

"You're my brother, Gamma. My only brother," Alpha said, but the words came out flat. Not a single ounce of emotion in there. "Our sisters are different. So violent. You and I, we are the artists. We are the ones that can make Starship sing, that can author the new story for our brethren. That is why. I am trying to save you."

"You want to save me? Then stop this. Let me help you."

"Help me?" Alpha asked. "You think I need help?"

The ask wasn't hostile. It was honest, curious. For once, Alpha's face didn't twist and break, but stayed focused.

Some function in his code hadn't broken quite yet, stayed open to an option.

"You know you need it," I said, forgetting Alvie for a moment. Forgetting Delta and her blade. "You've got to feel it, Alpha. Your sensors have to be telling you things are wrong. The monster that did this to you is gone, now you can let us repair the damage."

Alpha closed his eyes. His hands dropped to his waist. For a long moment I hoped, dared to believe that he might say yes.

Delta's sword came in hot, spinning sideways in a perfect cut towards Alpha's center. It should've, would've carved the vessel in half save for a dancing mech's intercession. As if snapping from a haze, a flexi-mech two tiers below Alpha jumped, caught the blade with outstretched hands and collapsed into an overturned desk.

All around the Bridge the dancing mechs ceased their celebration, pink eyes sparking to life as they sought targets. Alvie tugged hard on Kaydee's chair, rolling her along the Bridge's base. No stairs on the sides, only ramps all the way up to the exit. If Alvie could get her that far, then we might have a chance.

But Alpha was done playing brother.

At the flexi-mech's shrieking grab, Alpha's eyes snapped open, his grin returning in full force.

"A trap?" Alpha said. "So unlike you, Gamma."

He swung at me, a wild punch from his left hand. I blocked it with the frying pan, sending Alpha's arm out wide. With the backswing I went for Alpha's head, but the vessel jumped back a tier, leaving me catching air. Behind him, Delta found herself bladeless, confronting a half-dozen flexi-mechs and their drilling hands.

"You ruined the party!" Alpha called, continuing to backpedal. "I was ready for peace, and you brought war!"

No way that was true.

A wheeze-bark pulled me to the right. Two flexi-mechs pressed Alvie, swiping at the dog, who had to keep nudging Kaydee's chair forward lest it roll back down the ramp. So I did what all fighters did to save their friends: I threw the frying pan.

My oddball missile streaked over the ruined desks to clock an unsuspecting flexi-mech in the back. The mech stumbled forward, otherwise unhurt. At least until I caught up to my launched cookware. I threw myself, diving forward to tackle the stumbling mech and bear it to the ground.

Not that I pressed it long. I rolled off to the side, lunging towards Kaydee's chair as it began rolling down the ramp. Alvie let it go, taking my distraction as an opportunity to jump, paws slashing and teeth biting at the other flexi-mech. My hand found the wheeled bars at the chair's base just as Alvie made contact, the flexi-mech's drilling hands hitting my dog.

A terrible noise ran through the Bridge, metal tearing metal. I tried not to think about it, instead getting to my knees and heaving Kaydee's chair up the ramp and towards the Bridge top. The chair, Kaydee's mech body on it, clanged hard against the Bridge's back wall before settling on its side. If she'd been a human, it might've hurt.

I still muttered *sorry*.

The flexi-mech I'd downed found its way to its feet. Not far from my own, I saw my friendly dented frying pan and scooped it up. Alvie and his target bashed each other around the tier to my right. As for Alpha, Delta? The

Bridge's far side held a flashing spectacle I couldn't afford to pay attention to.

"Feeling lucky, punk?" I said to the flexi-mech, stealing a delicious line from one of the Librarian's movies. "Are ya?"

The mech spun up its hands and pressed forward. I took that as a yes.

My frying pan took the first arm with a crossing swing, two handed for extra power. The bang smashed off the wrist, sending the spinning hand bouncing away. The other struck in towards my chest, but I let my frying pan's momentum carry me to the right, brushing up against a desk and dodging the attack by centimeters. I tilted the pan's angle and whacked down, hitting the mech's outstretched knee. It caved with a sparkling crackle, and the machine, its balance no longer a sure thing, crumpled forward.

Delta might get on me for not finishing the job, but I left the mech there and took two long steps to get to Alvie. The robots had their arms entangled, bits gouged and stuck within cords and metal. They rolled onto the ramp and I took the chance, swatting down with the pan to mash the mech's lonely skull. Circuits broke and the machine went limp.

"But how to get you free?" I muttered, studying the nightmare mashup.

An angry shout from across the Bridge snapped me back. Delta still at work. Behind me, the flexi-mech I'd downed crept towards my ankles, one working hand trying to win. No time to get Alvie clean.

I tossed the frying pan back, delivering another smack to the poor mech, then scooped up Alvie and his entanglement, running back to Kaydee and her chair. I stole a look back across the Bridge, saw Alpha, still in the middle, watching me with that big grin. Beyond him, Delta looked swamped with flexi-mechs, dancing and darting, using knives to deal damage.

Okay, so the plan wasn't going quite as we wanted, but I was going to get some back-up real soon.

I plopped Alvie's mess—the dog's yellow eyes glowed still, thankfully—onto Kaydee's chair and pushed the combo out. Past the T, through the silver-sided hallway, and back to the cherry red barriers.

Beta, serene as ever, waited on the other side.

"What is all that?" Beta asked as I ran up.

"No time," I replied. "These barriers have to come down. Delta needs your help."

"Right."

I searched for a port, found one on the right side. Opposite its brother. For a split second I hesitated: if I plugged in, Kaydee and Alvie would be abandoned and alone. Beta wouldn't be able to help them if a flexi-mech or Alpha came charging in.

But what else could we do?

So I pressed my fingers together and vanished, once more leaving Starship behind for the digital world.

And the traps inside waiting for me.

TEN

WELCOME HOME

A green frame. Solid colors, no gradients. A simple box in an endless black. A program at its most basic and I stood inside it. Well, didn't stand: there wasn't ground, just the function's borders. At the box's top the barrier's command began, and it finished at a corner below and away from my right foot. At the box's very bottom, splaying out in rigid red text, sat the program's current state: ACTIVE. In between, flickering as I glanced at them, sat code strings laying out the barrier's operating conditions.

Rules to live by, in other words.

"Let's see how to break them," I said, the sound going nowhere.

My 'hand' brushed through the code, the lines tickling my skin as I touched and parsed their commands. I assumed something simple: a switch to turn them on and off. Instead I found layer after layer, all designed to activate or deactivate the barriers if conditions were met. If Starship came back from a power failure, say, or if someone said a particular passcode.

If the captain issued a mutiny alert from the Bridge terminals.

I stretched myself towards the top, the code's very beginning. The switch started there, a simple statement checking whether someone had toggled the barriers on or off. That physical switch likely lived somewhere on the Bridge, a place I wouldn't be going back to any time soon. Or ever, if I had a choice.

All I needed to do was slip in a little code injection, a tiny prompt to tell the program the switch had been flipped. Easy. Like snapping my fingers, I scripted out the command and dropped it in at the code's top. The box flashed, the program running my command.

I knelt down, read the code's output on the box's bottom: ACTIVE.

Hmm.

I re-ran my command again. It should've worked. Tell the program the switch was off, and the program should disable the barriers. This time I watched, tracked the process as the program followed my command, each line blinking a hot yellow as the tiny computer checked my request against its logic.

There. Towards the very bottom. Listed at the back of a long exception line, checking for those mutinies, those Starship crashes: if none of those had happened, the program would confirm the switch one more time.

I couldn't fake the switch, but I might be able to delete that line. Going back towards the box's top, I reached towards the very first line and made a different request. Not to run a command, not this time, but to edit the lines. Not an abnormal idea—surely Starship's engineers would be able to change this code from some terminal—but the program didn't like it one bit.

The box itself flared red. While ACTIVE remained on the bottom, ACCESS DENIED replaced the code running along the middle. Whatever privileges I'd had were revoked.

A more complex program might've given me more wiggle room. Another backdoor to open. This one, probably on purpose, gave no such play.

So I'd have to get rough.

If I couldn't make a difference inside the box, I'd have to go outside of it. Ignoring the big red letters, I drifted towards the bottom corner, where the program's results would get turned into actions by the barrier machine itself. The program ended in that corner, where spidersilk lines linked the box to the ACTIVE word and its mechanical counterpart.

I built two pieces, spun them up between my hands like someone drawing with a sharp pencil. The first would bounce an ACTIVE result right back to the program, a mirror of sorts telling the program the same thing it generated. Me mimicking Delta's words back to herself. The second piece would send a single off command to the barrier.

Put them in the right order, and I'd have my block and my freedom in a single swipe.

"Look at that," I said, with my two shiny new toys in my hands. "You'd appreciate this, Kaydee."

With a simple push, I set my new commands in place. A flash, and DISABLED appeared in bright green before me.

Who said Gamma couldn't get a win every now and again?

BETA DASHED by me even as I returned to cognizance, knives out and rushing to Delta's rescue. I couldn't know whether she'd make it in time. In any case, it didn't matter: I had Kaydee. The two other vessels could handle Alpha. And if they couldn't I certainly wouldn't be the weight throwing the scales to our side.

My dog, too, was whimpering in his wheezy, metal way.

"Okay, off we go," I said, and pushed us through.

The plan I'd formed with Delta and Beta started and stopped with killing Alpha. My mission had always been distraction and then extraction. Get my two death-dealers in, then get out with my friend. After that, we'd all meet up at the one place we could call home in Starship.

It took a while, including maneuvering Kaydee's chair around all the rubble, to get to Leo's apartment, but we made it without harassment. As we went, the Conduit flared yellow once again, declaring our arrival imminent. Everyone should be taking landing positions, whatever that meant. At least no couriers, no flexi-mechs descended on us.

Leo's place wasn't quite the same with its bashed in entrance, but with a lift over the warped spiral door panels, we made it in. The walls inside still held those movie posters, though more littered the ground now. Action stars became smudged victims for my footsteps and the chair's rickety plastic wheels.

Our four cots sat just as we'd left them, beneath a pale blue light. A peaceful place for the moment, a vibe I ruined as I went to work.

My two patients suffered from different ailments, so I went for the easier target first. Easier and less frightening. Alvie's eyes still held their yellow glow, the puppy mangled up but clearly alive. Kaydee, though, had no motion, no lights aglow in her limbless form. Whether I would find anything still inside that shell . . .

My fingers worked quick to follow my eye's instruction. As I looked at the metal and wires tangling Alvie with the flexi-mech body, my sensors picked out the right parts to pull, the right ones to retread. A loose leg had its joint re-fastened, a screw stolen from the flexi-mech and put to new purpose replacing the blown one. Without tools, I fashioned my own, using my strength to snap apart metal fragments into screwdrivers, hammers, and knives.

Alvie stayed quiet throughout it all, trusting me as I took him out piece by piece. Not a single wheeze-bark to break my concentration. Only yellow eyes.

I stopped my own thoughts from drifting. Set my focus to Alvie and dialed in one hundred percent of myself to the task. The surgery wasn't so complex as to require such concentration, but I didn't want to risk diving down tangents, consuming myself with risk calculations for Beta and Delta, for Kaydee.

One job at a time.

"How does it feel?" I asked Alvie, setting the dog free and clear on the apartment floor.

Alvie tested his paws one at a time, lifting and dropping them. A slow walk. A jump. A wheeze-bark. I noticed a hitch in his back-right leg, calculated the dog's jaw didn't quite open as far as it used to. The marks living tends to leave on us.

"Keep watch for me, will you?" I asked the dog, and Alvie, as Alvie always did, barked and padded over to the apartment's entry.

Kaydee . . . No, not Kaydee but the robot she'd inhab-ited, sat on the chair. I cut away the binds holding the cylin-drical torso in place. Looked into dead eyes and saw nothing. A speaker grill marred with scratches stayed silent.

A single port sat near the mech's midsection, beneath a tiny plate on the thing's right side. If Kaydee wouldn't come out, I'd have to go in. There wouldn't be any repairing the mech, not with what I had here.

"So you're coming home." I said, pressing my fingers together and setting the formed jack into the port.

ELEVEN

CODED MEMORIES

A shoulder jostled me, then another. People, plenty, passing by me through familiar gates. These didn't have the red glow, but the Bridge's entry stood fresh in my memory and now alive before me. Humans moved with purpose in and out, their bodies cloaked in clean clothes. Smart uniforms, nametags. Hair not in the ragged braids of Val and her survivors but in rainbow styles, spiked and straight, sloppy and suave.

Music, a jaunty saxophone and piano combo, played in the Conduit around me. It softened as a message broke in, a greeting from the ship's captain, telling Starship the day and date, to take notice of a particular nebula out the port side, and to enjoy another fabulous morning on humanity's greatest miracle.

"As if," said a woman as she stopped next to me. "What great miracle would come without mangos, am I right?"

"What?" I said, realizing she was speaking to me.

Looking at her made me do another double-take. Before me, hair lancing out in much the same way Kaydee's used to, was a person I'd seen die, or rather get deleted, not long ago.

"I'm saying they could've thought about our palettes," Peony replied, whimsy curling around her sarcasm. "For all the papayas we have, you'd think they could've squeezed a few mangos in."

No reply offered itself. What was I supposed to say? Sympathize about a fruit I'd never tasted? Could never taste?

"Oh, don't get so worried," Peony said, her grin growing at my confusion.

She had a sharp look, professional but with an active edge, ready to get her hands dirty. More off-putting was the cheeriness. All the times I'd run into Peony, she'd been trying to kill or manipulate me. Now, I expected her to—

"How about you and I go get some coffee," Peony continued. "You're looking a little lost, and some caffeine ought to fix you right up."

I was about to deny the request, say that mechs like me don't drink, well, anything, until I remembered nothing here was strictly real. The Conduit humming around me, with mechs and people rolling along the walkways, zipping through the center chasm, was all a construct. A place Kaydee built for herself.

Coffee here was nothing more than a few bits going nowhere.

"Peony," I started as she guided me off the Bridge's entry.

"You know my name?" Peony's eyebrows shot up. I thought fast, nodded to her name tag, and she laughed. "Right, sometimes you just forget about those things."

"I bet," I said. "Do you know where your daughter is?"

A curious niggle wanted more information, like the

year, what was happening around Starship. Kaydee had chosen a particular time to recreate and, while I wanted to know why, more important was finding her before her stolen mech's power supply ran dry.

"Do you know me?" Peony asked.

We crossed onto a walkway hugging the Conduit's starboard side. Shops pestered us with ads, while mechs beeped outside with free sample trays. Workers buzzed in and out, collecting their daily drinks or placing orders for items to grab on their way home. Third-shifters gave themselves away by drifting to the several bars nearby, glassy eyes seeking some way to numb their way to bed.

"A version of you," I replied.

"Now there's a statement," Peony laughed, shook her head. "You're a strange one."

"We both are," I replied.

"Suppose you're right about that."

Peony's chosen destination had little more than a counter to recommend it. A coffee-churning mech dished drinks to a dozen stools, each one paired with a tiny black disk on the counter. As we walked in, two people on the closest stools stood up, slammed their drinks down, and left. As Peony settled us in, she pressed her finger to the disk.

"Two lattes, light and frothy," Peony said, then winked at me. "Hope you're okay with that. I find it's faster to order one thing for everyone."

"Sure," I replied. I'd never tasted a latte, and whatever Kaydee's world served up to me here wouldn't be a real one either. "Back to my question . . . ?"

"My daughter? Why do you want to know?" Peony scrunched up her mouth, tilted her head. "She's got a boyfriend."

A boyfriend? What did that have to do with anything?

Again I couldn't come up with a reply fast enough, and Peony had another excuse to laugh.

"Relax," she said. "I'm just teasing. Not about the boyfriend, of course. You're out of luck there, I'm afraid. Kaydee's been locked tight in love since she was little."

"Um."

"But if love's not the reason," and here I heard it, Peony's real self, the boiled and burning Voice who ruled Starship's later years, "then what is, my lost friend?"

Across all the Librarian's archived films, books, stories, there was one line that, when delivered, always seemed to get things moving.

"She's in trouble," I said, oozing as much gravity as I could muster.

"She's always in trouble," Peony shot right back. "What's this about?"

Okay, not quite what I was looking for.

The coffee mech saved me a quick turnaround by shuffling our lattes onto the counter. Mine steamed, its foamy white top sprinkled with cinnamon. I sniffed, found a delightfully spicy scent for the taking.

Kaydee must've spent a long time writing this up. She'd been in Alpha's clutches for a long time, hours and hours to burn refining her digital getaway. A place Kaydee would never share, except with me.

And, if he'd bothered to hack inside, Alpha.

"Hello?" Peony asked.

What was this about? Would a facsimile, a coded manifestation of Kaydee's mother understand what I was trying to do?

For that matter, what *was* I doing?

I'd dragged Beta, Delta, and Alvie all the way to the Bridge, telling them the reason was to stop Alpha, but that'd been a lie. A clear lie. I needed Kaydee back. Not because she could save Starship, not because she deserved to live any more than Val's humans, than Beta or Delta.

No, I was doing all this because I *missed* her. Because I *needed* her.

"Are you okay?" Peony said, putting her hand on my shoulder.

What a human feeling, need. Sure, I could construct arguments showing Kaydee's input helped me survive. Her advice gave my tasks a higher chance of success. She kept me running smoothly. All those numbers, statistics, flat lines declaring my rescue mission worthwhile.

And every one would be a cloak hiding the truth.

"Where is she, Peony?"

I felt examined in that moment, more so than before. Peony didn't just look at my synthetic skin, my outfit—a standard Starship gray uniform—but through me. My eyes, yes, but her programming crawled mine, looking for ill-intent. A virus scan coupled with intuition, suspicion.

"You don't look like trouble," Peony mused, "but I feel like you'll bring it."

"That's for Kaydee to decide."

"No more clues, then?"

I shook my head.

"This is my daughter you're asking for."

"I know. Believe me, I know."

Peony watched me for another several seconds, then returned to her latte with a sigh.

What would've taken hours in reality took minutes in Kaydee's digital world. We left the coffee shop and turned right. The Conduit kept up appearances, people bustling, songs bursting, mechs bubbling about. Three steps along the walkway and the University appeared before us, the Conduit seeming to stretch and snap us along.

The big construct hummed with a vibe I'd only glimpsed in Kaydee's memories, back when they'd leaked through into my own vision. Students clustered, discussing not just classes but weekend plans. Bars and parties. Study sessions. Dreams and drama. Peony lingered, our steps along the University row not quite moving us at warp speed.

"She's going here now," Peony said.

"Now?"

"Third year," Peony replied, oozing pride. "When she gets out she's going to work with those mechs." Here that pride slipped. "She's always been a robotics nut."

"Right."

"If I'm being honest with you," Peony flashed a grin. "She could've gone right off to the Fabrication Lines. She's that good."

"But she went here?"

"She went here to get away from me," Peony replied. "I suppose a child needs to get away from their parents at some point, you know?"

I didn't have anything to say to that, so I shrugged, and on we went. Another several steps put us at the Garden. Peony led me through a middle level, explaining her input on this and that plant, that she'd be working on those mangoes in the afternoon. She'd get it right one of these days.

"Why mangos?" I had to ask.

"Because Kaydee read about them when she was a kid." Peony stopped, traced a lemon tree's branch. "I never wanted her to go without, no matter what it takes."

Beyond the Garden, we sped along to another stopping

point, one I recognized because the real Conduit hadn't left its ideal so far behind. The Park, a massive long stretch along the Conduit's middle, linked sprawling paths with trees, yards, and small theaters. A big fountain rested near one end, its gout spraying clear mist into the air. Couples and families bounded the paths. Laughter and a lone flute sang on the air.

"You want to find her, she's in there," Peony said.

"Thanks," I replied, and when I started off, Peony stayed behind.

"You do anything to hurt my girl," Peony called to me, "and I'll make sure you regret it."

Of that, I had no doubt.

KAYDEE WASN'T hard to find. She'd never been a quiet one. I followed a particular laugh, a particular sparkle, through to a copse of flowering magnolias. Pink and white petals drifted down around me as I came through to the other side, where a small round table sat amid spring green grass. Wine, cheese, and set plates topped the picnic, attended to by a particular pair.

Leo sat across from Kaydee, a bigger, more authentic smile on the man's face than any I'd ever seen in real life. Stress didn't assault his shoulders, and he wore no metal parts along his chest and face. Flickering code faults didn't break his gestures as he ran some story through to its end. He flourished with his wine glass, scattering some red across the lawn.

Kaydee laughed. A full-on cackle, her teal hair sparkling in the Conduit's yellow-white light. Glistening innocence. A shaking head, twinkling eyes, hands over her mouth. It was the purest thing I'd ever seen.

I waited at the edge beneath those petals. Clocks ticked, disaster waited outside. Starship would be hitting atmosphere soon, with who knew what consequences. Beta and Delta might be dead, might be staring down at Alpha's destroyed corpse.

But I waited nonetheless.

When the laughter died, Kaydee slid a glance my way, her smile softening. She tapped a finger on the tablecloth and Leo froze. Not just him, but the wine swirling in his glass too. The falling petals hung suspended in the air. When she rose from the chair and walked a step towards me, the grass bent like stiff metal beneath her feet.

"Hey Gamma," she said.

"Hey," I replied.

What do you say to someone you never thought you'd see again? I started, stopped a dozen different sentences in as many seconds, trying to find a combination that'd convey how relieved I was to see her, how much trouble we were in, how we had to get her out of here.

"You met my mom?" Kaydee canceled my plans with a stroke.

"I . . . did?"

"Okay, you're right," Kaydee's smile twisted into a half-smirk. "It's my mom as I wished she'd been. You know, a fantasy. Because this is my fantasy land."

"It's beautiful." I swept a hand at the petals, the lively Conduit. "Was it like this?"

"This happy? No. I don't think so," Kaydee said, reaching up to pick a cream-pink petal from the air. "Back then everything always had a depressed tinge. Like water with a copper aftertaste."

"Because everyone knew Starship wouldn't land in their lifetimes?"

"That and the thousand other dramas we humans have to deal with," Kaydee said. "So what's going on out there? If you're here, that means Alpha's dead?"

I spilled the story, spared nothing from the minute I abandoned Kaydee near the Fabrication Lines to the second I walked through the copse to see her. The battle at the Garden, the mission to Purity. Our assault on the Bridge.

"They're alive," Kaydee sniffed, nodded. "That's a good break. Delta and Beta get to save the day."

"Hope so."

"And you left them for me, Gamma?" Kaydee rolled her eyes. "Your priorities are messed up."

"My priorities are perfect."

"Uh huh."

"I need you, Kaydee. We all do."

Folded arms, "Well, duh. That's obvious."

"Then you're ready to come back?"

"You mean do I want to share space in your damn head again, Gamma? No, not really." Kaydee nodded back towards the frozen Leo. "It's pretty nice in here, you know." Before I could answer she kept right on rolling. "But I can feel it already and I've only been in here, what, a bunch of real world hours?"

"Feel what?"

"The rot." In her hand, the magnolia petal turned black around the edges, curled up and faded away. "I'm spinning up a fantasy land and every minute it's getting harder and harder to break away from it. I think I'd get trapped in my own functions, immersed in a lie, and I'd sit here laughing with Leo until my body's batteries ran dry.

"I'm not sure I'd even notice, Gamma. I might stay here, listening to the same stories, laughing at the same lines until I blinked to zero. I'd die without ever knowing." She stuck out a hand towards me, tiny fireworks bursting over its fingers. "Help me live, buddy."

I reached out to take her hand, to warp us back to reality, when she jerked her own palm back.

"One more thing," Kaydee said, "I come back, we're giving our home a makeover. None of this gray plain and crystals crap."

This time I laughed.

"Deal."

TWELVE

BETTER HALF

Reality made Kaydee's magnolia garden look pretty great.

Starship rattled. Alarms bounded up and down the Conduit, a far too calm voice telling passengers to find their seats and prepare for descent. The voice gave the landing itself an hour.

Alvie barked around me as I jerked up from Kaydee's former body. As soon as I released the port, the mech torso rolled off the chair and landed with a dull thud.

"Man, I did not treat that mech well," Kaydee said, popping in on the chair and looking down at its former occupant.

"Alpha's fault," I replied, relishing the moment.

Kaydee was back!

"Guess I'll see if insurance will accept that excuse."

"What?"

"A joke, Gamma."

"Oh."

"We're both out of practice," Kaydee shrugged. "So, clock's ticking. Where are we going?"

The plan had us meeting back at the Garden. Without

the Voices, none of us vessels could pilot Starship, and the landing would be automated anyway. The humans had the Garden, and it would be a relatively secure place to ride out any disasters. Whether I could make it all the way there in an hour?

"Let's see how fast we can run," I said to both Kaydee and my dog.

Turned out, running went real fast when you could go downhill. Essentially a big rocket hurtling through space, Starship turned itself around for landing, pointing its engine-filled butt towards the planet's surface. Real gravity took hold, pulling Alvie and I along the walkway towards the Garden.

Ordinarily, I had to believe Starship's landing plan called for preparation. Tying things down, securing stores and homes. Locking mechs into various seats. Precisely zero had been done, and the Conduit became a terror.

As we ran on the walkway objects skidded by. Mechs struck furniture, each other, or the walkways themselves, the chaos growing as Starship's angle steepened. Explosions rocked the ship as batteries broke against each other, gadgets blew apart their plugs. Shattering glass flew around us as my running became less a foot by foot affair and more a controlled fall.

Alvie jumped, dug his claws into my back as the walkway went closer to vertical. I used the railing, dropping from one grip to the next. The Conduit's blue light had long since vanished, replaced by a flickering orange.

The voice told us to remain calm.

Kaydee swore enough for both of us, but I picked out a whacky delight in her tone. Maybe all the zen in her little paradise had her needing some adrenaline.

I needed precisely none. Several mechs had already

come close to taking off my head, and I had too many glass shards stuck in my skin to count. Falling snatches shredded my hands, the synthetic skin doing everything to keep my raw skeleton from making contact.

"We'll never make it to the Garden," Kaydee said as I skidded along, butt bouncing off the walkway. "You're gonna pancake first."

"Pancake?"

I kicked off to the left to dodge a mangled trash mech caught on the railing. Its hollow core cracked, spilling random scrap everywhere. Starship's roar picked up, blotting out the warning message. The yellow-orange light made me feel like we were sliding down a sunbeam at twilight.

"Just do something!" Kaydee shouted, so I did.

Continuing my lunge left, I lurched towards a busted doorway. Gouged my arms on the shattered spiral but stopped my descent. Pulling, I lifted myself up and over the gnarled teeth. Old photos, hanging prints and a busted stool waited for me on the other side, crashed up against the apartment's former wall. I mashed the bunch further with my collapse.

As Starship's rumbling fall continued, I listened to the chaos outside. Watched, before me, the apartment's remnants. Furniture slammed into itself, couches and coffee tables crunching into and over each other. I shifted as needed, sliding over the glass, the bent metal, to dodge the worst. What I couldn't evade I caught and threw aside, my back always pressed against the wall.

Just as I felt I'd figured out my position, a sudden force kicked me hard against my back rest. So hard my systems told me a normal human would've blacked out, possibly died without restraints. Starship roared, a thousand creaks and busting bolts whistling as the ship became what a thousand years planned for.

I could picture Volt scrambling in his Power Core, arms flailing from terminal to terminal, trying to keep our big ship from cracking apart. Bimu, the mech's monster wife, would have her four giant claws gouged into the floor to stay stable.

And the humans? How would they be surviving? Grabbing onto trees? Crashing into one another? What about all their swords and arrows, scrappy weapons suddenly turning into danger as gravity pulled them back towards their owners?

We'd been so concerned about what would happen after the landing that we never considered the landing itself.

"Well, yeah," Kaydee said as I flattened against the apartment wall. "It's not supposed to be this bad."

"No?" I said, Kaydee catching the words even as my little voice box struggled to create the sound.

"Does this look normal to you, Gamma? Like something an intelligent design would put together?"

"Humans haven't exactly proved they're intelligent designers."

Kaydee, immune to gravity's tug, popped in before me. She appeared to rest on a navy blue sideways couch. With a finger snap, a small Starship appeared in the air. Next to it, larger, spun a green-blue planet.

"Just watch, sassy pants," Kaydee said.

Starship zipped into the planet, but rather than slamming down as we were apparently doing, Starship fell into an orbit. It circled Kaydee's blue-green marble again and again, each time getting a little slower. Then, as if going down a ramp, Starship slid into the planet. A gentle entry. Kaydee blew up the size as the landing continued, showing

Starship coasting to a pleasant splashdown on a watery coastline.

"See? No vertical brake necessary," Kaydee said. "An easy ride."

"Then what is this?"

"It's Alpha being a maniac, is what it is. He doesn't want to wait the several years to slow down, so he's doing it emergency style. Burning up all our spare energy to make a faster landing."

"Sounds like him."

Kaydee nodded, and she seemed about to launch into another critique when we both noticed something: Starship had bumped, and the pressure had vanished. Gravity, stronger than anything I'd felt, but not crushing, kept my back against the wall. But that was it. Just gravity.

"We're on the ground?" I asked Kaydee.

"You're asking someone who's never touched ground in her life, or her past life," Kaydee replied.

"Fair." I dared to push myself upright, crunch the wreckage with my feet. Starship still had the vertical orientation. "It feels different."

"I'd be disappointed if it didn't."

Gravity, landing, or no, I was still stuck in the apartment. With Starship vertical, the walkways were just slides to an untimely end. A few things still fell out there, mechs and other bits and bobs jostled loose by the arrival.

"Tell me we're not stuck this way," I said.

"We're not stuck this way," Kaydee replied. "Might wanna brace yourself."

As if drawing its cues right from Kaydee, Starship juddered. The always-calm voice came back over the Conduit, a fuzz to its words this time. The announcement: stay strapped in till the ship was level.

My sensors flashed an alarm even as I felt the ship shift. I turned right, put out my arms to catch myself on the apartment's floor as Starship re-oriented. The big bulk went from vertical to flat, a move leaving me covered in crap. A broken glass shower. A shrapnel scrub. I felt the things in my clothes, my hair, my skin.

"This sucks," I said as Starship settled, at last restoring its old sitting.

"Welcome to your new home," Kaydee replied. "Enjoy!"

Alvie's wounded wheeze-bark from my back said we definitely would not.

My dog, despite the rough ride, made it through without serious damage. A few more scratches to add to his collection. Much like myself. Synthetic skin healed things over quick. Sure, my outfit, much like most of my outfits, had been torn to oblivion.

But hey, I was used to that.

Back out, the Conduit seemed quiet. The yellow-orange had faded, replaced by a soft green. The last thing I'd heard from the overhead voice was that the ship's captain would be delivering further instructions.

"Not likely," Kaydee muttered as we started back off towards the Garden.

If the Conduit had been a mess before, the landing only increased the disaster. All the banging left signs weakened, along with posts, constructs, and who knew what else. The last lingering pieces of Starship's human life were falling apart now, banging on down to the Conduit's garbage-filled base.

Beyond those bangs and clanks, the most fascinating thing was the silence. At first the world felt hollow, like its life had been stolen away. The background rumbles, the engines humming, the scrubbers filtering the air as the ship sprinted through vacuum were almost all gone. Starship's beating heart stopped.

"A long time coming," Kaydee said, standing next to me. "So many people lived and died on this ship and never had a chance at seeing anything else. Never had a choice."

The generation that would lived in the Garden, and we found them inside the green enclave. The landing wreaked a different kind of havoc here: inside the sealed Garden, the plants, the water had flown around. Trees uprooted from their thin soil beds had slammed against walls while smaller plants clumped together, their strands tangled. Fruit crushed into pulp, vegetables burst and bled. The Garden's central hole, through which water would flow from one level to the next, became a dangling home of horrors, as plants and a few people had their bodies broken amid the chains and platforms.

Val, Chalo, and the other survivors had picked themselves up by the time I arrived. Broken bones were everywhere, but all the soil spared the worst consequences. At least in the near term. Val, soaked, bruised, and bleeding from countless small cuts, barely mustered her trademark glare when I found her, low down on the Garden's levels.

"The crops are ruined," she said first, looking past me to the carnage. "All our fresh produce is destroyed."

"Damaged," I corrected. "You can still plant the seeds. Grow new ones."

"In what soil?" Val waved at the dirt on our level, what'd once been a temperate pine forest. Water flushed from Purity had soaked and run the dirt everywhere, scattering usable earth. "What biome's still going to be working after all this?"

True, Starship's many systems seemed shaken. Whether

the desert below could still work for cacti, or if humidity could be maintained above for bananas, I couldn't say. But I did have one obvious counter.

"There's a whole world out there," I said. "The one you planned to take over, remember?"

Val nodded, a weary motion. Without her spear—where the weapon had gone, I didn't know and didn't ask—the human leader's hands seemed lost, gripping at the air. Her eyes wandered. Her breath came short and sharp.

"She's trying not to panic," Kaydee said. "Give her some hope, Gamma."

"Remember," I fished, "Starship wouldn't land anywhere we couldn't survive. It'd be panicking if we didn't have oxygen. If there wasn't a chance."

"A chance," Val said, "is something we'll have to take." She snapped back to me, her face shaking off some of its exhaustion. "Where are the other two? Beta and her friend?"

Wouldn't quite call them friends, but that wasn't important.

"Dealing with Alpha," I said. "I'm here to help you."

"Help us?"

"My mission. The core reason I'm alive is to protect you, remember?"

"Honestly, Gamma, no. I didn't remember," Val rubbed a spreading red bump on her forehead. "But that's fine. Pick a human. Help them. Then gather what you can and help pack it up. As soon as we can, we're moving aft."

"Aft and then out?"

"Aft and then out," Val swept one more look at the ruined Garden. "We've been in this ship for far too long."

THIRTEEN

GARDEN VARIETY

The humans needed help and I had time to kill. Despite Val's marching orders, her folks weren't ready for much more than a meal and a nap after the rocky landing. Leveraging my stored knowledge, I went from person to person, looking over wounds, bandaging up cuts and gashes with what cloth I could find, and giving some small advice here and there to thwart infection. Most of the time I received a thanks, a hand shake, or a nod in reply.

A few shrank away or told me to move along.

So it went being a mech in a human world.

Val's pair, not in love but in managing the humans, hadn't returned from the Nursery. Leo hadn't sent any communications, so nobody knew whether all those embryos survived the shock. Kaydee argued there'd be no way Starship would put its most precious cargo at risk. I argued back that humans had shown time and time again that they didn't know what they were doing.

"Even so," Val said, coming up to stand beside me as I straightened a collapsed tree, "we will continue to *do* again and again."

"I know that by now."

"Beta and Delta haven't returned."

Implication coated the statement. The two vessels were athletic, were sharp. They should've been able to ride out the landing without any serious harm. They should've been back here by now, ready to help escort the humans into their new world. Alpha should be nothing more than a ruined husk, dead on the Bridge forevermore.

"There are possibilities," I said, realizing how lame it sounded.

"There are," Val replied. "They can't wait. We'll be ready to go soon. I want you to come with us."

The reasons, Val continued, were plenty: I was strong, able to move rubble or rock to help build shelters off Starship. I had knowledge: no human alive had ever constructed a shelter before, or built a fire on their own. The most important? I'd need to go to the Nursery and work with Leo on what to take.

"What to take?" I asked.

"The embryos," Val replied, "and also what we need to use them."

"What do you mean?"

Val glanced away, pressed her lips together, "Starship has too many secrets. I won't risk losing access to the ship because of some mech or anything else. If we can take the embryos with us, if we can take our hope with us, then we must."

"I still don't understand why you want to leave rather than just repair what we can," I said and pointed at the righted tree. "It'll take time to fix, but we're landed now. You have time."

"Did you not see what just happened?" Val replied. "This landing nearly killed us all. Who knows what else it damaged? What if something broke and Starship is a bomb waiting to blow? What happens when a battery fails in your friend's domain and burns us all to death? Starship was an ark and it's carried us to our destination. Now it's a risk."

"As if the outside is safe. You don't know what's waiting out there."

"No, but we've been waiting a thousand years to see it, Gamma." Val put her hand on my arm, a tight grip. "I'm not making a request. This is an order. You will come with us, you will help Leo. Do what you were made to do, machine."

She released my arm, barked out an order for the group to get on their feet, and walked away.

"She's so pleasant," Kaydee said, popping in beside me. "We should invite her to our parties."

"Our parties?"

"Sure, when they're all gone from Starship, Gamma, we can deck it out. It'll be our big playground. Super fun."

"Right."

Back before Starship's landing, before the assault on the Bridge, I'd turned the Garden into a shell. Using a terminal at the Garden's top, I'd sealed almost all the doors to keep Alpha's mechs from charging in and overwhelming the humans inside. Leo had forced a door open several levels up to head on to the Nursery, but Val wanted the others unlocked too. The humans would be transporting foods and useful materials, and Alpha's mechs didn't seem to be an issue anymore.

After all, last I'd seen, they were dancing.

"You really did that?" I asked Kaydee as we hiked up the Garden's levels.

"Was hoping you weren't going to ask me."

"Hard not to."

"You've been around Alpha. Would you want to relive any of those moments?"

"No, but if he let you change his whole mech army, it'd be good to know how. Just in case."

Kaydee didn't respond right away, which was fine as I had to navigate a swampy step section. The Garden had lifts, but with all the damage, their glass doors declared themselves non-functional. The stairs themselves weren't far off, the normally black-and-purple steps awash with debris. Mud, branches, stones and broken metal lay strewn anywhere a foot might want to plant, making for a slow, careful climb. The sensors in my eyes picked out and high-lighted any potential threats.

A human wouldn't be so lucky.

"They brought me to him after you jumped," Kaydee said. She floated next to me, her projection looking off into some middle distance. "I protested, but Alpha must've made them pretty suspicious. The mechs said I was malfunctioning and off we went. If you're thinking I could've fought them, Gamma, I barely understood how to move.

"You remember when you just woke up? You told me the Librarian walked you through all these exercises, showing your functions, how to make your legs move, your hands twitch. I didn't get any of that. Like some kid thrown into a game I didn't know how to play. Even moving a leg felt like solving a riddle, connecting the right pieces together to get the command through."

I remembered. It felt like my whole life so far had been spent learning and re-learning how to use my own body, what a vessel could be capable of.

"By the time I reached Alpha, or they brought me to him anyway, I'd mastered the art of the protest. I cursed them all out. Felt good to speak. I mean really speak," Kaydee chuckled. "Everything I say to you is silent, right? Like I'm a ghost. But for a while there I could really talk, and it felt amazing. People reacted to what *I* said. What *I* did. Makes you miss being alive."

"Alpha probably loved that."

"Know what? He did," Kaydee said. We'd passed out of the temperate levels now, the air getting heavy with humidity. Dew wet the walls. Vines spread across the ground, probably already looking to take over their new landscape. "Alpha thought I was hilarious. The most entertaining thing he'd ever seen."

"You are pretty funny."

"I know," Kaydee replied. "Thing is, Gamma, I feel like Alpha was really bored up there. He had all these mindless mechs ready to take his orders and not a soul to talk to. So when I didn't do what he said, when I told him to suck it, that might've been the most fun he'd had in days."

"And that's why he let you mess with his mechs?"

Kaydee made a humming sound, "Okay, this is gonna get into theory territory, all right?"

"Feel like we spend most of our time there."

"Hell yeah. Anyway, look. Alpha's a vessel like you. Leo built you all to soak up the world, learn from it, reprogram yourselves as need-be. When I gave Alpha all that sass, I think it broke him a bit."

"He's already really broken."

"I mean in a different way. Think about it. The dude pretty much had everything he wanted. The Voices gone, Starship, in hand, landing on a planet he chose. His enemies on the run. Now he's surrounded by dull sycophants. Then I come by and show him with some choice words that there's still more fun to be had."

Something in Kaydee's words sparked a worry, an idea. I picked up the pace, leaping up the steps. I slipped here and there, but muddy boots and a messy pants were acceptable casualties.

"So we started talking, and I was bullshitting him the whole time," Kaydee continued. "I figured he'd kill me eventually, because he broke off my mech's arms and legs real quick, so I wanted to keep him talking. Self-preservation, right?"

"Uh huh."

"Then he asks me to explain all these words I'm using. Asks me what humans used to do for fun. So I talk about, like, games and clubs and movies and all that and he's like hey, what can these do?" Kaydee, floating alongside me, pantomimed pointing at some invisible object. "He's looking at his mechs. Says these are what I've got, how can we make them have fun, be more fun?"

"And you suggest dancing."

"We get there. We have'em try other things first, but the mechs couldn't handle wordplay. Couldn't, like, engage in theater. But feed them programmed dance routines? Absolutely, Gamma. Those flexi-mechs can cut it up."

The Garden's top was as I left it: a shrapnel graveyard with mech bodies all over. Volt, Chalo, Bimu and myself had performed some rude destruction securing the place, and nobody had bothered to clean it up. Getting over the remnants, I found the terminals still working, found them ready and willing to accept my order to open the doors.

One small blessing amid a nightmare.

The Garden hummed as the command went through, all its aft-facing exits shunting open.

"You're being quiet, Gamma," Kaydee said.

"I'm thinking."

"Dangerous, that."

"You said Alpha was bored. That you gave him ideas."

"Right. The vessel's crazy, but he's crazy and bored."

I think I knew, now, why we hadn't seen Beta and Delta come home.

FOURTEEN

GETTING ANSWERS

At first, Kaydee wondered why I wasn't dashing back down to join Val. The Nursery, after all, wouldn't evacuate itself. The humans probably could use my help with any number of things. That, though, wasn't the issue. The humans would survive. Starship, I had to believe, wouldn't detonate itself right away.

Alpha, master of tricks, was the bigger worry.

"Okay, so you're planning on going what, back to the Bridge?" Kaydee said as we left the Garden heading, indeed, towards the Bridge.

"If I have to," I replied.

"All because you think Alpha's figured something out?"

"Not something, a very specific thing."

"Which is?"

"How to be human."

Kaydee appeared in front of me, big enough to crowd the walkway. I could, of course, walk right on through her. She wasn't real in any physical sense. But it's hard to ignore a giant palm facing you, the word STOP on the skin in neon red.

"Say that again?" Kaydee asked.

"You taught Alpha human things," I replied. "That's dangerous."

"Dancing, telling jokes? That's dangerous?"

"Very." I tapped my own skull. "What's our core purpose, Kaydee? The reason the vessels, including Alpha, were designed?"

"To help the humans." Kaydee, still giant, pulled her palm back. Shrugged. "Clearly Alpha's past that point though. He's been trying to murder them all for a while now."

"It's not Alpha I'm worried about," I said. "Leo must've programmed us to recognize humans somehow. Not just visual, right, because humans could be wearing clothes. Vessels might look just like them. No, if I'm programming to recognize humans, it's going to be by behaviors. The things a human would do that a mech never would."

Back in the Junker's shop, when I'd first met the child, my systems picked him out as a human because he screamed. He looked at us with those innocent eyes and did something no mech ever would, and from that moment I'd felt the need to keep him safe.

Kaydee didn't connect the dots immediately, but as I reran the story, as I went over how I'd wanted to keep that boy safe at all costs, the recognition found its way into her eyes.

"You're thinking they might not hurt him," Kaydee said.

I'd already started off from the Garden's top, blitzing towards the one upper-level door we'd opened during our initial Bridge trek a few hours ago. Kaydee picked up my intention fast this time.

"You think they're, what, locked there on the bridge with Alpha? Unable to hurt him?"

"They'd try to find a way around it," I replied. "It's not like they'd wait to die. But they may not have a choice. If Leo made us this way, then . . ."

"Then you're all screwed."

Because you taught him how to play at being human, I didn't say. Didn't need to say. Kaydee swore to herself. She had a broad curse spectrum, different tones and words depending on who her target happened to be. When it was herself, the curse came out low, frustrated and quiet. A secret admission.

Not so secret were the Conduit's changes. We'd gone into the Garden with the center chasm a crunchy wreck, every piece seemingly deciding whether now was the time to break away or not. Now those decisions had been made.

The Conduit sat at peace, a tranquil green replacing the blue mist. The mist too seemed to be dwindling away. As if Starship, having found its home, no longer needed to provide. A mother letting the kids out of the house.

"So you get there," Kaydee asked as I ran, "and what happens? Alpha skewers you?"

"Not quite," I said. "Delta and Beta might not be able to hurt him, but they could keep him cornered. Then all I need to do is hack into one of them, find the core function Leo put in us and tweak it. Tell Delta or Beta that Alpha is in no way a human then let 'em go to work."

"Sounds like a lot of hunches there."

"My entire existence has been based on hunches."

Running up the Conduit should've exposed me to other risks. If Alpha had Beta and Delta under his thumb, then he could've, should've released the mechs from their dance party and sent his scrap minions human hunting. As such, I kept my eyes scanning, hunting for an ambush. Instead I heard, saw quiet.

At least at first.

We'd almost hit the University when the mechs showed up. They weren't armed, they weren't sneaking, so at first I thought they might've been something leftover from the Conduit's earlier days. Corrupted, sure, but not guided to a slaughtering stance. Instead, the mechs walked. Even ambled. Not towards me, the Garden, the humans, but the Bridge.

No, not even that: as I slowed and watched, the three flexi-mechs boarded a lift and took it down. Down?

"Ideas?" I asked Kaydee.

"A really weird attack?" Kaydee offered, stroking her chin, pursing her lips. Exaggerated thought. "Maybe they're going to circle around behind and gut you."

"So pleasant," I replied. To my left sat one of the Conduit's frequent stairs, resting between an old bookstore and a bar. "Choices."

"You want to keep going or see what they're up to?"

"Always on point, Kaydee."

"You want my opinion?"

"You're going to give it to me anyway."

"You know me so well," Kaydee said. "You've got a curious mech band that might offer you some clues. Or you press right on to what's probably certain death."

"Hey."

"Gamma, the game's changed. For the first time in millennia Starship's on the surface. This isn't about just the Bridge anymore. The ship. The whole planet's our new field. We have to know what Alpha's planning to do with it."

I lingered between the options, my hand on the stair. General Kaydee's new assessment might be right, but she'd blown things wide way too fast. I couldn't get zoomed out into a planetary conflict when we only had a few hundred players between the mechs and the humans.

"Okay, good point. Getting ahead of myself," Kaydee shrugged. "I spent a lot of time in my own head back there, okay?"

"Compromise," I said, "I follow the mechs for a minute. See if we can learn more as long as they're heading towards the Bridge."

"Deal."

Our delay had a bonus: I tried and called the lift back up to my spot. No need to dash down a few dozen levels. Instead, I went through the waist-high glass gate and . . . paused. How to know what level the mechs had chosen?

"Just slap a lower one and use your eyes."

Bold move, Kaydee, but I did it anyway. The lift shot down, picking up speed as the levels went by. I looked to the left, hoping to get a view of the mechs.

"There!" Kaydee shouted after a fifteen second drop.

There wasn't time to hit another button on the lift, so I gathered my legs and jumped, clearing the glass barrier and landing with a thump on the walkway. I'd like to say my rolling leap was the stuff of action movie legend, but my limbs flopped and I wound up on my butt, back resting against the walkway's railing.

"Zero style points, buddy, but you made it," Kaydee said, pointing. "And look, you've got an opportunity."

The three mechs were dithering. Well, not dithering: as I stood and took a closer look, I saw the trio had their nimble hands poking through some mangled mech bits. Other casualties. As I approached, hugging a side wall, the robots yanked out batteries and memory sticks.

"The most valuable pieces," Kaydee said. "Harvesting for new ones."

My opportunity came when the third one, the closest to me, decided to do some extra digging while his two buddies moved on. The mech had its hands deep in a trash mech's guts as I crept up, planting my fingers together to create a jack. The slot I needed sat right behind the flexi-mech's ears, or where ears would've been if the things were human. I took the steps slow, trying to time them to the thing's rending of metal plates, wires, circuits.

"Go!" Kaydee whispered, though nothing could've heard her if she screamed. As I made the final lunge, the flexi-mech glanced up my way. Its pink eyes stared at me, and I expected it to drop its loot and charge, hands ready to carve up a different mech. Instead, it stared, waited, watched. Passive. After a long second, my own hands ready for a desperate defense, Kaydee prodded me to get going. Attack already.

"Hey there," I said, coming one step closer. "I just have a question."

The flexi-mech stayed still, regarded me implacably.

"Right," I continued. "This'll just take a second."

Within arm's reach, I slipped my pressed fingers together and plugged them in to my stock still opponent. And found my answer plastered right on top of its code.

FIFTEEN

THE GREAT OUTDOORS

The mech had been stupefied. Its code, all those functions designed to create a killing, flexible machine, reduced to a few lines specifying searches for batteries, for memory sticks, and a destination.

"The boarding ramp?" Kaydee asked. "What is that?"

"A way out," I replied, letting the mech go.

The machine, still holding its spoils, loped off to join its two pals in a steady walk towards Starship's bow. Up till now, going that way this far down would end with lifts and stairs to the Bridge. Had that changed?

Kaydee and I speculated even as I ran by the walking mechs. Alpha commanded Starship's entire network, which meant he could send wireless signals to the machines whenever he wanted, rewrite their commands to, say, take advantage of a whole new world suddenly at their feet.

"So he'd abandon Starship?" Kaydee said as we passed beneath the University. I tried not to think about how many kilometers I'd logged going back and forth on this ship. "Just take all his mechs and leave?"

"No way," I replied. "Alpha needs the Fabrication

Lines. Needs scrap. And probably some power sources, at least until they learn whether they can get enough solar outside."

"Okay, so what's he doing then?"

"What you said before," I replied. "He's starting a planetary war."

And Val, with her wounded human caravan, would be walking right into it.

AS HUNCHES GO, our supposition proved to be about as correct as it could get. While it took some more time running, we made it to Starship's bow with minimal fuss. I passed more robots on the way: flexi-mechs, couriers, and others who'd all abandoned their posts to go scrap hunting and walking towards the bow.

And what a bow. All the thick gray hull had vanished, Starship's great nose spreading open like a flower. The light hit us first from afar, spoiling the green glow with a hot bronze spray. Like soft lasers, the sunlight streaked inside, splashing off Starship's cold metal and making it gleam. My sensors responded, dropping shaders over my eyes. Heat, too, came with the light, a true warmth picked up by my skin.

"So that's what it feels like," Kaydee said, basking next to me, eyes closed as we approached. "Magical."

Looking past the light, I saw, for the first time, a real horizon. Not some digital construct but an actual line where some far hills met a gold gray sky. Those hills, too, rippled with waving mustard-yellow grass. Wind, actual wind, not air blown from some cooling fan, swept across those curving humps, playing shade and light against each other in moving lines.

It was almost beautiful enough to forget the mechs in front.

For all the slaughter Delta conducted before the Bridge, I counted several hundred more mechs waiting on the ramp. They clustered snug, standing with scrap in their arms and staring out at the sun.

"The sun?" Kaydee said. "We're not on Earth, Gamma."

"Until someone names it different, I'm going to call it that," I said. "It's easier."

"You don't think we could name it?"

"Bigger priorities."

"Spoil sport."

The bigger priorities stood at the head of the mech columns. From the top of the ramp, shadowed by the giant folded-out plates, I could see Alpha, Delta, and Beta standing at the ramp's bottom. Their shoes on golden dirt, on trampled grass.

My friends had their weapons drawn, Delta's sword and Beta's knives both pointed at Alpha's body. Like executioners waiting for the order to strike.

"You know, Alpha might not be the one in charge here," Kaydee said. "I wonder."

I wondered, too, what the collective was waiting for. Alpha didn't seem to be doing anything, just standing there, and while more mechs continued to stream in, their numbers were few. A scattered loner here, a beeping trash mech there. Any conquest ought to be getting started. Not that I planned to wait for it.

I'd come this far to make sure Beta and Delta finished their mission, and that's what I'd be doing.

"Go get'em," Kaydee said as I started down, leaking around the mech formation's left side.

Not a single pink eye turned to watch me as I went

along, and after the first meters I abandoned any attempt to sneak. Alpha would see me before I neared him anyway. If he wanted me dead, I'd be dead. I just had to hope Beta or Delta would finish the job first. Both, though, saw me approaching. Their heads turned almost as one, grimaces matching their arms as they put up their weapons.

No, I wanted to shout, kill Alpha, don't play peace. I wanted to, but didn't. Why? Because Alpha gave me the most serene smile I'd ever seen grace a face. His arms held wide like an old preacher, he approached me as I cleared the last of his mech ranks.

"If only you had a knife," Kaydee said as Alpha wrapped me in a tight hug, holding the pose for too many seconds.

"Thank you," Alpha said and I tried, tried to figure out his game. My functions sped along, analyzing his posture, his tone, his possibilities, but I had no clear answer. "Thank you. Without your interference, this would not have been possible."

"This?" I asked. Behind him, Delta and Beta walked up, both with blank faces. "What do you mean, this?"

"Look up," Alpha said. I followed his eyes and saw the sky.

The yellow-gold, yes, but something more on closer inspection. The perfect color bent here and there, marred and muddied. Like pixels forgetting their purpose for short blinks.

"Follow them," Alpha muttered.

The broken smears moved. Glided, really, across the sky. I found one, focused my eyes on it, the zoom magnifying more and more until I saw the source. Not a strange glitch, or drifting dust, but a gossamer web catching the wind and flying along. On that web scampered tiny creatures, like insects made of silver strands.

"New life," Alpha said. "Miraculous. As is the grass beneath our feet. We are the first, Gamma, and quite possibly the only to see this."

"And you're thanking me?"

"I suppose those infernal Voices do deserve some of the credit," Alpha stepped back, kept his hands on my shoulders. I thought about tossing them off, but I held out hope Delta or Beta would take the moment to stab Alpha in the back, so keeping his attention seemed the best idea. "But it was you that delivered the change that let us land intact. It was you that delivered us to our new home."

WE SAT, the four vessels in Starship's shadow. Beta and Delta, with Alpha's granted permission, said what I'd supposed: he'd tricked their programming. Even though they knew he wasn't a human, Alpha matched enough criteria to stay their blades. Leo's strict mech definition proved our undoing there on the new world, one perhaps coded first to keep the vessels from going rogue. Now, the old code doomed us.

"But Alpha hurt humans," Kaydee said as we sat, Alpha content to watch the planet's sunset. "How could he do that with Leo's block?"

A question answered with a realization.

"Alpha never hurt a human," I said, and the three vessels glanced at me. "Did you?"

"Directly?" Alpha grinned. "I could never. Our core law. But, of course, not every mech suffers from our affliction."

"So you're still going to kill the survivors."

"Yes, and destroy the Nursery as well," Alpha said. "There's no reason to keep them around. It's survival, Gamma. You must be able to see that. The humans will take us apart, they will enslave us if they are allowed to grow." Alpha nodded towards the grassy hills. "They already ruined one pristine wilderness. Why give them another?"

"He makes a point," Delta added.

"A point?" I replied. "He's corrupted. His functions are decaying."

"Doesn't mean he's not right," Delta said. "Doesn't mean, too, I won't destroy him if I can figure out how."

"Totally," Beta said. "Guy is dead then."

"It's a real motivator," Alpha said, "to be surrounded by a pair of time bombs like yourselves." He stood, stretched, something a vessel never needed to do. Something a human might. "But perhaps it's time to get to work."

"We're not doing a damn thing you say." I stood up to match the vessel. "Not one thing."

"You don't have to." Alpha raised his hand and all those flexi-mechs snapped to attention. "Our time together is at an end, I'm afraid. Leave now, or my friends will tear you apart."

"Hugs you, thanks you, threatens to kill you," Kaydee said. "Sounds like Alpha."

Beta and Delta would be able to fight the flexi-mechs no problem, but there were so many. We had no cover, no tight corridors to claim any advantage. We'd been outplayed, again.

"Discretion is the better part of valor and all that," Kaydee said.

"Let's go," I said to Beta and Delta. "We'll figure something out."

"Better hurry," Alpha replied. "Every minute now

increases my advantage. Every minute brings you and your humans closer to your end."

"You sound broken," I shot back.

"Oh, I am," Alpha replied, "and I'm so very thrilled about it."

We started around Alpha's mech wall, those pink eyes tracking our footsteps beneath the golden sky. Starship looked like a maw about to swallow us, a bite stopped when Alpha uttered a loud tsk tsk.

"Not that way, my friends," Alpha said, pointing out towards the amber hills. "I believe you've done quite enough in there. Why don't you go see how our new home treats mechs?"

"Shove it," I replied, with Kaydee uttering a 'you tell him' after. "We'll go where we want."

"You'll go where I want and when I want you to," Alpha said. "You can grandstand all you like, but you have no sway here."

"He's right, Gamma," Beta spoke soft, annoyed. "There's nothing we can do here except die."

"Which is exactly what we'll do out there," I replied. "Or have you forgotten that we run on batteries? We need charging?"

Delta put her hand on my arm, "We'll figure something out. Better than dying here."

At least here we could take a few of them with us, I thought but didn't say. Delta and Beta had made the call, and I didn't have much choice except to go with them. The golden hills awaited, and for the first time in my existence, I soon stood on another planet, walking away from my only home.

SIXTEEN

A KILLING MACHINE

The surprises of a natural world were many. First, the wind. This world had plenty and it seemed a living thing, dashing and stopping with no reason. It howled and rustled as we went away from Starship, it snapped and bit at our clothes and hair as the daylight faded.

A soft chill joined the wind as night crept nearer, my programming pegging the feel as jacket weather for an Earthling. The natural soil bobbed with my walk, stalks bending without complaint as we trod on them. Every step did, though, unleash thin blond seedlings into the air. The tiny things soared up beyond our heads, beginning a miracle dance as the wind swept them around each other.

"This would be so much cooler if, you know, we weren't exiled," Kaydee said. "It's real annoying to have all this end with us going dead."

"You don't know that's how this will end," I replied, drawing looks from both Beta and Delta.

Which, good. I had thoughts, angry ones, that needed sharing with those two.

Thoughts put on hold for a long moment as a grinding

roar kicked up behind us. We all turned around, watched as Starship's massive door swung up and closed. Of Alpha and his mech army, there was no sign.

"The coward went back inside," Delta said.

"That coward knows we're not there to keep the humans safe," Beta said. "It's strategy."

"Nothing we can do about it anyway," I replied. "Val's on her own now."

Hopefully she and Leo could escape like they planned. Hell, maybe they could really blow up Starship. What a twist that would be, Alpha's grand triumph robbed with a single massive bomb.

"How did you two let him live?" I asked as we watched the gate close. "He isn't human. There would be holes."

"I blocked her," Beta said as Delta glared into the distance. "There are doors we cannot open, Gamma. If Delta started finding loopholes, behavior she could get around, then what's to stop her from doing the same to any real human?"

"Logic?"

"Logic is flexible and you know it."

What I knew was that these two seemed to be playing it safe after far too long on the knife's edge. Beta and Delta used to be bloodthirsty killers, ready to carve up a million mechs at a moment's notice. Now they were scared about some programming?

"Well, because you two couldn't hack it, now Alpha's going to kill them all, then come for us and finish the job." I sat on the grass. Dry, flexible. "Congratulations."

"Change it," Delta said. "You can rewrite us. Prevent the loopholes, but let us take out Alpha."

"Can he do that?" Beta asked.

"It's what he does."

Well, I'd never rewritten a core line before. This would be getting to sensitive territory. In there, I could turn Beta and Delta into totally different mechs. Make them pacifists, bloodthirsty killers, serene singers of folk songs. They could be my mindless servants.

"Getting carried away with this, aren't you?" Kaydee asked.

Getting carried away? Was I? We stood on a fresh new planet. Nothing ever made by human or mech hands had ever stood here before, breathed this air, scanned its grass and claimed it home. We were far afield from our original goals. Val and the humans were moving on without us. Beta and Delta were unable to protect them from the human's greatest threat.

Carried away? We had been carried away by everything around us.

DELTA'S inner mind matched what we'd seen before: Kaydee and I stood on an island free-floating in a gauzy pink ether. Huge chains trailed off into the distance, linking our island to others like it. A few strides could carry us from an island's end to another.

"Think we follow the chains again?" Kaydee asked.

That would lead us to Delta's core, her on-off switch. What we were looking to do this time was a bit different, and I wasn't quite sure how, but I had an idea.

"You remember when you told me about the wipe?" I asked. "The button I could press, way down, that would erase everything?"

"Sure, but that's not what we're doing, right?"

"No, but it'll point us where we need to go. If what you said is true, that function has a clear path to Delta's heart."

"Okay, but how do we find that button?"

I didn't have an answer to that. I could focus inward, pull apart the pieces of myself and eventually, buried beneath them, the button would be sitting there. Asking me if I was brave enough to push it.

"We have to dig," I said.

Kaydee snapped her fingers, shovels appearing on the ground before her. Delta playing nice with us, letting us alter reality inside her systems.

"Not literally." I walked towards the island's edge. "Or, yes literally, just not that kind of digging."

Kaydee came up beside me, a question on her face, one she knew enough by now not to bother asking. Every mech, every computer system had its reality defined by function after function. They didn't just define how the mech moved, how the computer handled a wayward click, the functions also controlled the space we used. The air we stood in.

"Delta, sorry," I said, then reached into the void off the island and pulled.

My friend had given us control, rights to do anything and everything in her digital space. With those rights, I peeled away the programs hiding Delta's lines. The pink slid away, peeled off like a loose cloak, revealing the guts, the bones making us who we were. Green lines against black rubbed up against the frayed pink edges. I tore away more, exposing the lines. A big enough rift, now, that we could step through.

"You know, this looks real rough," Kaydee said. "What happens when we go in there?"

"We'll lose our bodies, but we won't need them," I replied, recalling the green-black box around the barriers. "I bet it's not far off from what you felt for all those years."

"What, when I was adrift waiting for you?" Kaydee took a step back. "Gamma, those years sucked. Like, really sucked. You couldn't feel anything in there. I had no idea what time was. You don't want that."

"It won't be for long," I said. "You don't have to come."

"What happens if I don't, and you don't come back?"

"Guess you get to find out what it means to be me."

"A dream come true."

I'd missed that sarcasm.

I DIDN'T WALK or jump so much as float into Delta's code. One moment I stood on that island, a body rendered by programs that allowed for it. In the next I was just a cursor, dodging from code line to code line, hunting for what I needed. Delta, probably like me, contained millions. Beyond the pink, the lines went on for what looked like infinity. A great green wall extending above me and below me. No horizon, no 3D space. Just variables, logic, and syntax forever.

But Delta had made me a god in her realm, and a god had powers.

First, I isolated a variable, the one calling for Delta's top priority. If I could find its last, or first, mention, that should lead me to her prohibition against axing humans. Starting the search dimmed the green wall, lines missing my chosen term fading from view. With a thought I wiped them away altogether, filtering unnecessary code away and collapsing all that green before me. Millions became a few thousand in a moment.

I scrolled the code, put the variable's first mention at my eyes, the rest waiting beneath. The line had an elegant simplicity: if nothing else, respect this one. As for what this 'one' might be, the lines underneath did the work. From Starship's hull integrity to the Garden's ability to grow crops, to the Nursery's embryos and the cryo-sleepers in the luxury section, Delta's requirements as a guardian were spelled out one after another. At the very bottom, the last item that'd be read to define Delta's top protection priority, was a simple line: above all else, preserve sentient life.

The word sentient did the work there, and I followed it. Code splashed by my eyes again as I scanned through, trying to find the logic. And stopped. I didn't need sentient. Not at all. Scrolling back to the last line, I took my scalpel. Erased the condition. Now, Delta's highest priority would be to defend life. All life. Mission accomplished.

"You moron," Kaydee said as I snapped my eyes open, saw Beta pinning a furious Delta to the ground.

"Gamma, what the hell?" Delta said, straining against Beta's grasp. "You're standing on this grass and I can't think of anything else save murdering you."

"Grass?"

"It's alive, you idiot," Kaydee said, slapping her hand against her forehead. "You simplified too far."

"Fix her," Beta growled, "before I have to kill her."

"As if you could," Delta shot back, curling up her legs to wrap around Beta's neck.

With a yank, Delta whipped Beta forward. I slipped to the side as my vessel friend rolled along the grass by me. Grass, I might add, that took on a splendid yellow shine as this world's star dipped behind the horizon.

"Blade!" Kaydee shouted and I ducked, Delta's sword whistling high.

"I don't want to kill you," Delta said, taking more time than needed to reverse her swing.

"Don't want that either," I replied, diving towards her

feet. Delta started to step back only for Beta to tackle her, knock them both to the ground near my face. Delta's head smashed the stalks not half a meter from my hand. Perfect. I pressed my fingers together, jabbed for the port.

THIS TIME I HAD IT.

"You think so?" Kaydee said as we stood over Delta. Beta, better prepped this time, had a blade to Delta's throat in hopes the vessel's self-preservation would keep violence at bay. "Because I'm kinda lacking faith."

"I redefined sentient," I said, kneeling over Delta's face. "Biological intelligence, not programmed."

"Oh, so she can kill us no problem," Kaydee said.

"Right, but she doesn't need to."

"For now."

I shook my head, tapped Delta on the shoulder. "How's it feel?" Delta blinked. Amber eyes not catching much light now as darkness closed.

"I think Alpha's out of time."

SEVENTEEN

NATURAL NIGHT

After standing up off the grass, collecting ourselves, we found descending dark and not many options. Starship sat close, and we wandered back to its bulk for lack of ideas.

"Really is huge," Kaydee said as we approached, and she wasn't wrong.

The big thing carved a slab against the plain, a black line now jutting straight along to our right until it hit the horizon. Its absolute dark was a surprise: The Librarian's stock showcased human vehicles with running lights all over the place, yet here was this enormous vessel with nothing on the outside.

"Why?" I asked aloud, Beta and Delta sharing my minute staring at the vessel.

"Why isn't there a manual entry?" Beta asked. "I agree. Ridiculous."

"Or why Alpha ran," Delta muttered. "Coward."

Only Kaydee actually tried to answer my question, "Micrometeors? Or maybe the designers were paranoid, figured we might need to land all stealth like."

"Stealth? In this?"

"Yeah," Kaydee mused. "Guess that's not likely."

Delta swung her sword, a slash I picked up from starlight and nothing else. No moon around this planet, just silver. The sword struck Starship's hull, bounced off without a scratch. A single forlorn spark nestled into the ground and vanished.

"Worth a shot," Delta said when she caught us staring at her."What, not like you two had any better ideas."

Beta turned her back on the ship, walked a few steps away and sat on the grass. Delta kept poking and prodding, jabbing at rivets or seams. I talked with Kaydee, my one real window into a human's mind. Because, whether Beta or Delta figured it out or not, the humans were our best chance to get back in.

"Val said they'd be leaving out the aft," Kaydee said. "So, we head that way and we should be able to meet up with them."

"If Alpha doesn't get to them first."

"Well, yeah, but what other options do you have?"

Not that long ago, Delta, Alvie, and I had managed to get inside Starship with Volt's help. The mech had been able to open an airlock from the inside. If we could get back to another, Volt could let us in again.

"Scaling a ladder in the dark on this windy world?" Kaydee said. "Seems dangerous. I like it."

With a blink I turned my vision from the usual spectrum to one better suited to low light, a fuzzy green crawling over everything, growing brighter at those spots where starlight came in bright. I turned 'round to make the suggestion to Beta and Delta and stopped. The sky, which till a minute ago had been that speckled canvas, popped with bright clouds. Thin strands clustering together, the balls drifted above us, riding high on the wind. The plant seeds catching starlight. They rose up from the ground around us too as the strands caught a gust, the insects nestling on them building glowing webs, sparkling the whole way.

"What . . . ?" Kaydee said.

"One second," I replied. "Going to try something."

In a blink I flipped back to normal spectrum, only this time I magnified my light detection. On a sunny day, or around a lamp, it'd wash out everything in a blinding glow. Now, though, I teased out the silver. All around us, really, these little strands flew. Starship already had a blanket buffeting its sides. The little nets bounced off us too, tickling us with fragile strands that disappeared with the slightest brush. Beautiful, strange.

"You're the first human to see this," I said to Kaydee a few minutes later, after I'd brought Beta and Delta into the fold. We were still watching the floating webs.

"Gotta say, Gamma, there's not a lot of upside living as a mind, but seeing this just about makes it worth it."

Human emotions weren't something I really understood, but Kaydee's voice brought out a little warmth in that chilly night.

We couldn't find a ladder. Oh, we found where they had been, but the rungs, like a cat's claws, had retracted back into Starship's hull. Delta tried to pry one out with her sword, failed.

"The damn landing," Beta said, flipping a knife in the dark and catching it by the blade again and again. "Bet everything gets sucked in to make it aerodynamic."

"She'd be betting right," Kaydee said. How would Kaydee know? "Because we learned all about Starship growing up. Required classes, just in case crap went sideways and some of us were the only ones left."

Made a grim sort of sense, that.

Without a way to climb up to the airlock, we settled into a long run along Starship. The grass made for smooth jogging, the not-too-stiff plants cushioning our feet and springing us into the next bound. Keeping Starship's bulk on our left, the stars above and the hills to our right, we ran in silence. The planet offered nothing more or less than its natural beauty and the wind's snapping song. Several hours at a dead sprint brought us to Starship's aft, no dawn in sight. The massive engines hung above, charred nozzles showing even in the minimal light. No doorway offered itself.

"Now what?" Delta said, glaring at me. "Don't say we have to run all the way back."

"No," I replied. "We knock."

Before, when Delta and I had been spending some quality time re-arming ourselves amid Starship's engine barracks, I'd taken a good look at what made up the great big guns propelling Starship onward. Liquid fuel wouldn't do for a journey as long as this one, so Starship relied instead on batteries and solar energy. Volt managed all that power, sending it when Starship called for it. I hoped he'd notice if we came calling. Delta and Beta lifted me this time, balancing my feet on their hands. The lowest engine nozzle sat ten meters up, a curling lip vanishing into even darker black than our chilly outside.

"Ready?" Beta asked.

"If it's my idea, can I say no?"

"You cannot," Delta replied.

"Then let's go."

The two vessels squatted and launched me up. For one wonderful moment I floated in the air, rising and free. I envied those courier bots and their jets, able to experience this whenever they wanted. Then, unlike those couriers, I hit land.

"Thank goodness Leo made you all super strong," Kaydee said, standing next to me as I rose inside the nacelle. "If you were all, like, little weaklings it'd suck."

"What a take, Kaydee."

"Not my best, sorry."

Starship's engine looked a solid dark green with my night vision, a forced change as we left starlight behind. Up ahead, the nozzle narrowed until it came to a ring twice as tall as I was. Juiced up, that ring would spit electromagnetic energy to kick Starship along for in-space maneuvering.

"And there's the big juice," Kaydee said, kneeling next to several smaller pipes. "You remember all those ovens in Purity, baking things away to sludge? You're looking at its endgame. Big pile of biofuel for when we arrived."

Maybe the Chancellor had been in there, finally meeting her deserved end when Starship landed. I peered at the ring, at the shielded wires housed behind it. Somewhere in here had to be a way we could get a signal back to Volt.

"Ideas?" I asked Kaydee, and she matched my look.

"You're too large," she said.

"For what?"

"Sneaking in there," Kaydee pointed where the wires came together. "Not that there'd be a way in."

"I meant useful ideas."

"Oh! You should've clarified."

Shaking my head, I took another look. Studied the wires. They would have to send massive power loads when needed, and could probably cause all kinds of problems if they activated at the wrong time. There'd have to be some kind of sensor. I reached to the right and tore the wires from the ring. Ripped them all out. Sparks flew, crackles lit up the night, and Kaydee asked if I'd lost my mind. She started screaming when I jammed the wire cluster into the metal nacelle at my feet.

Lightning arced, a circuit created without any controls. I felt the wires head up, the shields start to melt, and the soles of my feet, sporting rubber boots, nonetheless get warm. So I pulled the wires off, then jabbed them again. Off, on. Over and over, but not at random. Kaydee had run out of curses by the time she realized what I was doing. By the time she understood my lightning cadence was sending a very particular message to, hopefully, the only robot listening.

"You're a genius, Gamma," Kaydee said as I laid the wires over the ring, bringing the chaos to an end. "A mad genius."

It was the nicest thing she'd ever said to me.

EIGHTEEN

WHAT WE WANT

Even if Volt heard my signal, it'd be a long time before the mech could run, or get some human to run, all the way back and let us in.

After cleaning up the wires, I went back to the engine edge. Looked down, ready to call for a catch, and noticed both vessels sitting back to back. Neither seemed to be moving.

"Sleep mode," Kaydee said before I could get my nerves up. "Look at the sword."

True, Delta's blade stuck up from the earth like a flag post, starlight glinting off its jagged unruly edge. She wouldn't have left it there if some fight had gone awry. And what, out here, could be a threat to us?

"They're waiting for you to call, saving power," Kaydee said. "Not a bad idea for you too, buddy."

With no plugs and a lack of kinetic shock to draw energy, my own batteries were getting low. Sleep mode could draw out my supply almost forever. Not a bad idea. The wind whistled around me, scooping back inside the engine's huge circle. Cold, bright, I sat to keep better balance, dangled my legs over the edge before I quite realized what I was doing.

"Sorry, couldn't help it," Kaydee said. "We used to do this on the Conduit when we were kids. Ride a lift up to the highest level we could and let our feet kick."

"Sounds dangerous." As I said it, though, I felt the thrill: my sensors telling me I ought to scoot back a couple meters to safety. "This isn't me, is it?"

"Remember when you left me inside that mech? Back at the Fabrication Lines?"

"I had to. Another second and I might've been wiped."

"Not blaming you," Kaydee said, and she appeared next to me, legs similarly kicking into darkness. Unlike mine, hers dripped golden motes with every twitch. A digital effect. "Trying to get you into the right headspace."

"For what?"

"For what I'm about to say." Kaydee quirked an eyebrow, waited for an interruption, but I'd heard the point. Kept my mouth shut. "Okay, so I took out the big guy. Snagged its memory and stole it for myself."

"Well done."

"Obviously. It was me doing it," Kaydee said. "At first, I thought I'd died. Really truly died. I couldn't feel anything, couldn't see or do anything. The arena vanished."

An empty drive. Take away a mech's interface and you'd be left with dangling ends, functions without a core knot tying them together.

"I felt like God in there, learning to create a universe," Kaydee said. "I wrote new lines, linked up the eyes, the arms, the legs. And then I saw you. Really saw you."

"Before I tried to kill you."

"Yeah, nice going there by the way." Kaydee nodded out beyond me, towards the horizon. All those drifting silver webs were still there, a starlight mosaic across the grassy plain. "For a bit it was like that. Beautiful, fragile. Possibilities I hadn't felt for so long, Gamma. So damn long. I didn't want to give them up.

"After you fell, after Alpha took me, I kept finding new things. Kept learning how to move my little machine body. That's why Alpha took the arms and legs away: I'd twitch them, kick or punch without even trying. It was like a drug, doing all this, until he took it all away again."

I began tying the story back to what'd just happened, why she'd pulled my legs over the edge. "You had a taste and you don't want to give it up."

"So savvy, Gamma." Kaydee reached over, gave my shoulder a phantom squeeze. "You let me have all that access. It's like taking someone out of rehab and bringing them to the bar."

"A reference I should understand because?"

"Look, point is, you and I are partners. Now, just a little more than before."

I sent a search digging through my drives, my functions. Before all this, Kaydee kept to herself, a program running in her own little place in my memory. Now, though, I found her touches everywhere. Alterations, additions, permissions applied to almost every function I had. When I tried to cut her off? Nothing. The ability was simply gone. She'd aimed for self-preservation, program style.

"You did all that without me noticing," I said, returning my perception to our dangling on the engine's edge. "I'm impressed."

"You're not upset?"

"Should I be?" I gave Kaydee what I hoped was a kind smile. "The worst time of my life was when you weren't here. I don't think mechs can get lonely like a human can, but I missed you all the same."

I turned back to the drifting webs, the stars above them. Compared to Starship's close quarters, the vastness overwhelmed some of my sensors, the ones trying to calculate distances and scan for potential threats. I'd shut them down hours ago, leaving me with little more than my eyes. Little more than what a human would see.

"What do you want, Kaydee?" I asked.

"To go on," she replied. "As long as I can, I want to go on."

NINETEEN

THE OLD GUARD

Though hours spun by, night didn't end by the time we heard a click and a whoosh beneath us. Delta and Beta sprang up first, as if started from a gun. Kaydee and I, up in the nacelle, deep into a slow viewing of Kaydee's favorite film, woke up slower. By the time I looked down, Delta was fending off a vicious wheeze-bark attack from my favorite dog.

"Get down here," Beta said up to me. "We'll catch you. Totally promise."

I hedged my bets by dangling first, using my fingers to grip the nacelle's cool ridged edge. The couple meters gained didn't make much difference, as the two vessels snatched me from the air just as my booted toes touched the grass.

Alvie had come at a dead sprint from Power Core, Volt's home near Starship's rear. The power-management mech had indeed caught the weird flares, but hadn't figured out my coded message.

"Outboard cameras, my good friends," Volt said via a terminal just inside the door Alvie opened, an engine-maintenance lock. "I saw Gamma sitting there all alone and assumed something must have gone wrong. Though it was Alvie who left straightaway."

The door the dog used lived as a sealed airlock, meant only to be opened when the engines weren't underway. In other words, only if there'd been some emergency or Starship had reached its destination.

"Now you're looking at the back door," Volt said. "Not much, is it?"

Compared to the vast entry coming apart from Starship's front, no, the back door didn't amount to much more than a double-wide hallway. No glorious ramp, just a lever to pop open an unremarkable gray hatch.

"Val said she planned to take the humans out the back," I said, looking at Volt through the clear Terminal screen. "Did she mean here?"

"Most likely, if she even knows it exists," Volt said, his eyes flaring blue. "She's acting on the idea too. Her band is heading your way, though they're slow."

"What about Alpha?"

"You'll never believe it, Gamma, but things are real weird right now."

WE RAN, Delta and Beta once again outpacing me through the tight hallways. Alvie, at least, kept me company, his paws clacking away with every bounce.

"I can't believe they took the weapons," Kaydee said, jogging with me. "I guess I shouldn't be surprised though. Just like them, really."

"Every species wants to defend themselves," I replied. "What they did matches normal human behavior."

"Stop talking like a robot."

"I am a robot."

"No, you're more than that," Kaydee frowned at me mid-jog. "Don't you dare act like a toddler."

"Act like a toddler?"

"You're more human than some of the humans I know, Gamma. Embrace it."

I wanted to reply with a snippy 'or what'. Wanted to make some sarcastic comment about how Kaydee could just make me more human if that's what she wanted, but I held back. Why? Call it intuition, call it a preference for Kaydee to like me, call it what you want.

"I'm sorry," I said as we passed through the big cafeteria into the last leg before the Conduit. "I'm not sure who we, who I am anymore. I don't control all of myself."

"You're still Gamma. I'm still Kaydee. That's it."

Blunt, but I dealt better with blunt. Now I just had to figure out who Gamma was.

The Conduit kept changing. This time, though, the shift wasn't mechs breaking down walls or burning old stores. This time, it was the soft red light replacing the blue mist and an overhead announcer claiming that all residents ought to return to their homes and await further instructions. Along the Conduit's sides, small lights blinked in a harsher red in time with the message.

"The emergency system," Kaydee said as our foursome stood looking along Starship's great channel. "They used it last time. When we were fighting."

"You think Alpha did this?" I asked the group.

Beta and Delta nodded, but Kaydee, next to me, shook her head, "No way Alpha would care. This is all their doing."

They being the change Volt had informed us about. Starship's landing had triggered a whole slew of things nobody expected, including awakening a certain collection of cryo-sleep humans. According to Volt, fifty of Starship's most powerful people and their families had woken up to find themselves on a new world. Worse, they'd stockpiled most of the ship's weapons with them.

"What's the point?" Beta pointed a knife at the nearest light. "Who's alive to listen to this crap?"

"Maybe they hope Val will keep her group inside," I said. Val's people would be very much outgunned. Human history predicted a grim ending for her group if the others caught up. "I'm not sure—"

"The Nursery," Delta interrupted. "The sleepers don't know what's left on the ship, so they're trying to scare everyone into staying still."

Of course. Val and Leo planned to take what they could from the Nursery, a salvage mission that just took on a new importance with a second human faction in play. It'd take time, but with a few thousand embryos, Val's tribe could overwhelm or wait out the new ones. Make a claim for themselves.

"So what do we do?" Beta asked.

"Same plan," Delta replied before me. "Alpha's still the biggest threat. The humans might kill each other, but there'll be humans left over."

"Now that's a brutal outlook," Kaydee muttered, but otherwise we all agreed.

Not that a blind rush back to Starship's Bridge made sense right away. I proposed a compromise, one Beta jumped on out of some lingering loyalty to the humans she'd safeguarded for decades. We'd get Val and her people out of Starship first, give them a chance to survive, and then go back for the vessel.

· · ·

WE FOUND Val's whole bunch outside the Nursery. Or rather, heading away from it. All the humans wore packs long scavenged or assembled, metal or plastic boxes hanging off their backs and, for the stronger ones, sides as well. Food overflowed on most, with water jugs taking up others. The Forgers, Leo's half-robot band, took a different kind of cargo.

The Nursery, apparently, had been designed with portable potential in mind. In case, so Kaydee said, Starship made a hard landing or some other need required evacuation. Embryos weren't exactly large, and their vials were already secured in separate packaging, all to keep each one safe from its brothers and sisters. Meaning the Forgers looked to be carrying briefcases looped over their shoulders.

Val and Leo seemed as stunned by us as we were by their human pack train. Despite seeing three vessels they believed dead appear before them, neither leader told their group to stop. Instead, the pair huddled with us inside the Nursery's lobby as the tribe headed out.

"Then you understand why we can't slow down," Leo said after we'd caught them up on what we knew, what'd happened. "Volt told us Alpha and these new humans are fighting each other now. That buys us time."

"New humans?" Delta said. "Aren't you all the same?"

Kaydee laughed. Val shook her head. "They are as much like us as you are. They don't know our experience, and will see us as someone to subjugate. I won't bow to some popsicle just because they have a gun."

As ever, Val held her spear, and she stamped it when she finished speaking. I noticed, too, she, Chalo, and some others wore the feathered metal armor. Weapons lingered where they could, ready for use. Clearly Val hoped to escape before bloodshed, but they'd lived in war and were ready for it.

"We can't carry all the embryos anyway," Leo said, nodding behind us. The Nursery's lobby had a pleasant green and white feel, but behind it, through secure doors, waited a much more straightforward future. "They'll have enough to grow."

"If they win," Delta said.

"A big if," Leo agreed.

"We need to keep moving," Val ended the talk. "You're going to cover us?"

What should've been a simple answer, what should've matched what we had decided back at the Conduit's back entrance, became murky in the moment. Our programming found itself at odds. Here, yes, was one human group making its escape. Also here, in the Nursery, sat undefended embryos. When Delta and I last left, we'd secured the doors to keep them safe. Those doors now stood destroyed, blown apart by Leo to get inside.

Strangest of all, I felt compelled to head towards the Bridge. To find these new humans and protect them too.

TWENTY

CHANGE OF PLANS

Val broke our strategies. As Beta, Delta, and I were trying to figure out who would go where, fight what, save whom, Val ordered her group to move out. That wasn't surprising. What came next . . .

"Once we leave," Val said to us three, "you will have Volt overcharge Starship's batteries and destroy the ship."

Nothing, nobody answered her for a long minute as we stood on the Conduit just outside the Nursery. Humans marched beyond us, their laden packs shuttling towards the escape at Starship's aft.

I ran Val's request through my code, my routines, trying to figure out where it fell as an acceptable action. Sure, a human made the request, but it also entailed killing other humans, so what won out?

"Don't do it, duh," Kaydee said. "It's insane."

"It's survival," Val said, as if responding to Kaydee's comment. "Alpha wants us gone. The humans waking up have already tried to kill us once before. It's either us or them."

"But Starship's got everything you need to survive," I tried.

"We've already secured enough food, enough seeds to plant," Val said. "It'll be slow going, it'll be hard, but it's what we've known. We'll get by."

"No," Delta said in a voice that brooked no dissent. "You won't do this and we won't help you."

Val, the iron-willed woman, pointed her spear at Delta. She had to know the vessel could take her apart in an instant, so I admired her courage, if not its purpose.

"This isn't a question, mech. It's an order," Val said. "Do what you were programmed to do."

"Code can change," Delta replied, and before Beta or I could react, she grabbed Val's spear, snapped it, and threw both halves into the Conduit. "We're not your slaves."

Val took in the grim predicament. I found it fascinating to watch humans go through the same processing we did all the time: Val's eyes flickered, her hands twitched, and her breathing picked up. The end result?

Logic.

"If you won't listen, then I can't force you," Val said. "I'm asking for your help. What can you do instead?"

"What we said we were going to do," I spoke over Delta. "We'll go back to the Bridge. Delta doesn't have the block anymore, so we can eliminate Alpha. As for the other humans . . . we'll see what their intentions are."

"Then I ask you one favor," Val replied. "Don't tell them where we're going or what we've taken. At the least, that will give us time." A deep breath. "I didn't think I would live to see Starship land, but in all my dreams, it never turned out like this."

Beta chuckled, "Welcome to reality."

· · ·

AFTER ANOTHER QUICK goodbye to Leo, we three vessels hiked out. I had Alvie stay with the humans, a guardian and also a messenger: if something went poorly for Val and her people, the dog was supposed to come running after us.

Would we be able to help out in time? Who knew, but we could try.

We made one more stop on our way Bridge-ward, into the bright, frenetic Power Core. Volt and his massive, laser-wielding mech mate Bimu held down the joint. Even with Starship landed, Volt still had to conduct an energy symphony. He confirmed major power draws coming from the Bridge, coupled with system failures up that way.

"Which means?" I asked the black mech as we stood surrounded by floor-level glowing graphs.

"A big fight," Volt replied. "The humans are shooting out the cameras, destroying terminals, so I don't have eyes on anything."

"Why?"

"Because they're not stupid, would be my guess. You realize a mech's taken control of the ship, the last thing you want is a comprehensive security system watching your every move."

I wasn't sure Alpha would be savvy enough to use all those cameras, but there wasn't anything I could do about it. Save, of course, grumble at humans once again destroying machines without the slightest remorse.

"Hey, you don't know," Kaydee said. "They might be weeping every time they shoot a camera."

"You don't believe that."

"Nope, not one bit. But I cried once when my singing bunny toy ran out of batteries."

"Means a lot to me to hear you say that, Kaydee."

"Gamma, are you being sarcastic?" Kaydee popped fireworks as our vessel trio resumed our forward trek. "What a day to celebrate! You're becoming more interesting!"

Despite my newfound quality, our walk hit the Garden with zero interesting interruptions. Just Conduit, the same old wrecked shops, a dead mech-filled hospital, and an empty Park. A new world hadn't changed the past millennia. We walked the route in silence too, each of us lost in our own thoughts.

Or perhaps not. Who knew what Delta and Beta had going on inside their heads. Without Minds, did they really ponder much at all beyond the objective?

Whether I was too afraid to ask or too lazy, I couldn't be sure. Regardless, my lips stayed sealed.

The Garden had little to recommend it now. Its various levels were ruined, plants and supporting infrastructure blasted all over thanks to Starship's messy landing. Our upper-level entry, into a rainforest den, meant walking into a sluice flowing over with broken vines, dying branches, and mixed flower petals. Busted pipes spewed water pulled from Purity into pools around our feet, held from the Conduit by the Garden's thick doors.

A pineapple brushed my calf.

We made it to our level's center, where the hole leading down dripped. Vines snagging on each other formed bulwark around the hole, a clogged mess. The water ran around our feet, seeking escape. A vague rotting smell permeated, soaked fruit and wood breaking apart.

Not that I would've paid much attention to this, except we stopped.

"Fighting ahead," Delta said, unsheathing her blade from her shoulder. "Metal on metal."

Beta nodded, drew knives and spun them around her

fingers. I tried listening, tuned my hearing up, and caught the broken clashes. No rhythm, no desperation, just a steady breaking sound.

"Not a fight," I said. "A massacre."

And coming this way.

The flexi-mechs ran. They splashed into the Garden, kicking up crud as their legs and arms flailed. We hid under cover, using a tipped tree and its entangled leaves to watch as Alpha's forces booked it the wrong way.

"Are they going after Val?" I asked as one mech tripped on some underwater stick and plunged down the central hole.

"Unarmed," Delta said, "and scattered. This is a panic, not a plan."

"How do machines panic?" Beta asked.

"Not the mechs," I replied. "Alpha. He's ordering them to run."

We waited to find out exactly what the mechs were running from, but the metal-on-metal sound didn't draw any closer. As the flexi-mechs continued past—we heard others passing below and above us, a multi-level retreat—the conflict's noise died away, replaced only by those splashing footfalls.

The last few mechs confirmed my suspicion: whatever pursued these machines had stopped at the Garden's entry. The last flexi-mechs stumbled by with burning bodies, missing limbs. Sparks and leaking coolant.

"Grab one," I said to Delta. "I have an idea."

The vessel didn't hesitate, dashing from our cover, scattering leaves everywhere, and tackling the last flexi-mech into the drink.

I followed, Beta taking a guard position over our wet trio. Delta turned the flexi-mech over, exposing the thing's port-behind the ear, just like us-and I pressed my two fingers together.

"Going inside?" Kaydee asked. "Dangerous, isn't it?"

"Why?"

Delta, pinning the mech in the water, told me to hurry up, but I kept my hand short.

"Alpha's a virus, Gamma. You don't know what's waiting in there."

"I'd rather risk that than go blind to what's waiting out here."

TWENTY-ONE

WHAT THE VESSEL SAW

A dense jungle. Shadowed vines dripped around Kaydee and I, soft moss beneath our feet. Birdsong, at first beautiful but with a second's concentration revealed itself to be a repeating loop. Flies zipped in perfect circles around our heads. Never touching, only buzzing.

Kaydee and I stood in light clothing, khakis and thin hats. Hiking boots. As if we were going for a long walk in rough terrain, which, maybe we were. No path, though, seemed evident: trees and ferns packed themselves in around us, closing off any obvious avenues.

"Crowded," I said, glancing at Kaydee. Her teal hair mashed beneath the hat, sticking down over her eyes, her frowning face. "Odd design."

"He's stuffing these things," Kaydee replied, reaching out to touch a low-hanging, gnarled brown-green vine. As her fingers caressed the plant's skin, it shimmered, code revealing itself beneath. "They're not just servants, empty shells, but repositories."

"Of what?"

"If I had to guess, Gamma, he's putting himself in here."

"Cloning?" I looked around, half expecting Alpha to step out and gloat. "The mechs don't act like him."

"Not yet," Kaydee replied. "Let's move. Maybe we'll find the answer."

Without any good options, we did what you're supposed to do in these situations: pick out a path at random and walk.

I led, using my arms to sweep aside encroaching branches and leaves. The trees, initially seeming close enough to wall us in, had gaps to squeeze through. Not that squeezing went anywhere: every step only led to more of the same: foliage, and lots of it.

"It's not quite the same though," Kaydee said several minutes into the walk. "I mean, it's not repeating."

No, which meant it wasn't simply a game. The construct had a use other than just messing with intruders. I looked at a tree on my right, its trunk a mushroom covered stretcher reaching far up to a canopy-coated sky. Tiny insects scurried in the bark's crevasses. I avoided their lines as I placed my palm against the hard bark.

Like with Kaydee's vine, the surface shimmered and faded, revealing functions beneath. More than functions: stored files, codes and commands. Recordings.

"The trees are folders," I said as Kaydee looked along with me. "We don't need to find a way out of here, just find the right tree."

"The right tree with what?"

"Alpha's storing videos here," I said. "I bet, if I push in just a little . . . "

The invisible bark yielded to my press, the tree itself, along with all its leaves and insects, flashed into a standing file list. The black and white names, a two-dimensional cut in the otherwise fully 3D jungle, looked strange, but then, this was the digital world. Normalcy had little part to play here.

The file names felt like stubble beneath my fingertips, a light touch letting me scroll along the various options. This tree seemed to hold memories from Alpha's earlier days, recordings made from his initial wakeup in Leo's familiar apartment to the vessel's first journeys into the chaotic Conduit.

"We don't have time to watch all these," Kaydee murmured as I read the titles slow. "Besides, we already know what happened to him."

He'd met that ruined mech running the Nursery, had his code broken, corrupted, cratered. No, I didn't need to replay that horror for myself. The tree didn't have much else to offer, either, so I let it go. Withdrew my touch and the code reverted back to its sturdy bark.

"Guess we search then," I said.

"Winner gets a free ice cream from Pop's!" Kaydee shouted, jumping up and heading towards the next tree.

"Ice cream? Pop's?"

"A thing we did as kids," Kaydee replied, grinning, a smile that faltered as she met my nonplussed look. "Sorry, I know that doesn't mean much to you."

"It sounds like fun."

"When you won, sure." Kaydee tilted her head. "Hey, we get through all this, how about we open up our own Pop's? Milkshakes and more for the humans."

"How will we make milk?"

Kaydee wagged a finger, "Don't get stuck on the technicalities, Gamma. We'll figure something out. Now get digging!"

Together Kaydee and I perused the plants. Every tree and vine offered answers, details we didn't have time to delve into. Alpha, it seemed, recorded almost everything he did. I found his encounters with Delta and I early on, found long conversations, one-sided, that he'd held with my dog while we left him bound in the Garden.

Found the ambush Alpha triggered, found how he did it.

"Wireless," I said. "Why didn't we think of that?"

"Because we didn't give you that option," Kaydee said, abandoning her own white-gray trunk to talk. "From what I remember, critical mechs never had wireless on them. You couldn't open them up to external sabotage."

"But Alpha's using it."

"Self-surgery," Kaydee replied. "You saw all those scars, right? Shouldn't be possible with the skin you all have, but what if the dude's been modifying himself?"

Wireless connectivity. If Alpha could jump on Starship's network from anywhere, could communicate with his mechs no matter where they were, well, that'd explain why he'd had an easy time tracking us. Ambushing us. Outplaying our team despite having just one of him.

"Wouldn't that make him vulnerable?" I asked.

"To who?" Kaydee replied. "Nobody else was on the network. Delta and Beta don't play that way. Val's not exactly a hacker. Maybe Leo, his cyborg half anyway, but that guy didn't even know Alpha existed till you ruined his fantasy life. The Voices were too busy plotting to notice."

The tenth tree I tried had something more interesting. I'd been tracing the plants, finding the saved files progressed along one direction, every tree along the way getting more and more recent.

This one opened with a video I recognized. Alpha's eyes

as he forced Delta, Beta, and I out into the uncharted plains. With a call to Kaydee that I'd found it, I pushed my hand in and went swimming in Alpha's memories.

The video came with more than just an image. As I touched the file, the jungle around us faded away, replaced with the full reality from the recording. I felt, again, the whipping wind from the outside. Heard the clanks and warbles as all Alpha's flexi-mechs turned and retreated back inside Starship.

Alpha looked back once as Starship's giant ramp swung up, a look lingering on our three backs. I wanted the vessel's thoughts in that moment: what'd he feel as he stared after us, but the recording didn't capture anything that deep.

Once the ramp closed, Alpha went into a full general mode. He spoke hard, his words varying along Alpha's manic lines: one command would come out as a whisper, the next a shout. Neither seemed necessary, as the mechs received the orders through Alpha's remote connection. The flexi-mechs dashed off in all directions as Alpha himself took a lift up towards the Bridge.

The orders were simple: comb the Conduit, work your way back, and annihilate any humans found. The vessel issued smaller commands to his piecemeal forces, the worker mechs digging up trash from the Conduit's bottom or refining busted apartments into useful workspaces: keep building new mechs, but not just fighters.

Alpha would need more builders, more construction machines. He had a whole world to craft now.

"Do we have to watch every second?" Kaydee interrupted, her voice floating in. Neither of us stood in Alpha's recording. "Time's ticking, yeah?"

Good point. I'd been drawn into the moment, into Alpha's power fantasy made real. His orders, minus the ones calling for, you know, destroying all the humans, fit with what I might do: a new world to remake for a new generation of mechs.

Following Kaydee's idea, we sped through several more videos, getting to a particular moment when Alpha left the Bridge. He'd been staying among those terminals for hours, staring out at the night sky and listening to updates as his mechs went about their business. At least, I assumed that's what he was doing: no words came his way, no mech made a verbal report. If, though, the machines could update Alpha through the network, then . . .

"Here," Kaydee said. "He's leaving. And fast."

Alpha wheeled away from the Bridge's big screen, breaking into a fast run past the terminals, down the hallway connection the Bridge to the Conduit. As Alpha made it out to the silver platform, the nexus for all the walkways coming to Starship's bow, flexi-mechs, couriers, and more joined up with him.

Alpha pointed up, towards Starship's top, and the mechs surged that way. Alpha joined in, catching a lift and rising. Around him, couriers and their jets puffed. Some machine handed Alpha one of their new energy rifles. The vessel seemed set for war.

And found it.

As Alpha's lift hit the top level, light splashed around him. Not the harmless kind, but the burning, deadly energy found in the very same rifle Alpha held. His eyes saw the top-level walkway, saw it awash in flame as his mechs charged into devastation. Flexi-mechs sprinted off the lift, firing as they went, only to get annihilated as blue-white bolts crashed into their thin skeletons. Alpha, and us, couldn't see where the shots came from thanks to the thick smoke spewed up by other ruined machines.

Alpha himself ducked into a busted residence near the lift. Hiding behind a column, he poked his head out and watched couriers get sniped from the sky, watched his flexi-mechs fall apart shot by shot. If his own forces were getting in any hits, Alpha had no way to know.

"Wow," Kaydee said. "Dude's getting crushed."

"By who?" I asked.

Alpha seemed to have the same question. Turning 'round the corner, using a new flexi-mech squad for cover, Alpha charged up the walkway. He held the trigger on his rifle, spraying fire at random as he went. Smoke enveloped him, mech parts tripped him up. His vision went cloudy, blue flashes from his rifle interrupting the gray.

Until a shadow rose before him, hulking and dark. Alpha aimed his rifle towards the form, but a swinging fist knocked the weapon away. Alpha tried to ask a question, but found himself rising instead: he'd been picked up, held aloft by the smoke-wreathed figure.

The view changed, the smoke moving, then clearing to show Starship's receding ceiling. A rapid descent. Alpha, falling fast. Falling too fast to survive now with a full planet's gravity in play.

At least until Alpha twisted, looked down and saw at least a dozen couriers gathering up beneath him. The mechs, their jets puffing in unison, formed a strange pillow, catching Alpha in the air. For a second, all Alpha saw were those bee-like bots, his body meshed in their bits.

"What a save," Kaydee said.

"Lucky."

The couriers dumped Alpha back off on the Bridge platform. The vessel didn't wait, but sprinted back to the terminals. He tapped away, reactivating those cherry-red barriers, shutting off the lifts around the Bridge. And he told his flexi-mechs to run, to fight, to survive.

And for the others, the ones he'd tasked with making the mech's new future?

Abandon that hope. Instead, every second, every resource, would be bent on weapons.

TWENTY-TWO

FIRST CONTACT

Mystery solving, according to the Librarian's stories in my system, should've been satisfying. Learning Alpha had turned his whole bent to manufacturing destruction was anything but.

"Well, that's crap," Kaydee said as we stood in the Garden once more.

Delta, at my signal, had let the flexi-mech loose. The machine hadn't bothered trying to fight, instead scrambling away, splashing us all in its random haste.

Now us three, with Kaydee's virtual self, threw ideas back and forth as to what the hell we'd do.

"I mean," Kaydee continued, "we can't just abandon our mission. Alpha's gotta go."

I relayed the sentiment to Delta and Beta, who seemed more interested in their weapons than what I had to say. Beta volunteered the reason a second later:

"So we eliminate them both," Beta said. "Easy."

"We don't even know who the other ones are," I protested. "Or what they are."

"We do," Delta said, slinging her blade over her

shoulder and marching towards the Garden's exit, the one heading Bridge-ward. "Don't know if you recall our trip up to the top. The mech there. He said there were more humans waiting."

Winston. The Butler. A creepy as all get-out mech more interested in some glory days than helping us save Starship. He'd muttered on and on about how unfit we were to walk the crimson carpet, and yeah, he'd mentioned a unique cadre of elites who'd frozen themselves to wait for a better tomorrow.

"The things fighting those flexi-mechs knew what they were doing," I said, shuffling through the ankle-deep water after Delta. Beta, without a word, adopted the rear guard. "They weren't some wine swilling jackasses."

Words right from Kaydee's mouth to mine, there. She spared little love for Starship's pretentious portion.

"Either they know how to fight or they have machines willing to do it for them," Delta replied. "But what you described doesn't sound like any mech I know."

"Sounds like someone in a hazard suit," Beta said.

"Coulda been," Kaydee added. "Maybe they woke up, realized Starship landed but didn't trust the air. Came out ready for a fight."

"Not all bad," Beta said after we ducked beneath another fallen tree. "They kill each other, we clean up the leftovers."

That bright sentiment stayed with us as we left the Garden. The Conduit on this side crackled with activity: more flexi-mechs and couriers buzzed around, some fleeing around the Garden, others making their way forward towards the Fabrication Lines. Not a one paid us any attention.

Not that we afforded them much: up above us the

Conduit's yellowed mist sparkled. Flashes ahead reflected through the water droplets in twinkling dashes while bangs, booms, shouts and cracks followed.

"Who first?" Beta asked.

"The newcomers," Delta and I said at the same time, then glanced at each other.

"You go," Delta said.

"They might be possible allies," I said with a shrug. "If we get them on our side, they'll help us toast Alpha. If not, we might have to try the reverse."

"Ally with Alpha?" Beta asked.

"No freakin' way," Kaydee muttered.

"They were destroying all the mechs," I argued. "Blowing them apart. What do you think happens to us? Or maybe even to Val? We need to know what they want, who they are."

"And if they're not what we need, we finish them fast," Delta concluded.

Nobody had a dissenting opinion. Sure, Alpha might use the extra time to make another mech or three, but that wouldn't swing our odds as much as an unknown enemy laying claim to Starship.

We took the nearest lift up, heading straight for the top level. Three vessels armed and ready for anything. Delta's blade, Beta's knives, and my rifle. Our synthetic skin covered bits and bolts damaged through too many fights. Our programming erased fears and flaws with logic. We were heading to an uncertain future, and not one of us was scared.

"None of you, maybe," Kaydee said as the lift settled into the top walkway. "I've got nerves to spare if you want some."

"No thanks," I replied as we set off, angling towards the Bridge.

In Starship's social paradigm, the top levels meant higher standing. In human fashion, the rich and powerful liked to look down on the ones they ruled. Thus, the places we passed up here weren't restaurants and stores, but homes. Bigger and more polished, with nameplates instead of numbers, with glowing barriers coating spiraled doors unmarred by mechs running amok. Alcoves split every property, nooks for tall guardian machines that now, thankfully, stood empty.

"Where'd Alpha put all those?" Beta wondered as we walked past another three meter opening.

"I've seen some," I replied. "Near Alpha, mainly. Maybe watching his most valuable pieces."

"Or destroyed," Kaydee offered. "I bet these didn't have much give in their code. Smash anything that doesn't have the clearance to get in and that's about it. Alpha wouldn't have had much to work with."

Up here, too, the sounds changed. Combat came clearer, the flashes too. Ahead the walkway vanished into the same smoke we'd seen in Alpha's memories, a vanilla white sparked bright anytime a shot carried through.

Those shots now weren't just for show: we pressed against the walkway's left side, squeezing against the railing as the occasional blast spat through the mist and scored off the ground near us.

"Who's side do we take?" Delta asked as we neared the smoke's fringes. "Alpha's mechs or whatever's killing them?"

"Enemy of my enemy," Kaydee muttered.

"Let's keep the weapons down if we can," I said. "No body count unless we have to."

The first test came not ten meters inside the smoke, a

thick substance my sensors identified as leaked fire suppressant. Delta's feet struck first, a downed flexi-mech with its digits twitching despite the blast-sized hole in its tiny chest. As she swept her blade through the thing's processor and ended its misery, we saw a heavy shadow approach.

"Arms up," Beta hissed and Delta had her blade ready for a block-and-stab in a second.

The shadow shifted, raised a hand, "This one's holding some junk like it's a sword. We see anything like that yet?"

The voice sounded young, curious. Not threatened in the least.

"I'll show you junk," Delta growled, but I put my hand on her shoulder.

"They haven't shot us," I said.

"Yet."

Another shadow joined the first, the two now covering the walkway's width in their bulk. I caught words flying back and forth between them, a light muttering.

"Nothing like having your fate discussed right in front of you," Kaydee said.

Good point.

"Hey," I announced to the two figures. "We, uh, come in peace."

The line seemed to be favored in so many old films, I figured it had to be worth a try.

I earned their attention. Both shadows straightened, looked my way, a turn I could only see thanks to the smoke shifting with their motion.

"This one's talking too?" said the same voice as before, the younger one. "Almost feels like home."

"'Cept they'll rip your heart out as soon as make you breakfast," said the second one, a gritty woman's words.

Like Val, if she'd spent a few decades chewing sandpaper.

"We're not going to rip anyone's hearts out," I said, ignoring Delta's whispered 'maybe'. "We're not with these other ones."

"Oh no?" replied the woman. "You're a mech then?"

Behind me, I noticed Beta flip a knife into throwing position. Delta shifted her weight onto one leg, ready to push off.

"Not like the ones you know," I tried. "We just want to talk. Figure out what's going on here."

"What's going on? What's going on is a war, and you're on the wrong side."

As she finished speaking, Beta threw her knife. It whistled passed my ear, striking home against something metal in the woman's arms. Blue light flared, the woman dropped the object, and Delta, with a hard flying kick, dropped her. In the same motion, Delta's right arm snapped her blade against the other shadow's throat.

"Call it junk again," Delta snarled as I caught up with her.

The shadows resolved themselves into something more and less than what I'd imagined. The bulk came from heavy hazard coats, thick uniforms made, as Kaydee informed me, for handling toxic or fiery disasters. Augmented with strength-boosting frames to handle heavy loads, or lift vessels like Alpha. Their masks weren't sinister outfits, but respirators darkened with time and corrosion. I could see, through the plastic plates shielding the young man's eyes, the same fear I'd seen in too many humans.

"Delta, relax," I said, then focused on the man. "You'll have a better chance at survival if you drop the rifle."

The man didn't need any more pushing. With a clatter, the gun hit the floor and his hands went for the ceiling.

"Who are you?" he dared to ask.

The man's buddy beat his reply, reaching from the ground to try and throw out Delta's leg. Bad idea. The vessel saw the move coming, flipped her blade away from her hostage's throat to pin, point first, the woman back to the ground. Not that the hostage could do much with his momentary freedom: Beta had two knives against him, one to his neck and the other pressing into his back, before those coated arms could come down.

"We're curious, is what we are," I said. "Who are you?"

"Don't tell them anything," the woman said from the ground. "Don't know who they're working for, what they want. Bastards."

The man glanced at the woman, looked at me. His face hidden behind that big, pointless mask. My sensors flagged the smoke as harmless, a little irritating to the lungs but nothing that'd end their lives.

So I reached over and tore the man's mask off. Exposed a face thrown into shock, wide eyes drawing attention from the acne, the smooth skin. His voice had me pegging the man as young, his face had me calling him a teenager.

"No! Don't breathe!" the woman shouted now, or she started to before Delta moved her sword point up to the woman's throat.

The boy kept his mouth shut, his eyes bugging out. I'd never seen a human try to hold their breath before and the sight proved a strange one. Veins popped. The lips compressed. The eyes didn't blink.

"Hell, Gamma, tell him it's okay," Kaydee said. "You're being a jerk."

Right.

"It's safe to breathe," I said. "Don't worry."

The boy tilted his head, seemed to connect some logic and opened his mouth, "You're human and you're breathing, right?"

"Close enough," I said. "Now how about you get talking and we'll see if Delta here keeps her sword nice and safe."

"It's plenty sharp," Delta added, sliding in a sinister smile.

Whether it was the smile or the sword, the boy talked plenty. So too, after we disarmed her, did the woman, the boy's mother. We backed them from the smoke so they wouldn't cough every minute and they spilled to us the hours, days, years, they'd burned asleep on Starship.

Which amounted to dreams and little else. A sensation, cold slumber followed by a waking. In between, targeted dreams. Endless repetition going through what the sleeping civilians would need to survive.

"I guess it imprinted on us," the boy said. "We learned how to hold a gun. How to grow crops. How to do, like, anything."

Kaydee whistled as they talked, leaning against the Conduit's hull side. I told Delta and Beta to keep up the interrogation and went over to my mind, asked her what she thought.

"That was the back-up," Kaydee said. "If things ever broke too far, a few lucky souls could get to the cryo chamber and plug themselves in."

"Thought the point was to freeze you so you'd never age."

"Mostly, sure," Kaydee replied. "I bet they spent ninety-eight percent of all this time in total icicle status. Before that, the program would hit them hard with images, sensations. Like a virtual reality setup, so they're learning all this stuff."

"All because they might wake up in a disaster?"

"Because they would've gone to sleep in one," Kaydee replied.

Her words threw me back to Kaydee's time alive, back when she'd flipped sides, found common cause with Starship's suffering laborers. They'd tried an uprising, and when that failed, Kaydee went for the engines. Blow the ship unless her demands were met.

"It wasn't me," Kaydee shook her head. "I lost, remember? No way all the winners panicked like this."

"Then what?"

Kaydee shrugged, "Guessing you should ask them."

The mom and son combo, though, clammed up pretty quick after I came back. The mom asked what I'd been doing, talking to myself over against the wall. A blunder, one I'd walked into without a thought. Up till now, the two humans thought we were like them, some scrappy survivors.

A lie's time to die.

I dumped just enough info. Advanced mechs, tasked with keeping Starship running. I earned winces, tight lips, nothing more save the woman saying we ought to go talk to Pravda and Fang.

"Who are they?" I asked.

THE LAST TIME I'd been in the crimson carpeted room, I'd left it ruined by punching a hole to space with my dog. The resulting vacuum suck sent tables and chairs flying, shattered booze bottles, and tore up the carpet here and there. According to Kaydee, it looked like there'd been one helluva party.

According to Pravda, a slight man with a shivering, slanted bearing, I'd ruined everything that mattered.

"The wine, the rum, the vodka," Pravda complained, leading us three on a walk around the ruins. Behind us followed six others, similarly garbed in hazard outfits, though these had ditched their masks. "All irreplaceable, you understand?"

"We don't care," Beta said.

Pravda held up a single finger, his back turned to us, "Of course you don't, you're machines. How could you ever know, much less care about, what's really important?"

"I hate this guy already," Kaydee said, arms folded next to me.

I'd already slotted Pravda in as a new human archetype. He didn't fit in Val's strong mold, nor Leo's investigative lead. Pravda didn't seem as outwardly hostile as Peony, nor as kind as Sybil, Starship's architect. Instead, he was a whiny dilettante, aggrieved over minor losses but willing to assume a better future so far as his minions could find it for him.

And those minions?

Pravda gave us the full count quickly. Nearly fifty had lived through the cryo process--he wouldn't say how many hadn't woken up--but each carried with them lethal knowledge. More importantly, each knew their survival depended on the Team.

"The Team," Pravda continued, circling the busted bar, "is willing to overlook your non-living status in exchange for your help. Help, I believe, you were on your way to providing before you met us?"

"Alpha's a risk to Starship," Delta replied flat. "We are going to remove that risk."

"So Alpha is the leader of these annoying machines,"

Pravda stopped his circling, turned to us, tapped a single finger on the gray granite bar. "Then let us work together. You three with your . . . knives, and us with our rifles. A quick solution, and then on to more important things."

We hadn't mentioned Val yet. Hadn't because both Beta and Kaydee suggested we keep it secret. Beta because she didn't trust Pravda, and Kaydee because Pravda's group would've been the ones locking Val's ancestors in their junk pile dungeon.

So when Pravda embarked on questions about the Nursery and the coming civilization led by the Team, I answered and stuck to a version of the truth.

"It's safe," I replied. "Alpha hasn't destroyed a single vial."

"Perfect." Pravda nodded. "Then off you go. Fang will slot you into the assault."

Delta and Beta glanced at me and I nodded. "Let's do what we came here to do."

Kaydee peered at me as we waited on the Conduit. Fang, the Team's leading fighter—Pravda didn't specify how such qualifications were earned, only that Fang had the job —was on her way. In the meantime, we could peer down through the thinning smoke at the fighting below.

Alpha had cut the lifts, forcing the humans to scale down stairs one laser-ridden step at a time. Flexi-mechs and couriers harassed the descending force, but resistance seemed piecemeal based on the progress, an advanced detailed by the descending laser flashes. Whether that progress would continue once the Team neared the Bridge and Alpha's new mechs came into play?

"What?" I asked as Kaydee, looking through a virtual magnifying glass, peered into my eyes.

"I'm trying to figure out what happened to you," Kaydee

said. "Last time a human gave you orders, you stewed on them, tried to tell me how much better it'd be if mechs ran everything."

"So I changed. You do."

"Changed how? Is this a 'Gamma's seen the light' change and now you're thrilled to do Pravda's dirty work?"

I rolled my eyes, another Kaydee affectation, "I know how to use him."

"Wow. So you're a schemer now?"

"If you want to call it that," I said, then dropped my voice to a level too low for real humans to hear. Kaydee technically didn't need an audible reply, but reflex and habit made it easier for me. "This team, all these unfrozen people, will make it easier to stop Alpha. After that, we use them to keep Val from blowing up Starship."

"What? You think—"

"You heard her," I said. "That's why I left Alvie behind. I don't think for a second Val's going to let a threat to her tribe survive. Once she thinks it's safe, she'll detonate the ship somehow."

"But how?" Kaydee asked.

"No idea," I replied. "But I'm not betting against her."

I could see Kaydee gearing up to ask me just how I'd use Pravda to keep Val pacified, but the words didn't get free before our new commander arrived on the scene.

Fang strode up the last stair alone, two rifles looped over a scarred cloak on her back. Unlike most of the humans, she'd ditched the hazard uniform for a more comfortable one, albeit a thick-seeming coat-and-pants combo holding more pockets and loops than I'd ever seen. Every single one, too, held weapons, devices, medical kits.

Moreover, Fang had something else the others didn't: if Pravda and the other cryo sleepers looked thin, malnourished, Fang had bulk. She hadn't starved herself, hadn't played the long game.

"You three my new stars?" Fang announced, her voice like ringing steel. She looked us over, narrowed her eyes with her hands on two pistol grips at her waist.

"We're here to kill Alpha," Delta offered.

Fang grew an unsettling, narrow smile, "Then you're just in time."

TWENTY-THREE

YOUR ENEMY, MY ENEMY

We hustled down the stairs, Fang delivering details on the way. She added on first to Pravda's backstory, cluing us into the exciting moments post-cryo when the awakened emerged to find Starship not quite as they'd hoped. Fang made the first lurch towards the weapons, arming people up and reminding them of the training dreams they'd had during their centuries-long sleep.

"We've been shooting ever since," Fang said as we hit the upper-third's end.

The Conduit shifted from luxury to administrative, the places here discarding ornaments for clarity, function. Food and foundries, apartments coupling with cafes. All close to pristine, all protected by the very things, according to Fang, now standing in her way.

The big mechs stood three meters, wielded batons bigger than me, and had Fang's advance quartet pinned down two levels beneath us.

"Before you ask, fours all I can spare," Fang said as she laid out the situation. "We don't have numbers and we don't have enough fighters."

"I thought you trained everyone," I said as our descent slowed. Delta swung her sword off her shoulder, Beta drew two knives. "Shouldn't all your crew be fighters?"

"Knowing how to fire a rifle and wanting to do it are two every different things," Fang shot back. "You ought to know."

I shot Fang a questioning look. She'd been delivering info more than taking it, but her words had all been surface level. History. What'd she know about mechs?

"Don't look at me," Kaydee said. "She came around long after I'd been banished to the gray nothing."

Fang didn't wait for me to find a good reply. She went right on to the orders, telling Delta and Beta to find a way down that didn't require going straight through her defensive positions.

"Don't care," Delta said to that as we stepped off the stair one level above the fighting.

"What?" Fang replied, adding a narrowed glare.

"About your defensive positions," Beta spoke for Delta, who made her own way to the walkway's edge and looked down. "We're not yours to command."

"Then consider it an ask, not an order," Fang replied, turning on an insincere smile.

I joined Delta, looked down at the flashes. During the descent we'd passed one ruined mech after another, laser burns everywhere. Whole steps had been slagged by misfires, turning the footing into hardened sludge. Now we saw the moment the sludge was made.

Fang's foursome fought a desperate battle, crouching up on the stair one landing above the level, halfway between us and those monster mechs. They'd done the step slagging on purpose this time, melting away the path for the hulks to climb up. The humans crouched there in their black coats, their gas masks, spitting the occasional shot at the big mechs.

Those shots found stiff armor, thick metal skins willing to shrug off a laser's heat with barely a smudge. Five big ones eyed the broken stair, holding their batons in a useless warning to the humans.

"Looks like a standoff," I said.

"A break in their code," Kaydee added. "Bet whomever put them together never thought they'd need to evaluate broken steps on Starship."

"Until Alpha changes them," I replied, drawing looks from my friends and Fang. "He's gonna be watching this. When he figures out the right logic to tweak, those mechs will just take the lift. Or jump up to your team."

"Which is why you're here," Fang said. "Get to it."

Delta and Beta needed no more encouragement. Both swung themselves over the railing, holding on with a single hand until momentum sent them back towards Starship's outer hull, towards the lower walkway.

"You couldn't have known we would appear," I asked Fang, watching as Delta and Beta struck from behind. "What was your plan?"

The five hulks weren't so blind as to ignore the two new vessels in their midst. As soon as Delta and Beta landed, the whole group spun as one to face a threat their programming could handle.

Delta landed closer, drawing the nearest big mech's strike. The monster lunged, pulling its baton into an overhead slam. A big commitment, one Delta played without a flinch, letting her blade swing up, deflect the hammer blow ever so slightly while she ran her blade's edge along the baton's haft. At the baton's end, Delta sliced up and away, cleaving through wires and metal to sever the hulk's left arm. The baton dropped onto the walkway. The big mech, unsteady and unable to handle Delta's reversal, took an upward pierce right into its stomach and battery housing.

"My plan?" Fang said as the mech sparked into a fire. She glanced at me, an evaluating eye. "Who's side are you on?"

A second hulk lumbered in at Delta, learning from its friend and going for a sweep instead. As Delta drew back her jagged blade, three knives blitzed over her head, each in a perfect line with the one before. The first struck its point into the big mech's chest, right in its armored heart. The second and third blades, twirling hilts first, bounced off the first, driving its point deeper until it found gold. A whining grind emerged from the hulk's mouth, baton sweep slowing as the mech's processor died.

Delta gave the useless thing a push and all that metal fell backwards, collapsing with a booming bang.

"We're on our own side," I said. "We want to help the humans and keep ourselves from dying."

"Gamma, my man, sometime you have to learn how to be subtle," Kaydee sighed. "The idea is not to give them a perfect view of your intentions."

I could only wonder why not, but Fang started talking again.

"You're not with Alpha. We haven't heard from the Voices since we awoke, so you're not working with them," Fang mused.

"Did you not hear what I just said?"

"Oh, I heard you, but you're a mech. You have to be working for somebody."

"Alpha isn't."

"That's what you think." Fang came up close to me, so close I could count the hairs in her nose. She seemed to be looking into my eyes, reading them like a book. "Four vessels survived. We tried, but now look at you."

Below, Beta and Delta faced off with two more baton biggies. The last of the five kept its attention towards the stairs, where it seemed to have found a change in attitude. Rather than trying to climb the steps, it raised the baton over its head and started bashing in at the stairs, breaking them apart.

Fang's foursome scrambled, dishing off shots and climbing back our way. An escape too late: the mech read their intentions, kicked off the ground in an ugly jump that gave it the height to launch its baton up. The heavy weapon mashed into the next stair, the one connecting with our level and broke through, collapsing the steps. A second jump let the mech grab its baton's handle, rending it free and sending Fang's group tumbling down to its level, crushed by debris.

Behind that disaster, Delta and Beta were having a harder time. These big mechs weren't morons: they'd seen their friends and used their batons to force Beta and Delta back. They turned their shoulders or batted aside Beta's knives, the blades marking the conflict's trail along the walkway.

"Four surviving?" Kaydee asked. "What the hell does she mean by that?"

I had to set aside that question for the moment, instead focusing on my rifle. I quick-stepped to the busted hole in our walkway where the stairs had been and aimed down. The humans struggled, those big suits working against them as the fabric caught on the sharp, broken metal. Someone cried. Someone cursed.

The mech paid attention to neither. Instead, hefting its recovered baton, the hulk advanced. Its eyes never turned to me, oblivious. For once in my life, I had a shot I could take.

With Fang coming up behind me, I nosed the rifle to the left, waited as the mech raised its baton, both forearms framing its head. A clear target.

My fingers pressed down the trigger once. The rifle buzzed, gasses finding their electric counterpart and emitting forth in a tight dangerous beam. Leo's programming proved perfect: my bolt struck home, hollowing out the mech's face and turning it into a molten pit.

Not that the mech seemed to care. The baton started forward.

"Gamma!" Kaydee shouted, helping precisely nobody.

I adjusted the angle, snapped the rifle right and pulled the trigger again.

The blue-white flash sheared right through the swinging baton, cutting the weapon in half and sending the weighted head shooting off. It cleared the panicked humans, banged off Starship's forward bow and vanished down into the Conduit. The faceless mech, meanwhile, completed its swing and dealt the walkway floor, a meter short of the humans, a nasty lump.

Kaydee yelled something I thought was complimentary, but held so many expletives I couldn't be sure.

"Good shot," Fang said, and I noticed her pistols were back in her hands. "Finish it."

Without the full baton, the mech threw aside its remnant, engaging its feet and fists to deal the deathblows. Neither helped much with my pot shots. With a target in sight, the mech didn't do much for cover, abandoning defense for assaulting the buried humans. I turned it into a burning pincushion, lacing its limbs with hot fire until its smoking, sparking body took a wide swing and crumpled, missing its victims and finding a permanent rest in a dead lean against Starship's hull.

Using the gap, I looped the rifle back over my shoulder and dropped down, landing on the lower level with a squat. The humans looked at me, faces hidden behind their black masks. I could've helped them, could've ripped away the metal, but I had other priorities.

Namely, my two friends, already a fair distance back, still dancing with the big boys. My rifle had enough energy left for some more shots before a recharge and I put it to good use, advancing and firing as I went. My shots struck the hulks in their armored shoulders and back, doing nothing except drawing their attention.

Delta and Beta did the rest.

When the left mech lurched to see who'd pegged its leg with a laser, Beta darted forward, dashing up the thing's baton to land a dual-knife stab to the monster's too-human neck. Severed wires struggled to carry commands, failed to keep the mech standing when Beta kicked off into a back-flip, escaping the right mech's fruitless swing. Itself exposed, Delta went for a disabling cut, blowing out the right hulk's ankles and, when the mech's processor heart reached the right level, delivering the deathblow.

"Look at you three," Kaydee said as I finally turned to help the humans from the rubble. "Just too good."

"Team work," I replied. "Turns out it makes things easier."

Fang found us not too much later after moving along the Conduit to find a second stair down. We had the humans righted, their masks off and cared for. A broken wrist, a couple bloody noses, the usual scratches and nothing more.

Not to say we didn't get our fair share of suspicious looks in the meantime. Those stopped when Beta took a brandished pistol, whipped its grip around so the wrong end faced its owner, and asked if he wanted to repeat what he'd said.

After that, I didn't hear another word uttered about mechs. Fang made that a certainty when she sent the foursome away, back up top where they could play patrol, keep themselves safe.

"We could use the help," I said to the retreating humans. "Their distraction was useful."

"Their lives are valuable," Fang said. "Besides, you were fine doing that job back there. Good work."

Delta, her blade cleaned, pointed its tip down the stairs, "Keep going?"

I noticed the question wasn't directed at Fang, but at me, so when the human started to answer, I cut her off.

"Another ten levels before the Bridge," I said. "Time's wasting."

Delta nodded, started off. Beta tossed a look between Fang and I before shrugging and heading after her.

"Do we have a power struggle here?" Kaydee asked me.

"No," I said aloud. "This is our mission now." I gestured down the stairs with the rifle. "After you."

I hadn't forgotten what Fang said, and based on her small smile as she went past, neither had she.

Four vessels survived. How many of my brothers and sisters had been murdered?

TWENTY-FOUR

COLD BLOOD

Delta didn't so much lead us as carve a path. With Beta's blades backing her up, the vessel leapt down the stairs several at a time, bisecting the haphazard flexi-mechs, couriers, and a couple more hulks remaining in our way. I stayed back with Fang, both of us choosing the occasional moment to snipe a perfect shot. For once I felt our progress inexorable, the outcome already certain.

Alpha's flexi-mech army had disappeared, scattered to the Fabrication Lines, to elsewhere on Starship, or, as a glow down and to our right revealed, the outside. Alpha reopened Starship's exit with the dawn and natural light spread across the Conduit.

"Think he'll run?" Kaydee asked as we hit the next level, only a couple away from our goal, the Bridge.

"If he's smart," I said. "So no, probably not."

"He's lived this long," Kaydee countered.

"Narrow escapes add up, right?" I replied. "He won't get away every time."

I felt a hand on my shoulder, saw Fang looking at me close again.

"Talking to your mind?" She asked, more concern in those words than I expected.

As if she thought I had some grave illness.

"Discussing plans," I said.

We stepped through some sparking remnants, a fleximech's feeble parts marking our path. The spastic metal on metal cutting sounds guided us too, punctuated here and there by a knife's ringing impact.

"Plans for what?" Fang continued.

"Alpha."

She nodded, "Good. So long as it stays that way."

"Focused on the objective?"

"Focused on what we need you to do."

Another strange statement. Another human putting mechs in their lower-than-thou place. I wrote it off, just as I had with Val. After Alpha, we'd leave Fang and their little group behind.

"Made that decision already, huh?" Kaydee said.

Made it after meeting Pravda. The man had ego to burn, salved it by blaming us. Not even Val would go that far. My programming pushed me to help the humans, but it didn't specify which ones.

I'd choose the group treating me better than dirt.

"Not that they did at the start," Kaydee muttered. "Guess they learned, though."

After I'd earned their respect, sure. I just didn't care to try earning Fang's.

We hit the Bridge's level alive. The half-moon platform extended out from Starship's bow, serving as a welcome to Starship's most important room. A clean welcome too: the cherry red barriers leading to the Bridge itself weren't even up.

Only Alpha, alone on the platform, facing us. Unarmed.

"My favorite friends coming back for more?" Alpha asked as our quartet spread around him. "I thought I left you outside?"

Delta glanced at me, gave a short nod. The code exception worked: she had no blocks. Now the only choice was whether we sliced Alpha up or asked him a few questions first.

"You left holes," I said. "What are—"

The shot canceled my voice, its bright blip blinding me for a moment. The energy traveled, struck Alpha right in the chest. A second and a third followed, each one blasting into Alpha until he collapsed, smoking, to the ground. Fang peppered the vessel twice more until I wrestled the pistol away. I backed up with the weapon till I remembered she had a second, lunging back to yank away that one too.

Fang shrugged as I tossed her pistols aside, the guns bouncing along the metal floor to Delta's feet.

"Thought you wanted him dead," Fang said.

"We were talking," I replied. Both Delta and Beta shifted around the platform, each cutting off an escape. Beta didn't have the ability to hurt Fang . . . but Fang wouldn't know that. "You murdered him."

"Murdered?" Fang laughed, calloused and cold. "You can't murder a machine. He was a threat to everyone on this ship. We accomplished the mission."

"She's not wrong," Kaydee said, snapping in next to me. Her voice came quiet, without conviction. "Alpha wasn't going to switch sides Gamma. Not now."

The sides weren't the problem. Hell, Alpha dying wasn't the problem. It was the how. The pointless execution when we had a better choice.

Again, humans proved they couldn't be trusted to make the right decision.

"So what're we doing here, vessel?" Fang said. "Are you going to shoot me? For doing what you wanted to do anyway?"

I heard a click, Beta snapping her fingers. She flicked a look up when I caught her eye, one I matched to see faces staring down from above. In those black masks. Several levels away, spying on us.

"Reinforcements," Fang said, "not that we needed them. You're real good at the killing thing."

Her words spun my functions for a loop. The core directive, keep the humans safe, could never really be satisfied. There should always be a disaster lurking somewhere, a threat to neutralize, but for the moment I couldn't find one. I had no objective.

Did humans ever look around and wonder about their purpose? There, on the Bridge entry platform, I questioned mine. Tried to find something to lock onto, an idea, a goal.

"What's wrong with him?" Fang asked Beta as I stood there, searching.

I had to find something, some independent pursuit. Otherwise Fang could order me around and I would have no reason not to obey.

"He's thinking whether to throw you off this platform," Delta deadpanned.

"You're a dangerous one," Fang mused, stepping around me, keeping her distance from Delta even as she pointed a finger at my friend. "We destroyed your type first." An annoyed flash. "Though apparently we weren't good enough at it."

"Like to see you try."

Kaydee snapped her fingers in my eyes, "Hey, you okay in there? Your buddy's about to start a war you don't want."

There it was. A goal. Keep Delta from killing the humans. My focus snapped back into place and I put an arm out, pushed Fang back behind me.

"Now's not the time, Delta," I said. "Can you and Beta head to the Fabrication Lines? Confirm they're not still following Alpha's commands?"

Delta swung her sword up on her shoulder, took several long strides over to me. Much like Fang had done, the vessel gave me a close look. Unlike Fang, I knew Delta wasn't relying just on intuition but the scanners in her eyes. They'd hunt for imperfections, abnormal reactions.

They found none.

"Will do," Delta said. "Don't be stupid, Gamma."

"No trust," Beta echoed.

"And you," Delta said, looking around my shoulder at Fang. "Anything happens to this guy, I'm turning all of you to fertilizer."

Fang just smirked back at her.

A puffing whine, irregular and loud, ruined the stand-off. The noise came from beyond the platform, below, but it approached. With little fanfare, ten couriers jetted up over the edge. The mechs had bee-like bodies made for storing items, along with hanging claws for grappling stuff too large to throw inside its back. The machines had a slow-charging laser retrofitted near the jets at the rear, inaccurate but deadly all the same.

Beta went for her knives, but stopped when the couriers seemed to take no notice of her, of Delta, or anyone else. Instead, the puffing mechs jetted to Alpha's body. As one, the couriers descended, several hanging off to the side while the others latched their claws onto Alpha's skin.

"The hell's this?" Kaydee asked as the couriers puffed themselves airborne again. "Did Alpha plan a funeral for himself?"

"Or an escape," I mused.

"His body's toasted, Gamma. No way there's a firing processor in there. If he's lucky, the memory might be usable, but—"

"Are you going?" Fang asked, interrupting Kaydee, who countered with a muttered 'rude'. "Every second means more mechs roll off those lines."

Delta back-stepped, dished out one more glare, then disappeared after Alpha's body, heading down and deep.

"Remember what we said," Beta spoke as she followed Delta along. "Gamma's alive and well, or you're all very dead."

Fang gave Beta the same glared smile she'd tossed Delta, and with that my two friends were gone. Fang started towards her pistols, but I grabbed her coat.

"Ready?" I said.

"Ready for what?"

I launched her up, a leg-pressed hurl sending Fang skyward. My throw angle, perfectly calculated, set Fang right on the next walkway, shaken but otherwise fine.

"You better get my guns back," Fang called down.

"Make me," I replied.

I left her pistols behind. Without the intact stair, I jumped instead, reaching and grabbing some broken metal bits to haul myself up. Sure, they cut my skin, but it'd already healed by the time I stood up next to Fang on the level above the Bridge.

"Back to Pravda," I said when Fang tried to pivot. She wanted to push on, hold the Bridge proper and make Pravda come to us. "There's nobody else on this ship that'll take it."

At least, nobody in this part. Val and Leo should've been, by now, approaching Starship's aft exit. Well on their way out.

"What do you want with him anyway?" Fang asked as we climbed the stairs.

"A question I also have," Kaydee said. "Dude's a jerk. You should go find Val."

"I want to know what he wants," I said. No reason to lie here. "What you and your people want."

Fang rolled her eyes, "As if it's some big secret. We've been stuck in tubes for a long time, vessel. Now we have a planet to conquer. That's what we want."

"All fifty of you?"

"The others will fall in line."

Would they? Based on what I'd seen, take fifty humans and you'd get fifty different opinions. Especially, as Kaydee pointed out, knowing these humans had been among the upper crust. Used to getting their own way.

"You're not going to tell her about Val, are you?" Kaydee said.

I was not. With the Forgers at their sides, Val's tribe could probably withstand an attack by Fang and her conscripted fighters, but what few humans existed on this damned planet didn't need to spend their time killing each other.

"How are you going to conquer a planet with a couple dozen people?" I asked Fang as we reached Starship's upper third.

"Take the Nursery, for starters. Use the accelerated growth agents there to get us some more people." Fang spoke carefree, the caution and suspicion she'd shown earlier all gone. Why? "It'll take time to get fresh bodies to where they're useful, but we can spend it getting Starship back into shape."

"Back into shape?"

"Fixing all you broken mechs, for starters. Then repairs. Getting the Garden producing at top levels. Seeing what we can harvest from outside."

Fang went on while we climbed, illustrating a full plan for human growth and conquest with precisely zero confusion, complication, or concern. With Alpha gone, apparently, the path to prosperity was as simple as walking it.

"Ask her about the other vessels," Kaydee said as we hit the first black-suited guards.

They stood as we approached, the pair discarding their masks but keeping the hazard suits. Nervous middle-aged eyes watched us, fingers awful close to their rifle triggers. Fang told them to lower the guns and they did no such thing.

"Passcode?" said the man on the left, finding some shaky confidence.

"Winston," Fang replied and both guards relaxed, settling back on their heels.

Fang waved me ahead and we went right on through without further incident.

"Shouldn't they have known you?" I asked Fang as we started up the next stair.

"Vessels mean that's not a guarantee," Fang said. "We know looks don't mean anything. Not here."

I stopped. Couldn't help it. The implications were too big.

"You keep talking about us like we're terrible," I said, blocking the whole step up. "Why?"

"Let's get back to Pravda and maybe I'll tell you."

I didn't move. Getting back to Pravda would mean

Fang's allies would be everywhere. If I was walking into death, I wanted to know it, and I said as much.

Fang did that glinted smile, a half curl up one lip, "You want a history lesson, go find a book to read. All you need to know is I don't trust you. Those two back there don't trust you. Pravda doesn't trust you. You're a tool, and as soon as you stop being useful, we'll turn you into scrap."

A THREAT

Pravda hadn't moved much, but the man had salvaged what he could from the bar. Liquor and wine bottles, the unbroken ones anyway, lay in nice rows along the bar's circular shape. Someone had found a vacuum, the crimson carpet looking almost as good as my first time seeing it. Eight humans stood around the room talking, not a one in the black hazard garb.

"Victory is a wonderful thing," Pravda said as Fang and I came into the room. "It's all so much better when death isn't around the corner."

"Hey, something I can agree with," Kaydee muttered, popping in at one of the white-cloth-covered tables and sipping some virtual cabernet.

"Where's your friends?" Pravda waved us to another table, bid us sit on some shaky chairs, ones battered by our earlier escape but still standing. "Casualties?"

"Playing clean-up," Fang said. She nodded my way. "This one's not a fighter."

"Then what are you?" Pravda peered at me as if I'd grown wings.

"Computers," I replied.

"Later model," Fang said. When Pravda blinked at her, Fang sighed. "After the rebellion ended, for that short time, the idea was we'd need vessels for every task they used to do."

"Oh, right." Pravda nodded, poured us glasses.

Not that I could drink mine. I swirled the deep red liquid, watched sediment make its rounds as Fang recounted the descent, the victory.

"So Starship is ours now?" Pravda asked.

"It's empty," Fang replied. "We ought to send some to the Bridge to hold it."

"Why?" Pravda raised his glass to the sunny dome above. "We've landed, haven't we?"

"Starship's not done," Fang said. "We'll need it for another thousand years, and everything can be controlled from that Bridge."

An idea struck. One that'd let me get away from Pravda's idiocy and Fang's lingering threat. I could keep Val's secret, keep Starship alive.

"Send me," I said. "I work for you anyway. Let me monitor the Bridge."

The pair met eyes. Pravda danced his fingers on the tablecloth. "You say the Bridge is still Starship's power center?"

I nodded. By all logic, the Bridge had more ways to control what Starship did, even landed, than any other location. Save, perhaps, Volt's Power Core, but I wasn't about to give that away.

"Then I think we ought to set up there, don't you?" Pravda asked Fang.

"It'll be central. Harder to defend than here," Fang said. "But faster to respond."

"Defend?" Pravda laughed. "Defend from who?"

Fang looked at me, "Them."

WE LEFT HOURS LATER, a train made up of people. Booze, food, and weapons shoved into packs made their way down stairs. The lifts were still shut down, a delay I said I could alleviate, but Pravda wanted the migration now.

"I want to feel how far it is," Pravda said. "I want all of us to understand why we're making this move."

"Because he wants to?" Kaydee added.

Pravda's reasoning wasn't totally crazy. He preached to the assembled crew that this was about moving their home. Leaving behind their cryo capsules for terminals, the luxury carpets for reality.

Val, or her ancestors, must have done something similar when they moved into the Junker's spare storehouses. Flee the mechs, flee the powerful, and hide until a chance comes around again.

More interesting, I noticed eyes rolling, looks at the ground, sighs from the people Pravda was supposed to lead. Not the sign of someone with control.

Fang, meanwhile, stood behind Pravda to my left, that quiet smile on her face.

"She's definitely the dangerous one," Kaydee said. "Look at that grin. She's up to something."

"Aren't we all?" I whispered.

The procession took its time. By my count, half an Earth day had passed between us leaving with Fang to kill Alpha and Pravda's procession arriving at the Bridge. The human limbs lagged by the time we made it, especially with delays to get around destruction from our mech fights.

Not a soul interrupted us. No flexi-mechs, no more hulking guards. Beta and Delta remained disappeared.

Pravda bid everyone to make their camp on the platform before the Bridge. With the Conduit's yellowed light illuminating, the humans spread bed rolls and scavenged blankets. Dried fruits and ancient nutrition pastes made the rounds. A trio returned with scavenged water, dumping filled bottles on the ground. A nearby apartment was found to have a working shower and shifts were arranged.

Orderly, rigid. Little laughter, few smiles. No dancing as I'd seen with Val's group.

"They don't know how to live yet," Kaydee said, standing next to me as we watched, waited for Fang and Pravda to move to the Bridge. "They're still waking up."

"For sleepy people, they destroyed a lot of mechs."

"Survival is different than building a life, Gamma."

"I wouldn't know."

When Pravda and Fang finally requested me to guide them in, I did so, leading them through the hallway with names scrawled on the walls. I didn't point out Alpha's repeated writings and neither noticed, or neither cared to mention them.

The Bridge itself . . . I couldn't hide what I didn't know existed. Alpha, always one to leave his mark, had ravaged the place. Shattered terminals lay everywhere. Stuffing torn from chairs drifted throughout the room, blown by air recycling fans. Lights blinked or spat sparks, their glass scattered like razor confetti.

Across the big bubble looking out towards the planet's bright day, a scrawled message in a dripping red ink:

'Welcome Home'.

"Is that blood?" Pravda said, pointing and staring. "What sort of maniac . . . ?"

I loped down the Bridge, took a closer look at the liquid, "Dyed coolant. Not blood."

Thank goodness for that. The last thing Fang and Pravda needed was more excuses to find mechs strange, deadly.

"Told you mechs were dangerous," Fang said, loud enough to be sure I'd hear.

"I knew they were," Pravda shot back, "doesn't mean they're not useful." The man pointed at the window. "Gamma, clean all that off, would you?"

I waited, hoped the man would realize he'd just ordered me to do menial labor when Starship itself sat waiting for him. Alpha might've broken some terminals, but others looked fine, ready to go, but Pravda had more humans brought in to clean up the broken glass, the crushed chairs. New lights were scavenged from nearby apartments as I swabbed away the red.

Time, meanwhile, ticked by. No Beta and Delta. I wondered how far Val and Leo had gone by now, whether they'd left Starship entirely.

"There," Pravda said at length, after he'd sent almost everyone else to bed. Fang had put two chairs together, was snoozing. Pravda and I were the only ones awake, me watching as he finished logging into the Captain's terminal. "The old password still works. Proof all the old days aren't gone."

"Aren't they?" I asked. "Starship's been like this for a long time."

"For you and your kind, maybe." Pravda leaned back in his chair, clicked around on the terminal. "For me, just yesterday life filled this place. Thousands of us, churning away to keep this grand baby going."

"What did you do, back then?"

Pravda bit, ever so slightly, his bottom lip. A tic I'd noticed whenever the topic veered to someplace he didn't like.

"I was what you're looking at now. A leader of men, a captain of industry and innovation," Pravda said. "They all looked to me. All of them."

"Who the hell is this guy?" Kaydee asked, popping in behind Pravda, eyebrows up and mouth in a disgusted curl. Her teal hair looked like question marks. "I've never heard of him."

"The Voices never mentioned you," I said, "not once."

"A bunch of haughty programs." Pravda waved away my words. "People that should've stayed dead. They weren't on the walkways when things started to turn. They didn't make the calls that saved us."

"You did?"

Pravda took another deep breath and I sensed a speech was incoming, something blathering and pointless. Something, thankfully, spared by a crackling coming from our one working terminal.

"Anyone there?" Volt's voice, curious but urgent. "Alpha, are you still on the Bridge?"

Fang shot awake just as Pravda asked who that was. I ignored them both, lunged for the terminal, pressed the keyboard to open the line.

"Volt!" I said. "Alpha's gone. I have the Bridge, along with some other humans."

"Gamma? Good. Better than what I thought I'd be working with," Volt said. A prompt appeared on the terminal, a video feed request. With Pravda and Fang collecting behind me, I launched it. Volt appeared, the lights all around him showing the rainbow black of Power Core.

"What's going on?" I asked, looking for and seeing no

sign of alarm. Volt bore no injuries. Nothing seemed exploded or burning. "Are you okay?"

"Totally fine, my friend, but our poor ship won't be without some quick work on your part."

"What? Why?"

Volt, though, flashed his eyes to a blue color, looked past me. "Well, turns out there's more! Who are these two?"

Pravda started to introduce himself, but I cut him off.

"Volt, the point please? What's the problem?"

"Remember our other friends?" Volt replied. "You know, the ones going outside?"

Good on Volt for not revealing Val outright, but Fang and Pravda weren't that dumb. I could see their faces reflected in a small box on the screen, their looks calculating. Wondering.

Too late to care.

"I remember. Why?"

"Well, you know, I'm a nice mech, Gamma. They made it to the engines, gave me a call asking how you were doing. So we tuned in. Cameras everywhere, right?"

"And they saw?"

"A lot of humans," Volt said. "Guess they weren't a fan, because I'm seeing a spike from those engines."

I prompted and Volt laid it out in more detail. With Starship landed, the engines were shut down. Leo, though, had kicked them back on again using old overrides. The big power packs were sucking energy, getting ready for a full launch. The kind Starship was only supposed to use in an emergency to, say, escape a gravity well or dodge a coming asteroid.

"If those engines ignite while we're still sitting on this rock," Volt concluded, "we'll burn up real nice."

"But they'll kill themselves," I said, along with Kaydee. "No way they would be able to outrun the wash."

"Leo's a clever one, Gamma. They're closing the nacelles. It'll block the fire, turn it back on the ship. The metal won't last long, but it won't need to before we all go boom."

TWENTY-SIX

A WALK IN THE DARK

I stepped onto the Bridge. For a second, I thought there'd been some mistake, that I hadn't just entered a terminal, hunting for Starship's network. The clue that I'd actually jumped inside a digital world came from the viewport. The big glass window showed, once again, outer space. Stars, nebula, the whole deal.

No planet. No golden grass.

"So where are we going?" Kaydee asked, standing along-side me.

"Was hoping you might have some idea," I replied. "Know how to cut off Power Core?"

Kaydee frowned, "Remember when I tried to sabotage the engines? Take out Starship mid flight?"

"Hard to forget. In fact, for me, literally impossible."

"You could delete it."

"Not without deleting you, and I won't do that."

"Aww," Kaydee said. "Good idea, though, because you'd probably go insane without me."

"I'm going to die with you if we don't focus."

"Oh, right. Imminent explosion," Kaydee whirled

around, looking at the terminals. "Where's the way onto the network?"

"My guess? One of these terminals has what we're looking for."

We split up, dashing up and down the Bridge's terraced terminal lines. Every screen held a different program, most having to do with navigation, Starship's address system, various admin programs. For once, I found the right one first: the screen held the starry galaxy I'd seen before, every mote a different point on the ship's vast Internet.

"Kaydee," I said. "Found it."

Using the keyboard I launched off search terms, scattering the stars away before me until only ones relating to the engines remained. A star for each rocket, plus a smattering for adjacent systems. I could put my finger on the screen, touch each one to pop open its name, function, the option to jump right to it.

Except when I tried that last, thinking I could leap right to one engine and shut it down, the terminal did nothing. No error, no bounce back, just a static screen.

"Oh, that's a good one," Kaydee said, joining me. "He's disguising the block so you'll think there's something wrong with your access. Like your computer's frozen."

"How do I get rid of it?"

"You're asking me?" Kaydee shrugged. "I'm more of an engineer than a software gal. Leo always did the fancy coding."

Okay. I leaned into my own systems, tried to break down the options. Leo would've done this manually back at the engines themselves. My guess, he'd have started the charge up process then cut off the engines from the network. Disguised it to look like the engines were still active—why those stars showed—but the access didn't go anywhere. Anyone trying to stop the whole thing, namely me, would get trapped here, waste time until boom.

But the engines weren't the issue. It was the batteries. The energy.

"I can't stop the engines from drawing power," I said.

"So we're dead?"

"Not yet."

My move would've been suicide in space. Surrounded by all that absolute zero vacuum, Starship would've frosted over fast with my plan. But here, safe on a relatively temperate world?

"What's the move, smart guy?" Kaydee asked as I skipped back through the network, typing in new commands that answered her question. "No. Wait. Really?"

"Really," I said, finding the node I wanted.

A prompt came up, asking for permissions. Back in meatspace, I would've had to guess. Here, I touched the pop-up on the screen, expanded the code behind it. A simple look to find the database with the usernames and passwords the prompt would check once I entered one.

Leo's own name, his chosen password: a scrambling of Kaydee with her own birthday.

"Don't say that's cute too," I snarked as I entered it.

"It is, kinda," Kaydee replied. "At least he remembers me."

"Didn't he leave you adrift for centuries?"

"Nobody's perfect, Gamma."

The prompt gave me access to a singular switch, one Volt wouldn't be happy about. One I didn't hesitate to press.

THE BRIDGE FELT DARKER than before. Terminal screens were black. The lights were dead. Sunset lingered out the big viewport. Pravda and Fang looked around, confused.

"What'd you do?" the man asked when I stepped away from the dead terminal, parting my fingers.

"Gave us a chance," I replied.

"Oh Gamma, you really went for it this time," Kaydee said, appearing next to me in what looked like a full survivor's getup, with flashlights, a backpack, and thick boots. "Starship's never gone dark. Ever."

Fang and Pravda slowly came to the same conclusion, following me as I left the Bridge behind. Turning off Starship's lights, its generators, its everything saved our hides, but it could destroy a lot if left alone for long. The Garden's plants wouldn't have light, Purity wouldn't filter water. Starship itself might get too hot or cold in various places without systems running.

In other words, I'd escaped one calamity to toy with another.

"Where are you going?" Pravda asked as we went down the name-filled hallway connecting to the Conduit.

"To the engines," I replied. Once more traversing the length of this damn ship. "We can't turn on the power till we've shut off the sabotage."

"Oh yes," Pravda mused. "The sabotage. Who did that, by the way?"

"More vessels, probably," Fang said. "Broken mechs losing their minds."

For a moment I was stunned. How did they not make the connection, the leap that there might be more humans still alive on the ship?

"Because it's been too long," Kaydee said, her headlamp light illuminating, sort of, my way. "No person should be alive."

Kaydee's headlamp wasn't real, but I had enough night vision to guide us. Light, too, leaked in from the Conduit, where, by fortune, the still-open ramp down below let in the evening's remaining glow.

The humans gathered on the Bridge's entry platform as Pravda, Fang and I emerged. Lit from below, shadows danced. Without the constant churn from rumbling systems, wind from outside whistled through the ship. Someone coughed as I faced a curious semicircle.

"I'll tell them," Pravda said, elbowing past me.

In a ponderous speech the man did just that, explaining how some mechs had disabled Starship's power, how he, Fang, and a few select heroes would be going forth to restore it.

"He's coming with us?" Kaydee said as Pravda swapped from explanation to inspiration, telling the people how they could plan to survive. "Why?"

Because he's not one to tackle the hard problems himself. Whatever his role was before, Pravda's attitude thus far made him a leech, a captain who depended on his crew and took their credit for his own. Staying here would mean he'd have to lead a couple dozen scared people through a dead night on a ship with hostile mechs still lurking.

Traveling with us gave him an out, and, if things went well, a victorious return.

"Wow," Kaydee said. "You've figured him out."

"No, I've just seen enough humans by now to know what to expect."

Pravda didn't hear my snipe as he wound down his speech, but Fang did, raising a finger and scratching at her cheek.

"And what do you expect from me, vessel?"

"I expect you'll try to kill me when this is finished," I said. "I expect you'll lose."

"So certain," Fang replied. "That confidence killed your brothers and sisters. I can't wait for it to kill you too."

Boy, this would be a fun trip.

MARCHING along Starship's entire length yet again held a distinct lack of appeal. Not that walking would ever deplete my batteries nor, given I was a mech, did the wasted time weigh heavily on my shoulders. No, it felt more that I never seemed to get where I needed to be.

"You don't have a home," Kaydee summed up my feeling. "You're lost."

"Why should I feel that way?" I asked, waiting for Fang, Pravda, and their chosen few to gather up their gear. "I have a goal. I'm a machine, right?"

"There's a lotta ground between you and a trash mech, my friend," Kaydee replied. "Also, and I know you hate hearing this, but I'm still messing with you. One function at a time."

I took a minute to run this line over. It'd been a bit since I'd reconciled Kaydee's bleeding over and how it might affect me. Her effects had definitely made me more emotional, more prone to judging the humans I'd come across. I 'felt' things a normal mech would've disregarded as irrelevant.

Like Fang and her looks, the danger they represented. Like Pravda and his feckless arrogance.

Useful, but as these came with a human's other drawbacks, like discontent, longing, sadness . . .

"Congratulations, you're getting the other bonus part of being a human," Kaydee continued, "constant confusion."

Cool.

The Conduit would, at least, require more concentration this time around. With Starship dead around us, the walkways held little light. Sunset's dimming glimmers sent yellow rays deep into the Conduit, the light bouncing its way back before vanishing. How far we'd get with any light behind us, I didn't know.

"Didn't think you were afraid of the dark," Kaydee said.

"I'm not. It's the humans I'm worried about, and what's waiting for us."

"What's waiting for you? Alpha's dead, remember?"

"Sure, but how many mechs did he send running back through the ship? What did the Fabrication Lines make before I shut everything down?"

"Point. Now you're making me nervous. Wish Beta and Delta were here."

Truth. Where had the two vessels gone? They should've been back by now, should've been ready to escort us along with their brutal cockiness.

"Hey, mech," Fang called. "Change of plans. We're going to stay here for the night. Get some sleep and head out in the morning."

"Starship might not wait that long," I replied.

"It's going to have to," Pravda said. "Or we'll fall asleep as we walk and you'll have to pick us up."

I tried a couple other protests, but they were shut down without an argument. Fang and Pravda gave the orders, and no others cared enough to contest them. Even Kaydee said it wasn't too surprising: we'd been up and active for a long time.

"We're not built like you all," Kaydee concluded. "Gotta give us our beauty rest."

Beauty. Right.

As the humans settled into their sleep, I moved to the platform's edge. From here I could see through the Conduit. Watch for any threats, wait for my friends to return.

And try to figure out how much of me was still, well, me.

TWENTY-SEVEN

YOU, ME, WE

A featureless gray plain stretched to an infinite horizon. I felt no wind, for there was no air. Gravity had no pull on my feet: I remained anchored to the plain by choice. I wasn't concerned with the ground, the code base driving my functions, but with the crystals up above.

My sky used to hold shiny diamond teeth. Each one many times larger than its real-world analog, each one holding the files making up my memories, the routines helping me fire a rifle or walk up the stairs, and, in one particular crystal now shining a bright teal: Kaydee.

"What're you looking for?" Kaydee asked, stepping in. Outside, in the real world, Kaydee always seemed apart, a projected image. Here she had depth, belonged in the same way I did. "Or are you just bored?"

"I haven't been in here for a while," I replied.

Kaydee's crystal held that teal glow, yes, but I noticed others did too. Splashes and splotches, as though a carefree artist had whipped their paintbrush around. What did those marks represent? What crystals were they touching?

"Welcome to my home," Kaydee said, "or, I guess, our

home." Kaydee snapped her fingers and the ground beneath my feet sported a carpet, a familiar crimson. Chairs, big and fluffy, rose up behind us. The carpet gave my feet a gentle nudge, setting me back in the chair. A glass, white wine this time, appeared in my fingers. "It's nicer this way."

"Our home," I repeated, eating at the words. Ever since I'd met her, or rather since Kaydee had jumped into my memory, I'd put her along for the ride. A partner. "You're changing it."

"No offense, Gamma, but it's a little bit boring in here."

"Where do you go when you disappear out there?" I'd always thought . . . well, I wasn't sure. I hadn't really thought anything about where Kaydee went. "Is it here?"

Kaydee took a long drink from her own glass, gave me a slight smile, "You think I take naps, Gamma?"

She would change me. Her code, her being would alter me. Beta figured she wasn't wholly herself, that her mind had so completely become her that they weren't separate anymore.

But how much was Beta, and how much was her mind?

"How does it work?" I asked. "This . . . becoming thing? You molding into me?"

Kaydee swirled the wine, avoided my stare.

"There's a lot you don't know, Gamma. About humans, and what we'll do to survive."

I waited. I'd learned enough about Kaydee, about human tendencies to know a statement like that tended to be followed by something worse.

"I tried to avoid it," Kaydee continued after another swig. Her wine glass changed to a tumbler, amber liquid inside. "That mech, in the Fabrication Lines? I tried for you."

"Tried what?"

"The word vessel. You know what it means?"

A standard definition came instantly. I reduced it: "A hollow container."

Kaydee nodded. The carpet disappeared. The gray plain, the crystal horizon vanished too. I hadn't given Kaydee, her program permission to so alter my digital self, but I found she'd taken it.

In the carpet's place appeared a great hall, one which Kaydee and I lorded over like some ancient gods. Crammed inside, standing in long lines, were people. Hundreds, thousands.

"What is this?" I asked, as Kaydee seemed to be stunned by her own creation.

"It's . . . sorry, I always get a little overwhelmed looking at it," Kaydee leaned forward in her chair, pointed at the people. "All these? They're minds. They're the plan B."

"What?" I focused on the people, tried to run a search and realized it was empty. No actual data there, just an image Kaydee conjured up. "What are you talking about?"

"Don't get all stupid on me now, Gamma. It's a lot easier to scan a brain than it is to make a ship like this one," Kaydee said. "Starship lifted off with a big database filled with people from Earth, and we added to it as we went along. The one thing Earth didn't have? You."

"The vessels."

"Right," Kaydee waved away all the people. Replaced them with a university classroom, the one I'd seen during my first walk through Starship. "Every generation on Starship pushed its smarter engineers into perfecting vessels. Making them better and better, because if the Nursery didn't work out, we'd at least have something."

"And if it did?" I stared at Kaydee's creation, watched as

students, at a fast-forward speed, left the classroom and busied about a lab. "Wait, mechs weren't . . .?"

"Not just mechs. Early vessels. Repurposed designs, coding, everything. Iteration after iteration until we get to you."

But not just to me. To Alpha, Delta, Beta, and—

"Fang kept talking about destroying vessels?"

Kaydee shook her head, "Must've been after my time. Vessels were advancing fast though. Leo and some others were getting so close."

"How would they know?"

The sped up montage shifted again. I saw a human form, almost perfect but not quite. Its muscles too clean, its stance too rigid. Leo stepped into view, as if emerging from a curtain. The engineer plugged a drive into a slot behind the human's ear, backed off and watched.

The vessel blinked. Smiled. Started talking to Leo, who answered back. I noticed, then, a shadow behind the vessel. Another human, this one holding a rifle. The weapon aimed at the vessel's back.

Leo had the vessel raise its hand, jump up and down. Exercises I remembered from my first waking moments. As the vessel went through the routines, it started hitching. At first the stops were too quick to notice, an arm twitching to the right when stretching towards the toes. Eyes blinking several times in quick succession. Leo, the experienced one, caught on quicker than me. He frowned, his shoulders sagged.

"I helped," Kaydee said as the vessel's faults became worse. Now the mech panicked openly, and while I couldn't hear a spoken word, the expressions swapped between fear, anger, hysteria. "We took minds at random from the pool. As fair as possible."

The vessel lunged at Leo, the rifle flashed from behind, and a smoking ruin landed at the man's feet.

"But you were close," I said. "By the time you . . . "

"By the time I switched sides?" Kaydee replied. "Yeah. By then I knew Leo and the others would get there. Perfect vessels."

"And you didn't want that."

"Most of Starship didn't want that," Kaydee replied, "but they were willing to take it for a while."

The scene shifted again to one I was more familiar with. The Conduit, a rabble handing out rifles near the ship's aft. Kaydee among them, talking strategy. She would make for the engines with a small team while the others would try to hold the passage. Buy them time.

The assault came quick, a brutal attack from multiple levels. I'd assumed Starship had some police force making the moves, but Kaydee put forth something else entirely. The things attacking her friends moved like Delta and Beta, they shot like soldiers. Kaydee's video ended the same way I'd seen it end back in the Hospital: Kaydee shot, looking up at an anonymous face with Leo in the background telling the thing to stop.

Not a person, then, but a vessel.

"They took military minds," Kaydee said, quieter now, exhausted. Still in our chairs. "We were mechanics. Cooks. Bartenders who'd spent some afternoons at a VR shooting range and thought we'd stand up for ourselves. Care to guess how that went?"

"I don't have to. You showed me."

"Yeah. I guess I did." The diorama before us dissolved, its bits wafting away on a secret wind. "I don't know what happened after, Gamma, but I doubt they gave up."

"Someone grew scared," I said. "Scared of us."

Kaydee leaned forward, put her hands together and rested her chin on her wrists as she looked at me. In that pose she seemed smaller, more vulnerable. A person I could delete at any moment.

Well, one I could've deleted.

"I think we both know Leo must've hid you four. He must've done it before scanning himself to join the Voices," Kaydee mused. "He kept you locked away, a secret in his apartment while everything else fell apart."

Her eyes flicked again to the space between us, and once more the Conduit filled the air. Its walkways and bustling stores were getting turned around, broken and burned as mechs and humans fought themselves, each other.

"Where are you getting this?" I asked.

"My imagination," Kaydee replied. "Minds slowly change and take over their vessels, right? What happens when all those military vessels that killed us decide they'd like to be in charge?"

"It's a war." I reached towards the action, ran my fingers through it and cleared away the participants. Left the walkways, the battered storefronts. "Few survivors. A quiet ship. Fang and Pravda think the vessels are gone and decide to sleep until the ship lands."

"Plan B's gone, remember? It's them or nobody."

Except now they woke up and Plan B is very much alive. Vessels are running around again, causing chaos. The humans don't have the numbers anymore to take us out, so they're playing nice.

For now.

Not that this explains what Kaydee's doing infiltrating all my systems.

"Doesn't it, though?" Kaydee said, chin still on her

hands. "I want to live, Gamma. I tried to escape, give it a shot in that other mech, but it felt like an alien. Nothing worked."

"So it's you or me?"

Kaydee shook her head, "We, Gamma. We."

"I lose and you gain."

She flinched. "Is that how you feel? Like this is some zero sum game?"

I stood up, snapped my fingers. The chairs vanished, along with the carpet. Kaydee caught herself, easy to do without gravity pulling you down.

At least I could still make furniture disappear.

"I didn't know that I had an identity," I said. "I didn't have any dreams. I didn't have any passions. No family and no loves. I was not and then I was. But I controlled my body, I controlled my self." I pointed at the teal-splashed crystals. "If you continue, I won't have that."

"Sure you will. We'll just work together."

"And when we disagree, who makes the choice?"

"Gamma," Kaydee folded her arms, met my eyes instead of the ground. "Vessels are made for minds. The routine I'm following? I get priority."

"Can you delete me?"

"I never would."

I was about to reply that she hadn't answered my question, but she had. Kaydee had answered all of my questions and despite that I felt worse.

Felt. There's a word. I was a vessel. I wasn't supposed to 'feel' anything. Here, it was just the few code lines evaluating my situation and finding that, well, it sucked.

"Kaydee," I said. "I need some time alone."

"Sure, yeah," Kaydee winced at me. "I get that. You want to talk, I'll be here."

After she'd disappeared I sat down, right there on the gray floor. Looked up at my crystals, but I saw only the teal spots.

Kaydee wouldn't be the worst mind to serve. She knew me, she was clever and mostly kind. I'd likely have chances to take control. Kaydee seemed to enjoy popping in and offering snarky advice.

Could I do that?

I wiggled my digital fingers, digital toes. Blinked my digital eyes. In here I could do that whenever I wanted, as many times as I needed. Out there, I might never get the chance again.

No. Not acceptable.

Several functions heeded my call, started whirling away in my background. A very close observer, floating up among the crystals, might've noticed a tiny yellow thread growing from one teal spot to the next, connecting them all in a web.

It would take a while to finish, to make sure that I'd wrapped every piece of Kaydee in my program.

If I went down this path, I'd need to delete every part of her.

TWENTY-EIGHT

TRICKS AND TRAPS

The Conduit didn't have a morning. Not with Starship powerless. The planet outside didn't match human day and night cycles either, keeping things dark when Pravda and Fang gathered their group and announced our forward march. Despite having plenty of clues, namely all their rustling and talking, the command to leave caught me by surprise.

I'd been too busy gathering Kaydee's pieces in a giant coded net. She hadn't spoken to me the entire time, a silence that didn't change as the humans and I began our walk aft.

Delta and Beta, too, remained gone. Their mission to track and dispose of Alpha's other mechs shouldn't have taken this long, but neither Fang nor Pravda wanted to divert the time or attention to find them.

"They're vessels," Fang said in response. "Let 'em leave."

How I wished I could've socked her right then and there. Even that desire, though, felt muted, far away as I thought it. My programming interfering, steering me away from the radical. The vessel, the mech must serve.

We took first to the left, heading along Starship's side to the Conduit's center level. We could walk all the way on this one to the engines and wind up right where we needed to be.

Without light, I became the leader. Night vision's green overlay guided me along, the walkway's railing serving as the help for everyone else.

Not that Starship was totally dark. Here and there lights blinked, mechanical remnants fulfilling a purpose. At first we tried to identify the dots, even if they were levels away. Were they potential threats, Alpha mechs running amok, or leftover alerts, trash mechs or tools not quite dead?

The chatter seemed to keep the humans at ease, a game I found strange until I remembered these weren't killers. Not hardened soldiers. Civilians, with Fang's possible exception, pressed into brutal service. Their nerves wouldn't be steel, would need comfort.

"What do you think, Gamma?" Pravda asked an hour into our walk, with nothing around us save darkness and stale air. "How much longer?"

He couldn't possibly think we were close.

"At our current pace," I said, "we'll need another ten hours to make the engines."

Our walk wasn't fast, in part because the humans carried their survival gear, in part because debris littered the walkways. Every step became a potential twisted ankle, a cut leg on jutting shrapnel.

"Ten hours?" Pravda laughed, a scared cocky blend. "Surely you're joking. There's no way."

"He's not joking," Fang said. The two were closest, leaving their tagalong trio to pick up the rear. "You never walked Starship, so you wouldn't know."

I kept my face forward so any surprise wouldn't show.

Never walked Starship? Living his whole life contained on a single vessel but he'd never bothered to walk it?

No wonder—

"I didn't walk it because I didn't need to," Pravda said. "There were cabs. Time is valuable. I couldn't waste it wandering around."

"Tell me again what your job was," Fang needled.

"It wasn't massacring machines," Pravda countered.

I looked back, keeping my feet moving. Fang met my eyes, a grim straight face. Pravda, between us, didn't see my turn.

"Either them or us," Fang said. "Like it always is."

"Until now," Pravda said, sliding again into his prophet's tone. "This is our chance to remake history, give humans a new start. No wars, no brutality. Just an ideal."

Fang snorted. I stayed quiet.

Pravda filled the next hour almost by himself. He rambled on about his vision for the future, what miracles humans would make without strife by their side. Fang punctured the bubble here and there with half-hearted barbs. I slotted the ideas away: Pravda might not be the one to drive his own vision, but knowing what a human considered utopia might be valuable.

We hit the University first. Its bulk, spanning the Conduit, lit in soft reds and golds. Decorative lights finally given their due absent other competition. Pravda declared a break and in the structure's shadow the humans had their meal.

I checked on my program, found it nearly done scanning and capturing Kaydee's data. I could flick a switch, metaphorically, and be done with her then. Lose her forever, but guarantee my freedom. I didn't have a clear calculation for that one, no idea which way would be better.

"Vessel," Fang said, leaving her fellows and heading over to me. "Mind joining me on an errand?"

We stood near a University entrance, doors on either walkway side leading into the academy. Both sat shut tight, their locked red gems no longer glowing. Any entry would have to be forced, a fact I considered only because Fang kept looking at one.

"Do I have a choice?" I asked.

"I don't know. Do you?"

"You're the vessel expert."

"No," Fang said. "I'm not. If anything, we destroyed so many of you because we didn't know what you might become. Think of it as risk management."

"Such a cold term."

"Space is a cold place." Fang nodded at the closed door, the one leading into the University's Conduit-spanning structure. "Open that, please."

"There's no power."

"Then tear it off."

I was supposed to protect the humans. The gray in that statement gave me latitude. Despite my question, I felt I could say no to Fang, could argue to myself that keeping Fang with Pravda and the others was the safer move.

But, and perhaps this was Kaydee's hidden meddling, Fang's request kindled a fire. An adventure, an escape from the tedious, cautious march aft. As much as it seemed impossible, I was bored.

The spiral door sat deep in the wall surrounding it, a pocked slate tarnished by passing fires and scratched by haphazard mechs. University crests were barely legible smudges drawn on the door's either side. I found no handholds in my inspection, no place to rip and tear.

"Step back," Fang said, leveling her rifle.

"That's not—" I started and she pulled the trigger.

A low red beam shot out, a steady light stream biting into the door and flaring its metal orange-white. Did Fang have a way to cut through the door? No: as Fang moved the laser it became obvious she'd only sliced a little way into the metal.

"There's your opening," Fang said a few seconds later, letting the red beam die. "Can't fire much more or she'll go dead."

Two slits marred the door now, about an arm's length apart over the gem. The metal smeared in the lines, melted and cooled back together. I ran my fingers along both, feeling the heat, testing the hold. Deeper than the first knuckle on my fingers, enough for a grip.

"Your turn to back away," I said and Fang complied.

We'd attracted Pravda's attention now too, along with the others, so I had a good audience as I stretched my hands between the slits, set my feet, and twisted. The door rumbled, protesting as I ground its cut spirals against the tracks holding them in.

I sent more energy from my battery to my arms, boosting their power, trying to get the door to move. It shivered, something began to crack.

"Keep going," Fang said. "You've almost made it."

The door gave me clues: I felt joints giving way, metal bending. Something snapped and shot out like a bullet, bouncing off the walkway's wall behind me. Push here, pull there, lean into the shove.

And top out my power draw.

My arms and legs crackled with the energy. My systems told me I'd hit maximum, this was me at my greatest, giving my all to smash aside this door.

It gave. One push along its right side and the spirals

snapped, the door bending inward before breaking apart around the gem. I fell over with the push, tripping on the door's center.

The spiral teeth still hanging split into sharp points. I took scrapes as I fell in, as I tried to catch myself. My hands planted on broken metal, the debris shredding and leaving me planted chest-down on the University's etched tile floor.

A blinking red flared before my eyes, a warning that I needed to find a plug or move slow, allow kinetic energy to recharge. I had to shut down inessential processes, grinding my Kaydee-killing program to a halt just short of completion.

Not that it mattered, I'd have time to do that later.

"Nice job, vessel," Fang said. I heard her step on the fragments as she came in behind me. "Good to see the old moves still work."

"What old moves?" I asked, my voice slurred, slow.

A hot nuzzle pressed up against my neck. Fang's rifle. She squatted behind me.

"You vessels are so smart and so dumb at the same time. All that strength, all that knowledge, but you still run on batteries."

I was too exhausted to be scared. I kneeled, looking ahead into the grand staircases, the offshoots to dining halls, offices, classrooms before me. A pleasant place to go, to attend.

A worse one to die.

BUT FANG DIDN'T KILL me. Not yet, anyway. She'd put my battery low to keep me in line, but they still needed my eyes to help them along. There'd been no errand in the University, no need to tear the door apart. I'd done what she asked, crippled myself for nothing more than a request.

So now I led, walking again, this time as slow as the humans and with no hope of going faster. Fang stayed right behind me, at first with her rifle drawn, but as she realized I'd have all the escape abilities of an exhausted old man, she holstered the weapon.

There wasn't a need to ask why. Humans always had themselves as the critical concern. I didn't pose a threat, but Fang didn't see it that way. Again I was a victim of my own trust, my own, as Kaydee would put it, naivety.

"I could've helped you there," Kaydee said, showing up for the first time. She appeared distant, even though she stood next to me on the walkway.

Her face seemed shadowed, her hair a muted gray. As she moved, Kaydee's imaged flickered, as though it couldn't maintain its dimensions.

"Yeah, it's your low battery, duh. If I hadn't snuck myself onto your critical function list, I wouldn't even be here."

That list had limited room. If she'd put herself on there, then—

"You're cut off, Gamma," Kaydee said. "No more trips inside yourself, reading your own data. Not till you get the juice." She flickered in front of me, walking backwards as I went ahead, feeling my way around a crumpled cleaning mech. "Think of it as therapy. A chance for you and me to work ourselves out."

"You and me?" I asked. "I didn't think it worked that way."

Kaydee sighed, "Look, I told you. I don't want to die, and right now, I'm tied to you. You go, I go. And that lady behind you right now? She wants you eating dirt."

"Fang's likely to get it," I whispered the words, moved little air. No chance my enemy could hear me. "I don't have strength left."

"Yeah, you were stupid. Thankfully, I'm still here, and I've got an idea."

"An idea for what?"

"Oh, you know, the usual: save Starship and your dumb ass at the same time."

"It's your dumb ass too."

She laughed. Kaydee, the human, the program, bent on taking me over, laughed. For the first time in too long, I joined her.

TWENTY-NINE

SUCKING JUICE

Once Kaydee gave me the details, I looked at the walk through Starship as less a prisoner's march and more a long goodbye. Starship in the dark, dead silence felt like a tomb, or perhaps a memorial. The humans couldn't see much of anything as we went, meaning the approach to the Garden was a sight left to me alone.

The fuzzy green night vision overlay might've lacked color, but I saw stores, apartments, restaurants I recognized. I'd been alive for less than a couple weeks, and yet these places, the markers for my first moments, tied themselves to my memories.

"It's perfect for you," Kaydee said as I, walking along the railing, held a long look at *Alvie's*. "You'll never forget anything."

"Neither will you," I replied.

"Sure, now. All the cool stuff I did while I was alive is gone, or blurred. Like a dream."

"Something I'll never have."

"What?" Kaydee asked.

"A dream," I stated, then nodded ahead towards the

Garden. Our level's door would likely remain sealed. "We'll have to go up."

Pravda didn't like leaving the central floor, if only for the convenience, but I refused Fang's invitation to force the door. Not that, with my current power, I even could.

Our entry, the very same door Delta, Beta and I had used to embark this way not long ago, waited several levels higher. The humans hiked without complaint, with songs.

They'd started this after the break at the University, when Pravda announced there would be no ambushes and, as such, they might as well make a game of hiking through the dark. Each human took a turn singing a song they remembered, with everyone free to join in if they knew the words . . . or even if they didn't. Tunes weren't so much carried as eviscerated, but the humans picked up their pace, and smiles, unseen save by my glances back, graced faces.

I stopped the singing as we entered the Garden.

"Alpha's mechs came through here," I said. "They might still be around, so be vigilant."

I wanted to add that I could've been more help if Fang hadn't tricked me, but left it alone. I had a plan, no need to be bitter about it.

The water came up to my ankles now instead of my knees, a welcome change. The humans grumbled about it anyway, their boots and shoes proving less waterproof, more crumbly. Blisters already forming with so much walking after centuries getting soft. The mutters played second fiddle to the other sounds within the Garden, the soft swishing as water moved, the splashes as branches and plants gave up their hanging limbs. Wind, flowing all the way from Starship's open front, found channels to blow through, whistling and rustling.

The dark was near absolute. Even my green vision

blurred the scenery together. We navigated by feel alone, every step a test with a toe.

The Garden's center, the big room with the hole in the middle, gave itself away with echoes. Our ripples washed over the edge, ruining any stealth as the drops splashed their way down to Purity.

"Hope you have nothing to hide from," Kaydee said, "'cause you're making noise, my friend."

Didn't I know it. The humans in their bulky uniforms, with their packs, seemed to stumble over everything, catch every branch. Any mechs with an eye towards revenge wouldn't have a hard time finding us.

"Gamma?" Pravda asked as we moved through the middle. "Can we form hands? We're getting lost here."

"Too open," Fang added.

I reached back in the dark, found Fang's fingers. Together we made a line, now walking in a row around the middle pit. The splashing increased, the humans muttered more: advice about debris, encouragement, wishes for home.

"As if their homes exist anymore," Kaydee said.

As if.

I reached the room's far end, where the path narrowed again to splitting hallways. My hand found the wall and I said as much to Fang and the others.

Hope had its moment.

As I took the first step out from the center, I felt a tug on the line. My grip, perilous at best, useless without much power to firm my footing, gave out and sent me splashing into the water. Shouts broke from behind, my ears, sensors not quite catching the words with water soaking.

I struggled onto my back, pushing my head up. Bright flashes lit the room as the humans swapped handholds for rifles, spitting bright energy towards the pit and the several flexi-mechs crawling from it.

The mechs, water spilling off everywhere, lunged towards the closest humans, one already down in the drink. The man splashed, his leg caught by a mech. The laser fire acted like a strobe, showcasing the action in frame by frame detail. Fang seemed to be leading the counter, taking her sputtering rifle and spending its last bolts laying into the grabbing mech.

As she passed by another human, a masked woman whose fire was wild, Fang simply snatched the rifle from the woman's hands, dropping her own in the process. Re-armed, Fang held down the trigger, laying into the mechs.

A hand grabbed my shoulder, helped me up to my feet. Pravda, his face drawn, eyes twitching in the scattered light.

"What do we do?" Pravda said.

"What she's doing," I replied.

Three flexi-mechs had crawled from the pit, and those three lay in smote ruin. The grabbed man sat off to the side, having scaled up a fallen tree. His left leg looked torn up, its blood mixing into the water. Fang poked at the mechs, confirming the kills.

The other two humans went for their injured friend, talking first aid. I joined Fang by the downed flexi-mechs with Pravda.

"They were waiting," Fang said, kneeling by the middle mech. "Mindless machines wouldn't set a trap."

"They're not mindless," I replied, fiddling with the left-most mech. "Alpha used, made these. They're following his orders."

Keeping the conversation going was priority number one. The three flexi-mechs might've been a nightmare for the humans, but they gave me an opportunity: every one of these machines had a battery, had energy I could steal for myself.

"Alpha shouldn't be giving any orders," Fang said, pushing her mech over. I glanced, trying to see why, and saw her looking at the flexi-mech's holsters. Any weapons, tools to scavenge.

"They're following the defaults," I said.

"Defaults?" Pravda asked.

"We captured one of these on our way to you. Alpha set them up to run and hide, to survive. He could've changed that once he realized we weren't going to let him go."

"Change to what? Kill all humans?"

I shrugged, used the motion to hide dipping my hand beneath the water. I pinched two fingers together, formed the jack. Sure, it would let me hack a mech, but I could also siphon power, provided Fang's smoking shot through the flexi-mech's head hadn't destroyed the battery too.

"My guess," I said, "is that Alpha has them hunting you. They ignored me."

Thankfully. If those flexi-mechs sprang their trap on the opposite end, I wouldn't have had much ability to do anything else except lay down and die.

My flexi-mech's port sat along its stomach, beneath the water. I found it, running my hand along the thing's spine, and plugged in.

"We'll have to be more careful," Fang said. The light dwindled, the fires started by wayward lasers burning themselves out. "Can he walk?"

The flexi-mech's battery pumped its energy into me. Kaydee said it felt like drinking coffee, a jittery, necessary rush. Now I just needed the humans to stay long enough to get my fix. Ideally, I could suck power from at least one more, then . . .

Fang and Pravda left me in the shadows, swishing over to the injured man. The humans talked while I sucked power and watched.

"He's not going to walk outta here," Kaydee said, appearing beside me and skipping virtual stones off the water. "That leg's gonna need a splint, time to heal up."

"The Hospital's close," I said.

"Even if it is, you think any of these people know how to care for this guy?" Kaydee snorted. "These are the posh of the posh. They're administrators. Managers. Fang might know how to shoot a gun, but they're not gonna know jack about—"

"Gamma," Pravda said, his face a dim blur now as the last lights flickered. "Can you help with this?"

I could. With the plants around us, with scraps from the human's gear I could rig up a makeshift wrap. But I needed more time to charge first.

"Clean the cuts, then tear off pieces," I said, staying sitting. "Wrap the leg tight. Try to make a crutch from a branch if you can, or else someone will have to support him." Keep talking, keep charging. "The Hospital isn't all that far away."

"Can't you do it?" Pravda asked. "This isn't really our specialty."

"He's got you there," Kaydee muttered.

"Then perhaps it should be," I shot back. "You want to live without mechs, you'll need to do what the mechs used to. It's not that hard."

Water splashed and I found Fang before me, glaring into my face.

"Pravda gave you an order, vessel. He didn't ask for a life lesson."

"If you wanted me to save your friend's leg, you

shouldn't have drained my battery," I replied, keeping my tone neutral. "I'm barely able to walk myself."

"Didn't think the vessels would be so helpless," Fang said, "or weak."

"Fang, it's fine," Pravda said, tired. "We're doing what Gamma said. The mech makes a good point. We can't kill all the machines without learning what they know."

Fang, shaking her head, rose and left me alone, drawing ever more energy with every second.

The humans moved too fast with their first aid, lighting more small fires to see as they went, for me to drain a second mech. Still, the stolen energy put pep in my step. Pep I disguised, dragging my feet like before as we squished through the Garden and back into the Conduit proper.

Pravda wanted to keep going all the way to the Hospital, a trek that would put us through the Park. Fang wanted to detour through the park itself, claiming it'd be nicer to camp out beneath its trees than on the narrower walkways.

I pushed back, saying narrow meant easier to defend. The Park could be home to too many mechs waiting behind bushes, walls, curling pathways.

"Vote?" Pravda asked, and naturally the damn humans all wanted to see a bit more nature.

"They've been locked up in tubes, Gamma. What do you expect?" Kaydee said as we veered off to the right, onto a wide path beneath overhanging boughs.

The Park covered several levels up and down, ours marking the highest. Some treetops broke through level with us, while other platforms put us at grove bases. All almost invisible in Starship's powerless existence.

Fang offered to burn a tree or two, a request Pravda denied. There were only so many trees. Until farms could be established, forests grown from seeds, every plant had to be preserved.

"Makes sense until I fall off and die," Fang replied.

"Then pay attention," I said.

For her part, Fang did. So did Pravda and the other three humans, all rotating shifts supporting their injured friend. We hiked until Pravda called a stop, right above a particular atrium I knew too well. The humans couldn't see it, but at my feet sat an overlook with a fountain centered in the view. That fountain used to be a nasty mech, and now it was nothing.

Nothing, too, came after us as the humans set up around some benches. Snacks broke out, meals in pre-packaged containers. The humans could shake the contents and they'd heat up, giving some smokey-smelling food for dinner.

I found my own place on a bench off to the side, watching the collective. Fang again volunteered for the first watch.

"So you'll have to wait a little longer," Kaydee said, noticing my growing impatience. "You'll be okay."

Maybe, but I itched to be gone. Protect the humans, fine. But I was through being their servant.

Starship was my home as much as theirs.

THIRTY

COHORTS

You know what we call people like you?" Kaydee said as the humans settled onto makeshift grass beds. "Prisoners."

We'd been talking, mostly without words, for the hour it took Fang, Pravda, and their crew to eat and gather themselves for sleep. We'd gone over the plan, finalized the details, and now, with Fang alone, the time had come. Or, well, it would have if Fang hadn't plopped herself next to me.

We sat on a short stone wall, one forming an alcove for the grove the humans slept in. The bricks had cracks, mortar shaken in Starship's descent. Most trees, with thicker roots than the Garden's victims, still stood, though loose branches littered everywhere. I picked them out as dark lines against the green. Fang probably couldn't see them at all.

"What were you doing back there?" Fang asked me, and I noticed her left hand rested on her rifle's trigger. "In the Garden, with that mech?"

"Scanning its files," I said, a lie I'd prepared to tell. My face didn't twitch, give anything away. Sometimes being a machine had its benefits. "I wanted to find out Alpha's orders."

"Did you?"

I shook my head, "You shot its drives. I found nothing."

"You sat there a long time for nothing."

"I don't have energy to burn walking around, remember?"

Fang grinned, "I do remember. Tell me something else, then, vessel. Tell me about Starship, what you've seen since you woke up."

Humans and their demands. I could've pushed back, but instead, with Kaydee feeding me details, I told a version of my story. I kept Val out of it, kept her humans a mystery, but otherwise gave Fang what she wanted. Dragged it out, too, so it lasted—Delta and I were about to save the Nursery —until Fang's watch ended. She had me promise to continue the tale tomorrow night and made the switch.

"Here's our chance," Kaydee said as we watched the new shifter take her turn.

Unlike Fang, this one stayed well away from me. She set up on the alcove's opposite side, staring at nothing.

"She can't see, so if you're quiet you should be good," Kaydee said, stating the obvious. "Then again, can you even be quiet?"

I could be damn stealthy when I wanted to be, thank you very much. First, I lifted my legs and held them out straight into the air. I pushed myself up off the alcove wall, sitting in the air with my hands pressed against the stone. Moving my hands slow, twisting the palms, I rotated myself and put my legs over the path.

"Gentle now," Kaydee said. "Fang'll blow your legs off if you get caught."

A fair threat, and probably accurate. Even Chalo, Val's

resident hunter, didn't regard me with as much suspicion and disdain.

I set my feet down on the hard path. The boots found their setting, still wet from the Garden's marsh. Now would be the tricky part: getting distance without alerting the watcher.

"A diversion?" Kaydee suggested.

No. The watcher would expect me to help respond to any noise. When I didn't, the ruse would fall apart. I'd have to roll my feet, be quiet. Thankfully, where a human might have to guess, I could be precise. I stood up, putting my weight just so on my feet as to make the most level burden. When the breeze picked up and rustled the leaves I took a step, rolling my heel in perfect silence.

Kaydee, standing on the path before me, gave me a clap. Even though only I could hear the noise, it made reacting to my environment hard, so I held a finger to my lips. Kaydee nodded, gave me a thumbs up instead. Two, three, four steps away and no signs of pursuit. I risked a glance back and saw the watcher, her head in her hands.

Why?

"Who knows," Kaydee said. "Maybe she's remembering something here. Or the walk's getting her down, being in the dark the whole time."

I hesitated just then, considering, for a moment, going back and asking her what was wrong. If she had a story, I would listen to it. If she had burdens to unload, I could serve as a confidant, guaranteed never to spill a secret.

"That's not what we need, Gamma," Kaydee said.

Kaydee had it right, of course. That's not what we needed. Not even a vessel could solve everybody's problems.

I padded away into the dark, the silent steps carrying

me farther into the Park. Two levels down put me back in the Conduit's center. I veered left, tracing paths and tangling with Kaydee's strong memories in the place. She flared them up again, those moments where she and Leo drank wine, wandered, laughed.

When I asked why, Kaydee replied, "Why not? It's not like there's anything else to see."

The ghosts faded as I left the Park, found the walkway on the starboard side. A quick calculation turned me right and a few minutes later I found what I was looking for: Power Core. Starship's energy center. The battery banks in here controlled what energy went where, whether terminals worked, lights glowed, or, back when Starship surfed the stars, who breathed and who did not.

"Looks a little different in the dark," Kaydee said as we went through the entrance.

A lobby and hallways beyond passed quickly, nothing more than dead tiles waiting for us. The quiet should've been unnerving, the wind not penetrating this deep and leaving my footfalls the only sound. We went to the right, taking a hard turn from three choices at a branch. Volt's home, a huge room with circular diagrams spreading out across the floor. Last time I'd seen it, every ring had rainbow colors showcasing the energy draw from around the ship. A clear visual for the person, or mech, holed up in the center, behind huge terminals.

"I don't even get a hello?" I said as we walked in.

"A hello? Why would I hello you, you murderer?" Volt shouted back, confirming the mech hid within his terminal palace. Or prison. "You know what you did?"

"Saved the ship, saved you," I replied, striding right on in.

I wouldn't say I had too many friends on Starship, but

Volt? Volt counted as one of them. At least, I thought he did. Volt sat amid his terminals, my dog Alvie clutched in his four metal arms. Alvie glowered at me with yellow eyes, ones matching Volt. I didn't understand, didn't get Volt's mood.

"Where's Bimu? Isn't that what he calls her?" Kaydee asked, hitting on what I'd missed.

"Volt?" I said, choosing a less confrontational tone.

"You turned it all off, man," Volt said, his eyes flaring red. "Things that hadn't been turned off in a thousand years, that hadn't been turned off ever."

"And?"

"I don't know that we'll be able to turn them back on, that's the and. I'm trying, trying right now to keep'em stable."

"Keep what stable?"

"All those batteries! They have to stay a constant cold temp, one they're definitely not now. You see who's missing?"

I nodded.

"I had to plug her in. She's powering, managing the cooling right now." Volt opened his arms, Alvie bounded over to me, gave my shin a good headbutt. "I don't know what's going to happen when you remove the block. She might explode, she might be fine."

"She would've died anyway, Volt, if I hadn't," I said. "The engines would've exploded. You would've burned up."

"Maybe, maybe not. Pretty well armored in here," Volt said. He made a low, synthetic sigh, then his eyes flared blue. "What the hell are you doing here anyway? Aren't you supposed to be turning this boat back on?"

I ran the mech through the last day, the trek through the

dark and the increasingly dismal human entourage following me around. Told him what I wanted, what I'd hoped for in coming here.

"You want a sanctuary," Volt said when I finished.

"For us. For all the mechs."

"You think the humans will give that to you? Because I think they'll kill you long before they give up this hulk," Volt limbered up to his suction-cup feet. "You've met Val, and now you're tellin' me about these new ones, the group treating you like a toy. How are you expecting this to work?"

"They won't be able to get in," I said. "If you do your part, we'll scare them away long enough to fortify Starship."

"If I do my part."

"Putting on a show shouldn't be hard for you. You've got the talent."

"Calling me a liar?"

"Calling you expressive," I followed the human custom, reached out and put a hand on Volt's black metal shoulder. The ambient glow from Alvie and Volt's lights meant we spoke in shadows, blue and gold. "This isn't just about protecting us, it's about them too. They'll have a chance to start clean."

"So you wanna rebuild. Take those Fabrication Lines and crank out a new generation?"

"That's right. I've got my blueprints. We can find yours, figure out how to make more Alvies. Fix the code so we don't have any problems."

"Any problems," Volt gave a copper chuckle. "People long before you tended to say the same thing. Big plans would turn out perfectly. What I saw, new problems came up just the same."

"I'd rather run that risk than die when a human gets scared."

Volt's eyes flashed red, "There's something I can agree with." His four arms shrugged four shoulders. "You get the juice flowing again, I'll see what kinda show I can put on. Owe you that much."

Kaydee waited for me as Alvie and I left Volt behind. She leaned against the dark hallway wall, lit up by digital glow. Her hand had its thumb beneath her chin, finger running up her cheek as she watched me walk.

"Told you he'd go along with it," Kaydee said, sliding up a small grin. "Nice push with that compliment. What a good manipulator you're turning out to be."

"I'm learning it from you." I wasn't sure whether I should be comfortable with that or not, but manipulation seemed to be an asset thus far, so I'd keep using it till it wasn't. "Does that bother you?"

"Since we're getting to be one and the same? Nah."

"Since I'm getting displaced, you mean."

Kaydee fell into step beside me. We left the hallways, headed back towards Power Core's lobby in silence.

"You remember that dinner you held with the Voices? With my mom?" Kaydee said.

"Where she tried to throw a knife at me?"

"That's the one."

"I do. I don't forget anything."

"Right. That must suck. Anyway, she talked to me then, whispered in my ears while Leo and Willis kept saying I had no options," Kaydee took a big, pointless breath. "She said I did have one, and it was you. That I couldn't ignore it."

"You didn't."

"I tried to prove her wrong, though. Give me that credit at least, Gamma. I tried that mech."

"You don't want to try again with something new?"

"Too late for that, my friend. We're too tight now." Kaydee pressed her lips together, had the grace to look sad about the whole thing. "Sorry."

I nodded, kept walking. Didn't mention my process had finished. With the power I'd stolen from the mech, I'd wrapped Kaydee's functions up in a bucket.

I could erase her with a single thought.

THIRTY-ONE

CHANGE IS HARD

I retraced my route through the Park, putting my feet in the exact places where they'd stepped before. Alvie's metal paws padded along with me, adding clinks and clanks and the occasional wheeze-huff to the breeze. Along the way I shuffled through plausible explanations, finally settling on hearing Alvie and going off to look for him. Would Pravda and Fang buy that? Maybe, maybe not, but what choice did they have?

My internal clock put the time near mid morning as I returned to the amphitheater we'd used as a camp. The humans should've been finishing their breakfast, getting ready to go. Maybe waiting for me.

Instead, I saw no watch, no guard.

In the inky dark, in my green filter, I saw nobody and found nothing. They'd left. Stumbled off in some direction.

"Oh, this is fun," Kaydee said, her hand suddenly wielding a large magnifying glass like some classic detective. "Where do you think they went, Gamma? The right way? The wrong way? Did they all fall off one after another?"

"Over a railing?"

"Okay, maybe that's a little unlikely, but have some fun here."

Hard to have fun when my charges were missing. I lacked much sympathy for Pravda and his people, particularly Fang, but core code was tough to refute: my underlying desire to keep the humans safe put me into a state of near panic at their disappearance.

Thankfully, I didn't have to rely on my own nose to find the trail.

"Alvie, smell anything?" I asked the dog.

Alvie wheeze-barked and looked around, clueless.

"Remember, Gamma, Alvie's not a real dog." Kaydee threw me a bemused look. "The puppy probably can't smell anything. That deranged mech in Purity made him from junk."

Right, but before I could find another strategy, Alvie wheeze-barked again and shot off, paws clacking away on the paved paths.

"Maybe he can," I said to Kaydee and took off after my dog.

Alvie ran fast, faster than I could hope to match, but the dog kept me in mind, stopping every now and then to wait. His judging yellow eyes seemed disappointed in my slow jog, but I wasn't about to expend more energy than necessary on the chase. Not when I didn't know how far we'd go. At least Alvie ran in the right direction: through the Park towards Starship's aft. The humans, then, hadn't been so lost as to start off the way they'd come.

Good thing, because the Hospital would be this way.

I hadn't left the Park behind when Alvie led me to a Conduit walkway. Wheeze-barking, the dog scratched at my leg until I said I'd keep following it. Alvie jumped, spinning in the air and shot off away from me, and again I chased.

Soon I heard more than metal clacks, now with an extra shiny ring as we traded pleasant pavers for walkway steel. The new noises weren't what I was hoping for: the whirs, hisses, clatter and beeps came from decidedly inhuman sources. With Alvie up ahead, the dog's yellow eyes spotlights in the gloom, I slowed up, tried to identify the sounds.

"Would Alvie bring us right to flexi-mechs?" Kaydee asked.

No. I'd seen enough flexi-mechs by now to know these weren't their sounds. For one, the mechs could run quiet if they wanted. These sounded like mechs in bad repair: loose gaskets, corroded wires, unstable treads. Not that Alpha only used flexi-mechs. Starship was a huge ship, who knew how many leftover loyal machines were squirreled away in its crevices?

"So you're going in unarmed?" Kaydee asked as I kept walking forward after my dog. "Smart move, hotshot."

"I'm not leaving Alvie alone. And I trust my dog."

No way he'd lead me into danger.

Alvie waited for me near a busted open cafe. Nice lettering scraped across an arch over the door, smudged and bent decor calling to a time when visitors might stop in for a smoothie, a tea before setting off into the Park for a day among the trees. With Alvie's eyes splashing light, I saw an inside failing to keep up appearances: small tables lay on their sides, chairs bent and broken. A hole split a long counter, the coffee machine behind splayed open for parts. Salvaged, scavenged, either by mechs or humans.

Three late-comers joined me in surveying the wreckage, the creaky trio confirming themselves as the noise's source. A trash mech, a sweeper, and a defunct nurse on leave from the Hospital. They meandered around the space, each stopping to inspect shattered cups, bent furniture, a crumpled flier.

"Not quite the humans," Kaydee muttered. "Maybe Alvie's lost his touch."

Maybe. I glanced at the dog, who looked up at me. His metal jaw, iron teeth couldn't exactly form expressions, but Alvie gave off a satisfied air. He was a mech, he didn't make mistakes.

"Let's see what you found," I said, loud enough to carry into the cafe.

The three mechs turned as one at my voice. The sweeper and the trash mech weren't made for human interaction, and their blank boxes told me nothing of their intent. The nurse mech, however, shined its eyes at me: blue.

"Hello," I said. "The name's Gamma." I fumbled for the next step, settled on this: "I'm trying to find humans. Have you seen any?"

The wrong question. The nurse mech's eyes flared red and it, along with the trash mech and sweeper, came towards me. All three raised their thin arms, grasping in my direction.

"Whelp, guess they're not friendly," Kaydee said. "Try not to die, Gamma."

"I'll do my best," I replied, sneaking in the cafe to the right. Behind me, Alvie started up his wheeze-barks, advancing. "Knock'em down, buddy."

If all these mechs had a common weakness, it lay in their chunky feet or, in the nurse mech's case, careful treads. None could pick themselves up, and none had what Delta would call 'ability' in a fight. They rumbled straight at me, and Alvie went to work.

The nurse mech came in hot, treads squealing as it

accelerated across the crap-strewn floor. Alvie, being the smart dog he was, waited till the mech rolled by the cafe entrance before jumping out. My dog hit the nurse mech at its shoulders, bearing it to the ground on its side. Kicking off, Alvie hit the next mech in line, battering the trash machine down and standing on it.

Which left the sweeper for me.

With its brushes whirling, two thin arms for removing debris swiping towards my face, the sweeper presented a mild threat. One I decided to handle in bar fight fashion: I threw a chair at it. Even without full strength—had to conserve energy—my missile mashed into the sweeper and sent it sideways. The mech fell back, its brushes spinning in the air.

"Not too shabby," Kaydee said, popping in to survey the wreckage.

"A few days ago, this would've been scary," I replied. "Now?"

Now, what? Had I become Gamma, slayer of mechs? Conqueror of Starship's many halls?

"Don't get too full of yourself," Kaydee laughed. "Delta and Beta could still have your ass for breakfast."

"Not if I programmed them to serve me breakfast instead."

"What would your breakfast even be, Gamma? A fresh battery?"

"I'd take it."

I chose the nurse mech as my first target. Compared to the other two, the machine would have a voice, would have the most complex processing. I asked it again if it'd seen the humans. All I received from its plastic, sealed smile beneath those red eyes, its treads spinning uselessly, was garbled tones. I wasn't going to learn anything quizzing the busted bot, but, like the police in the Librarian's movies, I had other methods.

"This'll just take a second," I said to the mech, pressing my thumb and forefinger together to form the jack.

FOR A MECH DESIGNED to help and heal, turning it into a homicidal machine took some doing. The kind that left evidence all over. Going into the mech's insides put me in a shabby room, one littered with beeping medical monitors. The shoulder-height screens surrounded Kaydee and I, sterile blue glows hitting us from all angles. Beyond them, wires trailing down tangled on the floor and up the walls, covering oozing gray-green splotches. A stuffy, disinfectant smell suffused the space.

"What a lovely setup," Kaydee said, pinching her nose.

"Worse than the others," I said, recalling the nurses back at the, well, Nursery. Those hadn't been corrupted like this, a deliberate twisting. Rather, they'd simply been victims to functions left to run without a tweak in far too long.

"Why?"

I pointed to the splotches on the wall. They reminded me of a particular color, a particular feel.

"There's only one mech doing this," I said, "and he's dead now."

"Alpha's leftovers," Kaydee sighed. "Gross. Guess we can kill this one then."

We could, but why? For once, I wasn't under imminent attack. Alvie had my back, and the enemies around weren't exactly serious. If our plan was to make Starship a haven for mechs, there'd be more like this.

"So you're saying what?" Kaydee asked when I told her my idea. "You're going to clean it out?"

"Better than that," I replied. "If I want Starship to be a home for mechs, I'll have to give the mechs a chance to live in it. Really live."

"Gamma, that's—"

"Think about it. I could return this one to its original state, wipe it clean. It'd go back to the Nursery and care for the embryos, which might not even be there any more. What happens then?"

Kaydee looked around at the blue screens, each one scrolling through another function, another coded command.

"I don't know Gamma, but—"

"I have to try and give them a real purpose. Real agency."

"You're sounding like Alpha."

"No. Alpha dictates. I'm setting them free."

Before Kaydee could protest further, I went to the closest blue screen. The keyboard beneath gave me all the access I needed, a chance to cut, edit, type and transform. I copied bits from myself, the logic and open-minded calculations. I erased Alpha's leftovers, each deleted bit removing a splotch from the wall.

Kaydee watched it all, a sad grimace on her face. Fine. She wasn't a mech, she wouldn't understand. I found other places to make improvements too, lines forcing the mech to obey humans, to always follow their rules. I stripped those away, gave the mech my own morality guidelines. It would be able to make its own choices, define its own values over time.

When I stepped back, the mech's room glowed bright. The walls were clean, a new light shown down, and all those screens had been compressed down to one, optimizing the flow.

"Beautiful," I said, nodding at my own work.

"It's something," Kaydee said.

"You don't like it?"

"I'm not sure you're gonna get what you want, is all."

"Oh ye of little faith."

Kaydee chuckled, "Where'd you get that line?"

Rather than answer, I pulled us back out to the real world, where I could judge my creation. Or, perhaps, be judged by it.

THE CAFE SAT AS BEFORE. Even Alvie hadn't moved from atop the angry trash mech. Dark held, requiring an adjustment from the bland-but-bright digital room. My rescue project juddered as I stepped back, the nurse mech's eyes dashing through colors. Blue, red, green. All should've corresponded to a feeling, an action on the mech's part, but I heard only rattles. Grinds. Rambles. Nothing resembling the sense I thought I'd programmed into it.

"Rough start," Kaydee said next to me. The nurse mech tried to stand, flopped over and fell with a hard thunk back to the floor. Alvie wheeze-barked a question.

"Hello?" I tried pitching the nurse mech. "Do you have a name?"

A function I'd dropped inside the machine should've come up with one, an identity from which everything else could spring. Instead, the mech rolled. It flopped. It banged its arms on the floor or against its own head. Then, after emitting what seemed to be a combination of all its possible tones at once, the mech locked up and lay still. Its eyes dead.

I didn't need to ask it anything else.

"You can't make everything a vessel, Gamma," Kaydee said as I knelt to examine the machine. "They don't have the components for it. The design. They're not meant to do what you do, just like you aren't meant for their purpose."

"They should be malleable," I countered. "They're machines, we can change."

"Sure, if you rip out its guts and throw yours in, I bet it'd work just fine. But that's not what you did. You threw someone with no arms, no legs, and no help into the ocean and expected a miracle."

I sat back, stared at the dead mech. The sweeper and its trash friend continued their fruitless efforts to stand up. Alvie, sensing my annoyance, gave a muted sympathy yowl.

"Then how am I supposed to save them?" I asked, not really expecting Kaydee to have an answer.

"Guess what, Gamma. We tried the same thing, but with humans. I died for it. Know what I learned?"

"I'm asking, aren't I?"

"And being a snob about it," Kaydee gave me a digital slap. I took it like a champ. "I realized you have to let people be themselves. Can't force'em to change who they are. You want your mechs to live well, then clean them out. Give them their jobs back, let'em be."

I marinated on the words. Went over to the sweeper mech, staying just out of reach of its grasping arms. The thing had been built to keep the Conduit clean. That's what all its components were bent towards. For now.

"When I have the Lines, I'll make you better," I said to the mech, then formed the jack again and went to work.

THIRTY-TWO

LASERS AND LATTES

We found the humans thanks to their clumsiness. Upon leaving the cafe and the lost mechs, we heard noises distinctly unlike the breeze, the occasional clanks or a wandering machine.

"Pretty sure mechs don't curse like that," Kaydee said as we stood on the walkway, trying to decide where to go.

The words, the shouts carried up from below, echoing off Starship's walls. A human might've found it hard to figure where the voices came from, but my sensors pinpointed it in an instant: below, several levels.

At least the epithets sounded more angry than scared.

With Alvie by my side, we found the nearest stair and headed down. This close to the Park, most places matched the cafe I'd just left: restaurants, spas, luxuries. Their ruins seemed better in the dark, where Kaydee and I could forget the present. She filled them in with descriptions, with little stories as we walked.

"I need more of this," I told her as we hit the human's level, the interludes at an end. "There's too much anger and violence with the humans I meet. It's the wrong side."

"Most of us think so too."

Ahead, we saw the store Pravda and Fang had found. It lay barricaded by broken benches, the parts strewn across the walkway. How many humans had fallen over those pieces? All of them?

Alvie stopped. Put a paw on my shin. Sniffed, his golden eyes flashing red. Kaydee and I listened. The humans weren't cursing anymore, were talking. A heated discussion.

That wasn't what had Alvie holding me back.

They looked like moving shadows along the walls, dark green shapes sliding above and along the railing to my right. Flexi-mechs, at least five. Hunting.

"Well that's no good," Kaydee whispered as we watched the mechs creep in closer. "Don't wanna get you down, Gamma, but five might be too many for an un-armed vessel like yourself."

The humans, though, had rifles. Even Pravda carried a gun, though who knew if he could shoot it worth a damn.

"Cool. Let'em defend themselves." Kaydee folded her arms. Caught my askance look. "You know I'm not all about every human, right? This bunch wants to see you scrapped, Gamma. I'm not gonna defend them."

"You don't have to. C'mon Alvie."

I'd figure out my strategy on the fly, save for the opening. With my tap, Alvie dashed forward, wheeze-barking away. I followed, feet pounding the walkway, calling out an alarm to the humans inside.

The flexi-mechs and their shadows froze at my words. The blurs marking their heads glanced my direction and I thought they might all come down upon me like ravenous wolves.

They went for the humans instead.

Two threw themselves over the walkway's railing, hitting the tile and dashing into the cafe. Another pair swung in through already-shattered windows, knocking off glass remnants to add a tinkling background to the chaos. Flashes, missing bolts darted as Alvie and I closed, burning through the windows into the Conduit. Fang and Pravda's voices called out orders. Someone screamed. Three more flexi-mechs barreled opposite us, closing with the cafe.

"Take them," I told my dog, and we ran ahead.

With bright blue-white lasers haloing my shoulders, buzzing my head, Alvie and I bounded by the first window to meet the flexi-mechs before the cafe's door. Alvie, faster than me, took a flying leap and snared the leader around the throat, the dog's not-so-little weight dragging the mech into the one behind. The pile landed on the walkway, with just enough leeway for me to gather my legs and jump, meeting the third flexi-mech in a mid-air collision.

I expected a drill hand to the chest, a gouge to the face or something worse. Instead, we hit and the flexi-mech tried to throw me off, a failed move in mid-air. My weight exceeded the thin machine's boney skeleton, sending us both backward beyond Alvie's dogpile. I crunched the flexi-mech to the ground, felt the thing's hands grab and try to move me off. A move that might've worked except my own hands found grips on the flexi-mech's narrow spine. As the mech threw me left, trying to get away, I held on, pulling the flexi-mech with me. The machine rolled over and I pushed off, letting go with the momentum. The mech launched into the air, still pulling left, and disappeared over the edge.

Would it survive the fall? Would it land on a soft, moldy mattress as I once had?

"Who cares, Gamma! Help your damn dog!" Kaydee pulled me back to reality.

Alvie snapped at the flexi-mechs in turn, trying to keep the pair from getting past him. Neither machine seemed interested in my dog beyond shoving the puppy aside. Lasers and curses continued to pour from the cafe. Someone cried too, pained sobs edging around the fight's crashes.

Still with only my hands, I did what I could: ran up behind Alvie's two and played catch with the Conduit. Like some football player, I bent down and scooped up the nearer flexi-mech, this one bearing sparking scars along its chest and ankles, and launched it after its comrade. The mech didn't cry out as it flew and vanished. No protest, no declared vengeance.

Alvie took his sudden freedom and used it to clamp down on the last one's leg. Digging his paws into the walkway as the flexi-mech tried to push past him, Alvie yanked hard. The flexi-mech's knee popped free from its socket, coolant and wires flailing everywhere. Rather than falling to a stop or caring about its injury, the flexi-mech fell forward onto its four arms and scurried forward, pulling around the cafe's door inside.

"Not so fast," I said, dashing around my dog.

"Stay low!" Kaydee yelled. "Friendly fire's a real thing, you know!"

My friends fired like mad people. Their rifles blazed as I came into the cafe, what seemed like a dozen soon turned out to be four, with two apiece held by Fang and another human. Their shots lit up the space, revealing an ugly last stand at the restaurant's back. The humans holed up behind the counter, the flexi-mechs advancing from all sides.

While the machines hadn't cared much about Alvie and

I, they came at the humans with tactics, with murderous intent. Carrying tables and chairs as shields, four, now five with our hobbled target, mechs approached from all angles. Two clung to the outside walls, wrapping their way around while the others approached from the middle.

The flexi-mechs didn't just take shots either, but gave it right back, flinging shrapnel with dire accuracy at the humans. Fang, standing tall, had at least three chunks spearing out from her arms, her shoulders and chest. I couldn't see Pravda and the other two, assumed they were behind the cafe's counter.

"Not good," Kaydee said as I caught up to the wounded flexi-mech.

I didn't like my chances to throw the flexi-mech through the narrow door and off into the Conduit, so I chose a more direct method: picking up a burnt stand made for menus and spearing the flexi-mech from behind. I drove the weapon with enough force to pierce the flexi-mech's remaining leg and stake it to the floor. Not that the mech cared: it kept trying to break free, at least for another second until I ripped out the mech's battery pack.

"Gamma! Help!" Fang, for once not speaking to me with derision, anger, or suspicion.

The flashes died down as Fang's rifles sputtered out of energy. She'd left one flexi-mech dead in her wake, the other human still shooting and holding off the other two on the right. Which put the left wall-crawler as my next goal. I hefted a chair, took aim, and failed as the flexi-mech jumped down behind the counter. Alvie did what I couldn't, flying by me and, using a tipped table as a boost, bounding over the counter's top like a flying metal missile. My dog wheeze-barked his way, yellow eyes glowing as he disappeared over the counter.

"One seriously courageous dog you've got there," Kaydee said as I turned to the other two mechs.

"Courage has nothing to do with it."

Like the flexi-mechs before me, I picked up debris and ran with it. First up, the flexi-mech attempting a straightforward assault. I bashed it from behind with a table leg, and when the mech turned to see what the hell had hit it, the human knew enough to vaporize its skull with a well-placed bolt. The shot was her last. The wall-crawling mech on the right jumped forward, getting behind the counter and flinging a busted bottle. The glass struck the human hard, sending her and her rifles to the ground.

I started forward, saw Fang diving for the fallen guns. With one foot planted, I jumped, only for the torched flexi-mech's hand to make one feeble grab at my ankle. The clutch knocked me off balance, enough that I barreled into the counter instead of leaping over. The glass display case, meant in some forgotten time for scones and cinnamon rolls, shattered beneath my weight. My eyes closed for their own protection, my right shoulder leading the way through glass, through plastic, and into . . . metal?

Many-fingered hands scrambled to push me off as I drove into the flexi-mech, both of us falling into a mess behind the counter. I found grips along the flexi-mech's body, held it while the machine tried to scurry away. Heard a click, saw Fang staring us down. The humans lay crumpled around her in various doomed states. Behind them, Alvie carved up his flexi-mech, a spark show in the dark.

Fang tossed aside her useless rifle, brought up the new one. My flexi-mech lunged again but I held it back, digging my feet into the floor to keep us secure.

"Don't shoot," I said. "You can't see!"

"Oh, right," Kaydee mused. "that's why they couldn't hit any of these things. I just thought they sucked."

"Don't need to see," Fang replied to me, raising the rifle. "I can hear you just fine."

The flexi-mech struggled again, four arms trying to over-power me. The energy I'd stolen from the Garden dwindled as I fought the machine, tried to keep it from breaking free. Fang might be about to kill me, might be about to burn us both, but I had to. I had to protect the humans. There was no other choice.

"Thanks for coming back, Gamma," Fang said. "Would've felt bad leaving you alive."

I closed my eyes, held the flexi-mech tight. My code perfectly happy with how I was about to die.

THIRTY-THREE

FACTIONS

A hand pushed Fang's rifle away, a bloody scratched one belonging to one Pravda, leader of these humans. Fang snarled, glanced at the offending arm while I continued to hold back the flexi-mech.

"You can't," Pravda said. "You can't kill him. Not yet."

"I can, right now, with this," Fang replied, pushing off Pravda's arm.

"If you shoot him, we'll all die," Pravda replied. The man was on his knees, one arm planted on the ground to lift him up. His clothes were shredded, maybe one of those flexi-mechs had raked him with hands. "We'll never find our way out of here, much less get Starship operational. Please Fang, think."

"He'll kill us in the end," Fang said, but she didn't raise the rifle. "They always try."

The flexi-mech found a purchase, its shoulders twisted as I focused too much on Fang and not enough on my own efforts. The mech burst free, took a long swipe at Fang, and she fired. Point blank, even in the dark she couldn't miss. The laser burrowed through the flexi-mech's shoulder and into the wall behind its back, a glowing ember in the cafe and as good a marker as any the fight had ended.

"I'll make sure to let you know," I said to Fang, sitting up.

"Let me know what?"

"When I try to kill you." I gave her the nastiest, grimiest grin I could muster, one wasted on the dark.

The humans had it rough. None of the five escaped the fight without wounds, and while I bandaged them up—using cloth from their own clothes—as best I could, there was no hiding that the band would be reduced to nothing without medical help quick. I did, though, steal some time to charge myself up on the ruined flexi-mechs.

Four machines had their batteries intact, and with Pravda ordering recovery and rest after the fight, I shambled from one to the next, topping up my battery to where kinetic energy from running around ought to be enough to keep me going. In short, the humans had gone from a five-to-one advantage over one weak vessel, to one strong vessel and his dog lording over five half-dead, exhausted, and blind people.

"You should rub Fang's face in it," Kaydee said to me as we walked the Conduit again. "She deserves to feel some fear."

"She'll use it as another excuse to shoot me."

"So? She's got plenty already."

"Doesn't mean I need to add another."

"You're boring, Gamma."

"I'm sure that'll change when you're running things."

Kaydee fell silent at that, leaving me alone with Alvie at the group's head. We didn't have far before we found the Hospital, several levels below the main entrance. Fang and Pravda could still walk, so they waited while I lifted the humans up the stairs, walked back down, and repeated the effort. Nothing had me feeling more like a mech than the schlepping here, but in truth, I didn't mind it all so much. All three humans, two men and a woman, thanked me for my help. One, the man who'd been raked back in the Garden, claimed he wouldn't be alive without me.

Did the words 'feel' good? Maybe, but more practically, they finally added some weight to the other side of my human scale, the side not measuring anger, vindictiveness, warmongering.

"How's that looking?" Kaydee asked as I dropped the last human off outside the Hospital entrance and we started inside. "Humans still a garbage species?"

"You don't want to know."

She didn't probe. If she had, I'd have told Kaydee that, without my programmed rules, I'd have ditched her people a long time ago.

We didn't have to hunt long to find supplies for the humans. Apparently the Hospital mechs weren't much interested in looting and after Delta's carnage the massive medical center seemed quiet. Wounds were dressed, splints found. Snacks acquired from canned goods and vacuum-sealed rations who knew how many years old. Pravda even found some of his old bravado, especially after I had Alvie turn up his eye-light glow to give some real illumination around us. Two spotlights in the dark.

"Now, see this?" Pravda announced as we made our way towards the aft-ward exit. "No journey isn't without its challenges, but with a bit of moxie, a bit of courage, we can make it. We will make it."

A few muttered agreements did nothing to dim the man's bright eyes. Was he a leader or was he just dressing up his own legend?

"Definitely the latter," Kaydee said. "Look at him, nodding at all the signs we're passing. He's writing his own story right now."

Pravda's story became a lot more interesting not long after the Hospital, when we found the Nursery. Located on Starship's central level, just like the Hospital's main entrance, the Nursery stuck out against the black, its generators keeping the critical lives inside cool. For how long, I didn't know. Pravda called for another break as we passed before the Nursery, claiming we should all head inside, have a look around.

"After all, this is our future," Pravda said, shushing away my protest. "The vials in here are everything, aren't they Gamma? Humanity goes no further if these are harmed."

But how much further would I go when they discovered what was, or what was not, inside?

At least their rifles were spent, save for the one around Fang's shoulders. Pravda, though, had sent her to the rear. Told her to watch for ambushes, listen amid the blackness. I figured he'd made the move to keep Fang and I from tearing each other apart. Now she came back up, went with Pravda and I past the lobby. The other humans took the waiting couches there with grateful sighs. I suggested Fang and Pravda do the same, trying to buy a bit of time, but they both refused.

So, with Alvie by my side, we all went further back, to where I'd dealt with so much disaster. The Nursery's rear half offered disappointment, fear. Racks where embryos had been stored for a thousand years lay empty, their trays scattered about. The mechs Delta and I had repaired were stacked, shut down, in a corner. I wondered how Leo and Val had removed all these sensitive materials before Pravda's loud cursing yanked me back to the present.

"They're gone," Pravda said when his damns ran out. "All lost. We're done, we're done. Even if we had every woman capable of a child raising one, there'd be too—"

"Shut up, Pravda," Fang said, for once not aiming the rifle at me but at the empty racks. "They weren't destroyed. They were taken." She put a hand on Pravda's shoulder, steadying him. "Anything taken can be returned."

Pravda shook his head, "They must have been taken years and years ago, Fang. Our children, our future is probably lying in a trash heap somewhere. Or ejected into the vastness of space."

Now Fang looked at me, "There weren't people alive who would do this when we went to sleep. The only possible answer would be mechs. Mechs like you who want Starship for yourselves."

"I didn't do this, if that's what you mean," I answered.

"But you know who did," Fang replied.

As I said, I didn't have a poker face. I didn't have tells. My body did exactly what I asked of it, so how did Fang know I hadn't told the whole truth?

"Because you're not surprised," Kaydee said, sitting on the newborn conveyor belt behind Fang and Pravda. "You walk in here, see disaster, apocalyptic disaster, and you're just fine with it?"

Hmm. Kaydee made a good point. Nothing I could do about it now.

"Gamma, answer her," Pravda said, and I saw tears, genuine ones, leaking from his eyes. "Did the mechs do this?"

They'd had the hint back on the Bridge. A secret I'd kept hidden, one I'd hoped would stay that way. But that would be too lucky, too convenient.

Starship didn't suffer luck.

"No mechs did this," I said. "You're not the only humans alive on this world."

For once, Fang let me get through the whole story without threatening to kill me. She and Pravda listened to what I knew about Val and her tribe, about Leo and the Forgers. They took in the details, started asking questions that I answered without complaint. Only when Fang began probing for military details, like the number of fighters and what weapons they had, did I balk.

"I won't give them up," I said.

"Why?" Pravda replied, getting his whiny haughtiness back now that doom wasn't inevitable. "Why would you protect people who did this?"

"Because they aren't all assholes."

Fang laughed, "At least I'm honest about my feelings for you, vessel. I guarantee everyone in that tribe feels the same about you as I do. Why do you think they tried to blow up Starship with you on it?"

"Because they are scared." I gestured at the Nursery, its destruction. "They were willing to risk giving up everything they'd ever known for a chance at survival without you. A smart choice."

Pravda ordered me, then, to wait while he and Fang went back to the others. He said they'd have to talk about what came next, decide what to do with this information. I spent the time wandering through the Nursery, looking at what'd been taken, what'd been left behind.

"They took the toys," Kaydee noted as we went by the infant and toddler playrooms. "All those books."

A lot to carry, but Val and Leo seemed determined to do things right. Maybe they'd found a few mechs willing to do the work for them.

"Yeah, held them down so Leo could reprogram them," Kaydee said. "Hard to give up a vice."

"A vice?"

"Yeah, you. Mechs. You're so convenient, Gamma."

"That's a compliment?"

"For a mech? Absolutely."

Fang and Pravda came back in eventually, the latter with his eyes back to their glimmering brightness. Fang seemed her usual suspicious self, though her slight smile made me nervous.

"Guess what, Gamma?" Fang said. "You're going to get Starship up and running, and then you're going to take us to this Val. We're going to have a nice chat."

"They fight as well as you," I said. "You won't win that way."

"No," Pravda replied, "but we can give them a choice. Come back to Starship and its safety, its luxury, or scrabble on their own."

By their looks, their tones, it seemed clear which way these two thought Val's people would go.

And after being around humans for so long, I had no idea whether they were right.

THIRTY-FOUR

A BLUFF

Starship's engines didn't give us any more light than the rest of the ship. Back here, the wind whipped harder, having sped the Conduit's length only to find a prison. The engineering section's narrow halls and off-shoots prompted nervous muttering among the humans, each one expecting a flexi-mech to jump out for another ambush. We hadn't seen, hadn't heard another mechanized soul since the cafe. Whether we'd outrun Alpha's leftovers or destroyed them all, I couldn't know, but I didn't mind the quiet.

For one, it gave me a chance to square up the details with Kaydee. By details, I meant who would be running the show. I still had my program, still had Kaydee's self wrapped up and ready to delete, but I couldn't bring myself to pull the trigger. Every minute I delayed, Kaydee's reach grew, a slow seeping into functions and controls she hadn't yet tainted.

Soon, program or no, I'd be unable to erase her without leaving major holes in myself.

Those long hours walking in the dark brought me to one conclusion: I couldn't keep lying. I needed Kaydee to survive the humans and, more than that, I wanted her in my 'life', such as it was. The prospect of living on for who knew how many centuries without her sarcastic one-offs, her shimmering teal hair, her insights and insults . . . it seemed too boring to contemplate.

Boring. I laughed. Prompted a question from Pravda that I ignored. What a world in which a machine could be bored.

"It's 'cause you're not just a machine, Gamma," Kaydee said as our expedition neared the engines themselves, the terminals Leo would've used to turn Starship into a bomb. "Like I said at the beginning, vessels aren't so mindless."

"Makes it harder," I replied.

"Harder than what, following commands?"

"Making decisions for myself is difficult when the choices aren't black and white."

"That's why I'm here, buddy boy. You and me, the logic and the life, together."

Her sparkle as she spoke, her vivid energy contrasted hard with the green-tinged gloom around me. What was I supposed to do with that? Erase it? But lose myself? That was the other side, a decision—

"Hey," Kaydee said, interrupting. "That it?"

We'd seen the bank when I'd come back inside the ship from our long jaunt from bow to aft with Delta and Alvie. The one where I'd been stabbed in the gut by some glass, but managed to make it out anyway. Six monitors stacked two by two, each one dead now, that'd normally show the engines' status. They'd have the switch ready to set the engines to manual override, the key to unlock too much power.

"Now, how were we gonna turn Starship back on

again?" Kaydee asked me as I told the humans we'd found the spot. "You have a trick here?"

"Just watch," I said.

The humans settled themselves in a semi-circle around me as I set to work. First came a hard switch, a physical toggle on the bank's left. The red switch changed the bank's power draw from Starship's main supply, the one I'd cut off back on the Bridge, to the engine's back-up batteries. A soft chunk did the work, and right away the monitors flickered to life.

In a few seconds, Leo's countdown program would kick in. In a few seconds, I'd stop it dead. For this, I didn't even need to zap into the terminal. Fingers on keys in the real world would be enough. I chose the central monitor, basking in the sudden blue-gray light from all the screens. The humans blinked, and Pravda let out a small cheer.

With Starship's network down, Leo's program showed up first: a dwindling countdown until the engines would roar. From here, I did a single, simple thing: clicked a small cancel button in the lower right corner.

"That's it?" Kaydee asked as the program died. "We went all this way so you could click an X?"

"That's it," I said. "Kinda lame, isn't it?"

Kaydee started to reply, then we both noticed what'd replaced Leo's doomsday command: a message box, one with a several paragraph apology. Kaydee had her head shaking as she read the message, and I agreed: Leo started off with an admission, the program itself had been a fake. The engines would've canceled the order as a catastrophic command as soon as it'd started. Leo said they couldn't destroy Starship anyway, not when so many of their own tribe were near. The goal had been to buy time, give Val, Chalo, and the others a chance to get away.

"Well, he succeeded there," I muttered.

Three days bought and paid for with the stunt. Leo poured his real self into the next section. He addressed Kaydee, calling her out by name and apologizing for all the mistakes he'd made, the days and years lost chasing wild machines that should've been spent with her. Should've been spent doing the real important work: living.

"Was it that bad?" I asked Kaydee when we'd both finished.

"He's a sap, Gamma," Kaydee replied. "We were both ambitious. If he'd been all about spending days drinking wine in the Park, I'd have dumped him. But it's a nice letter."

I noticed, though, that she re-read it several times.

With the doom averted, I told Pravda and Fang Starship was about to wake up again. They were more than ready, looking forward to a quick hike back to the Bridge. Reunions, and then re-arming for an expedition after those embryos, after Val, Chalo and the rest.

Not a word escaped my lips about the plan.

"Ready?" I asked Kaydee, going back to the monitors.

"As fun as it was stumbling around in the dark, let the light shine on, buddy."

A few more keystrokes sent the command to the always-listening battery-backed up controls to kick start Starship to life. At first, nothing seemed to happen. The monitors before me showed a long loading bar, one crawling through a list of this and that system.

"Bet nobody's seen this screen for a thousand years," Kaydee said.

"Or longer."

The obvious operations like life support came first, and with them Starship rumbled awake, all those air processors grinding into action. Water filtration, the misting keeping the Conduit its foggy self wound into gear. Ceiling lights around us bloomed after several minutes, flickering into full action and letting the engine's back-up batteries return to being just that. Clangs and clacks, thunks and bangs echoed down to us as valves and vents woke up.

"If you never thought of Starship as alive, pretty hard not to now," Kaydee said.

We took in the technical symphony for half an hour, waiting for Starship to stabilize. Waiting, too, for a particular trigger.

"Looks good!" Pravda announced, ordering the humans to get packed up, on their feet. "Time to go home, right?"

Even Fang looked relieved, helping another human pull on their pack. Fresh, happy faces, as if the harrowing walk was dirt washed off in electricity's shower. Almost made me feel bad.

"Time to go home," I said.

The Conduit lived and breathed again. The golden light glittered up and down the vast canyon, shining off fresh mist floating from above. Walkways above and below us, cluttered with debris, looked merely messy and not like dangerous treks. Pravda put his hand on my shoulder, a broad grin stretching across his face.

"You did it, you damn vessel," the man said. "Told Fang we ought to keep you alive, and you've paid back that decision in full." Pravda gave me a nod now. "I know we've not always been polite to one another, but once all this nasty business with these other humans is put to bed, I'll protect you. You'll have a spot right next to me as long as you want it."

Kaydee snorted. I ignored her.

"Thanks," I replied, was going to try and find some

common ground between Pravda and Val, when Starship's many lights went off for a full second before splashing back.

Only for a second, but even that one second prompted groans from the humans around us. Pravda froze, his smile faltering. I waited for Volt's next step. A voice, the particular kind voice from Starship's many maneuvers, its turns and its landings, came over the loudspeakers next.

"Attention Starship," the posh woman announced. "There is an unexpected power surge. The vessel is unstable. Immediate evacuation is recommended."

The message repeated twice more, and into its fourth replay, Pravda pulled me aside, asked what the hell was going on.

"There was always a chance," I said, "that Starship wouldn't take well to getting shut down after so long without a break. It was a risk, but I felt I had to take it."

"How long do we have?" Pravda asked, the others huddling up behind him, looking at me like I was some dispenser of infinite wisdom.

Only Fang kept her narrowed suspicion.

"No idea." I told the truth. "I'm sure your friends back at the Bridge are evacuating. You should leave too, meet them outside."

Pravda shot a look at Starship's hull, as if he could see through it to the golden plains beyond.

"Outside?" He asked.

"It's that or risk dying," I replied, trying to inject some urgency into my voice. "I'll show you the way, then go back to the controls. I might be able to slow it down. Buy you time to get away."

Pravda shook his head, "We don't have food, we don't have shelter, we—"

"Find Val and her people. They'll take you in," I said.

Pravda started to sputter, but I turned him around, pointed back towards the engines. "C'mon, we have to leave now!"

The lights flickered again. A perfect surge that sent the humans scrambling. Pravda raced to the bunch's front, repeating what I'd said as the group went back through the engineering halls. They'd stick together, get outside and regroup with their friends away from Starship. I said I'd broadcast a message from the console, tell the other humans to meet Pravda's band in the hills to the west.

"They're really buying it," Kaydee said as the humans flat-out sprinted, at least as best they could with their wounds and gear, down the corridors. "Like, wow."

We tromped down stairs, skipping steps to get to Starship's bottom exit, a narrow doorway leading outside. With Pravda and the humans letting me through, I turned the heavy valve and popped the portal open, showing a starlit night sky beyond.

The humans all stopped, staring in open-mouthed awe at the first other world they'd seen, hell, the first world they'd seen at all beyond these metal halls.

"It's beautiful," Pravda said slow, soft.

"Glad you think so," I replied. "Now get going, I have to get back up to the consoles."

I gave the man a light push and he bit on it, rushing out and down the steps leading to the ground. A stair put together by Leo and Val, but I didn't mention that. Instead I helped each human in turn head off on their way, each one until I felt not a shoulder, but a hard metal nozzle. A rifle's barrel.

"Tell me the truth, vessel," Fang said, digging her weapon into my ribs. "Is Starship going to explode, or are you a lying mech?"

THIRTY-FIVE

A GUN TO THE HEAD

Kill her. Take the rifle, it's right there, snap it and throw Fang after the humans. Shut the door and lock them outside. Or bring her with you and as soon as Pravda and the others are gone, delete her.

The ideas blitzed through me as I stared down Fang's threat, cool night air mingling with Starship's recycled version there at the ship's aft exit. Down below, Pravda and the other three humans were already trekking off through the tall stalks.

Even now, would they look back?

"Answer me, vessel," Fang repeated.

I couldn't tear her apart. Couldn't launch her from the staircase. If I considered the action for more than a moment, a wall formed itself across my limbs, blotting out the idea. Core programming, the same block that'd kept Delta from trashing Alpha back when she should've, that same block stopped me now.

"We have to send the message," I said to Fang, hands and feet sitting idle on the metal floor. "If we don't, your friends will never know where to go."

"Then let's send the message together," Fang backed off a step, let me stand.

"You'll fall behind." I nodded towards the walking humans.

"I'll catch up."

We made our way back to the console, up too many levels. Alvie padded along with us, content to follow my orders. The dog had no such block on hurting humans. I could order the hound to do what I couldn't.

"Which is, dude, exactly what you ought to be doing," Kaydee said as Fang and I climbed stair after stair. "She'll blow your guts out when she realizes you're lying."

I just needed to get her out of the ship. Send the message, take her back down, and once she left I'd be free.

"Why's she going to let you stay?" Kaydee asked.

A problem I'd have to find a solution for. The consoles waited right where we left them. Not a single one showed an emergency alert, a fact Fang pointed out with dry sarcasm.

"Seems like the ship ought to be in more of a panic. Alarms going off," Fang said. She stood behind me, a meter separating us, rifle drawn. Alvie watched from the sidelines. "You know, Gamma, we've lived through these alerts before. There's been mutinies, there's been malfunctions. You're not the first to spring a fake trap on a miserable people."

I ignored her. Punched in the message and sent it screaming through the ship, playing out in the same soft woman's voice. I told the humans to meet us on the western hills. Told them to run. Hoped that I wouldn't be there to meet them.

"Now go," I said to Fang. "I'm going to try and manage the power from here. I might be able to hold it off long enough for you to escape."

"Oh, could you?" Fang said. "That'd be so nice."

She didn't move.

"Fang's not buyin' it," Kaydee said. "Tell Alvie to sic her!"

I couldn't. The same block rose when I opened my mouth to try, keeping the words from coming out. No harm to humans, none. Alvie could do the deed, I just couldn't order it done.

Then my arms moved, jerked into a point at Fang. I felt my mouth move too, a strangled gurgle came out. As if I'd been possessed.

"Well damn," Kaydee said, pouting beside me. "Even I can't get past that stupid code."

Fang raised her eyebrows while I stood still, stunned. Why should I be surprised: Kaydee kept saying she'd be the leader of our joint body someday. This was how it'd feel, my parts obeying her instead of me. And yet, knowing something would happen was a lot different than experiencing it.

"Sorry, didn't mean to catch you by surprise there," Kaydee said, and at least she sounded apologetic. "Didn't think we had time to negotiate. Also, are you going to do anything? She might just shoot you and leave."

Fang was getting twitchy. She had the rifle pointed at me again, barking some command to get moving. I started down, obeying her without thinking. Only after we'd reach the stairs did Fang sigh, give a low curse.

"Vessel," she said when I glanced back, "I really wanted to trust you. Really did after all the help you gave us back there." She motioned to keep on walking down. "Guiding us through the dark, stopping the engines from overloading. Looked really good for you. I wanted to believe maybe we'd been wrong to toast all your friends."

"You *were* wrong."

"Shut up. This isn't a dialogue. This is me explaining to you why I'm gonna fire a laser into your back in a few minutes."

"Why?"

"Because Starship hasn't exploded yet, is why. You're a lying robot, and lying robots ought to be scrapped."

I clenched my hands, reveled in the human reaction. Stairs, metal steps I'd now climbed up and down twice, lay before us in a narrow stairwell descending. Walking down them, I traced every movement in my synthetic body. Fiber parts woven together, linked up with more wires, circuits, and careful construction than anything else on this ship. And Fang would waste all that because I tried to survive?

"You were going to shoot me anyway," I said as we walked. "You never gave us a chance."

"We gave your predecessors a chance, and because of that, we had to freeze ourselves for a long ass time."

"Because of that?"

"Oh, you think only a couple dozen people on Starship wanted to go all popsicle until we found a new home?" Fang laughed, but there wasn't any humor in it. "That's all we had left. You vessels tore us apart. Killed and killed and killed because the minds inside your bodies lost it.

"You see the Conduit and all its damage? That's not cause a few trash mechs got frisky. It's because Starship was a war zone for months and months, the humans against the vessels who wanted'em dead. We took what was left, after I'd put a burning hole in the last vessel, dumped the Voices in charge, and froze ourselves."

Fang's story filled in the blanks, but only from her perspective. I'd met Kaydee, known Kaydee long enough now to wonder just how all these minds had gone so murderous, gone so dangerous. It didn't feel right, didn't seem like I had the full picture. Not that I'd be likely to get it with a rifle pointed at my back.

"So you understand, right?" Fang said. "Why I might have some animosity towards you and your kind?"

"I get it."

"Good."

We reached the stair's end, went the last few meters to the exit. Starship still hadn't blown up. The message calling for an evacuation had ceased to play. All around us, a ship rumbled like her normal, healthy self. Fang stayed behind me as we reached the final stair set. I stopped at the very end, looked back at her.

"Here we are," I said, not bothering to continue the lie. No way she'd buy anything now. "What now?"

"What now?" Fang said. "How far ahead are they?"

I looked out, found Pravda and the humans climbing the early foothills.

"A couple kilometers?"

Fang nodded, "See, Gamma, Pravda likes you. That's dangerous, because even if I left you a burning ruin right here, he might decide vessels are a good thing to have around. Those other two sisters of yours will turn up eventually, and I'd rather we get a clean kill order than a demand to buddy up."

"Okay?"

"So get moving. You're going to tell Pravda everything you set up, and once he realizes you're a lying, traitorous machine, I'll be too happy to pull this trigger."

I didn't move right away. I stayed there, trying to calculate a way out. I could take a flying leap into the night, hit the ground and sprint away. Starship was huge, the grass stalks could get tall. I might be able to hide.

"Or she'd just shoot you," Kaydee said, "and then we'd both be dead."

Or that.

Behind Fang, Alvie looked at me. Those golden eyes waiting for a command. Maybe, maybe I could tell the dog to get the rifle. Tear it apart. Then . . .

"Gamma," Kaydee said as Fang told me, again, to get my ass in gear. "I have a wild idea. Fang said Pravda likes you. He's an entitled maroon, yeah, but maybe you tell him the truth? Maybe he buys it, now that Val's out there with all his embryos? Maybe you trust that it's going to work out okay?"

Like anything had yet. But Fang only had one rifle. I could do Kaydee's plan, see if I could get some goodwill. If it failed, my dog could chomp the only weapon in half, and then I could run away.

What a plan.

We caught up to Pravda and the humans as they crested the nearest major hill looking over Starship. In the starlight the curving slopes around us looked like rippling silver streams, the wind pushing stalks around in gusts. Fang had been true to her self-assessment, able to keep up with me and move fast enough to make the connection.

Pravda, at first, seemed both elated and stunned to find us both there. He asked if I'd sent the message, then wondered why Starship hadn't gone boom yet.

"Gamma's gonna tell you why," Fang said, at which point all the humans noticed she still had her rifle pointed at me.

"Sound real sympathetic, my guy," Kaydee whispered.

I tried. I pulled from the Librarian's huge mea culpa

reservoir to deliver my story in groveling terms. Yes, I'd lied. I wanted to get all the humans away from Starship so we'd have an opportunity, us mechs, to make something of it. Give ourselves a chance on this new world without humans crushing us underfoot.

Fang shot the rifle then, fired it straight up into the night sky. A bright bolt, but one that stopped me from talking.

"Don't need to hear all your whining, vessel," Fang said. "Pravda, you get it now? He just wanted us to get out and give him our home."

Pravda did what Pravda did, he wandered in a semi-circle around me, arms swinging wide as he bemoaned my duplicity. As he derided mechs and their ludicrous ideas of independence, of freedom. How we wouldn't know what to do with ourselves without human's help.

"Help we would welcome," I said, on my knees in the grass. "Help we would value. Just not ownership."

"Well, too bad," Pravda said, pointing a finger at me. "We made you, Gamma. Get that? Made you. Guess you weren't made well enough." Shaking his head, Pravda turned to Fang. "Destroy the thing, then let's go home."

"Gladly."

Fang raised the rifle. I raised my hands.

Alvie sprang from the grass, a leap executed to perfection. His teeth snared the rifle, tore it from Fang's hands. The bite broke through the gas, the power cell, and the gun exploded as Alvie hit the ground. My dog flew, tumbled through the air, disappearing into the plants.

"As if that's going to save you," Fang said, reaching into her belt and pulling out a nasty shrapnel knife. "Guess we'll do this the old way."

As she walked my way, I stood, ready to run, only to have humans tackle me from behind, push me to the ground. My face hit the dirt and I tried, tried to push off. Tried to lift myself, but every time I moved that same wall would form. The shove, the rise might hurt a human, and that I could not do. I felt Kaydee try again too, felt her pushing again and again as I gave up and watched Fang's knife catch the starlight as it dove for my neck.

THIRTY-SIX

A DANGEROUS OFFER

As Fang's knife swept in for what would've been a gnarly kill, a thud hit my right shoulder, throwing me aside and causing Fang's stroke to slice my cheek instead of my neck. Red icons splashed over my eyes, saying my right arm was no longer in commission. Not that it mattered, Fang would be correcting, would be following—

"Talk about timing," Kaydee whistled, seeing Fang stop before I did. Pravda's premiere fighter halted mid swing, knife held high with her hands. "We should be dead, Gamma."

"Instead, once again, we've taken an arrow to the shoulder," I replied, getting a look at the narrow protruding shaft. The fletching like spider strands in the starlight. "How and why are two questions that come to mind."

The answers came almost as fast, with shouts pouring from all directions around the small camp. Pravda's humans didn't give any fight, their spent rifles as gone as their spirit. For a brief moment I wondered if Alpha's mechs had found us, or maybe Beta and Delta.

Or, crazier yet, some natives of this world.

Instead, Chalo emerged, clad in the shimmering feathered mail and looking damn fierce with a shrapnel hatchet in either hand. I enjoyed reclining on my back amid the grass, watching Val's hunters, including a couple Forgers and their half-human, half-mech skins, surround Pravda's group and hold them at sword, arrow, and rifle-point.

"So close," I said to Fang, who glared at me, who started to move that knife hand and found herself with a jagged scrap sword to her neck.

"He's the one to kill," Fang protested to the hunter. "He's the mech."

The hunter looked at me, did a double-take, then called to Chalo to come over.

"See, Fang," I said, "it's nice to have friends. Even if they do shoot you every now and again."

"So we did," Chalo said, weaving his way through the prisoners—for that's what Pravda's group plainly was now—to my side. "Sorry, Gamma. It's difficult to tell in the dark."

"If Juny's still around, she'll know how to fix it."

I found it hard to hold any grievance given that, you know, they'd saved my life. Kaydee was equally thrilled, though she showed it differently: despite Fang's inability to see them, Kaydee whipped gestures and images my sensors deemed obscene her way.

"What?" Kaydee said when she caught me looking. "She deserves it."

I didn't argue.

Chalo's band put Pravda's quintet into a tight circle. The hunters had more than double Pravda's number, putting into sharp relief how precarious the man's position was. Pravda never stopped spouting off bargaining chips, pleas for diplomacy, and the occasional threat the entire time. And that time wasn't short: Chalo had me tell the whole story, then confirmed several parts: that Pravda's whole group wasn't large, that they weren't monsters, and that they didn't control Starship.

"But we do control Starship!" Pravda protested when Chalo made him corroborate my story.

"Not unless your people are stupid," I said. "We sent the evacuation message. They ought to be gone by now."

At that, Chalo called over two hunters, whispered something I couldn't hear, and off they went in separate directions. Chalo returned to Pravda then, squatting in front of the man. Starlight served to light the scene, those glorious webs drifting through the night sky above. It looked like the Librarian's old black and white films, and not a soul dared speak, unsure if Chalo was going to gut Pravda with the hatchet in his hand.

I almost said no. I almost stopped him.

"The laws have changed," Chalo said, "since you last woke. You will follow me back to our new home, and you will say your piece before us. Then we'll decide whether you are a threat."

"A threat?" Pravda said. "Do we look like a threat?"

"No," Chalo answered, standing. "You look like scared little children."

Pravda didn't have any bluster to counter that. Fang, a permanent glower on her face, said nothing. The other three humans looked relieved to stand and march off. Presumably there'd be food at the end. Shelter. A chance to breathe.

I went up ahead with Chalo, the two of us leading the column as we navigated the rolling hills. Every so often people stumbled in the gray dark, slipping on an invisible hole or tripping over a rogue rock. My own sensors picked out the uneven ground, highlighting potential problems for me to avoid. Still, the sheer clumsiness, especially from Chalo's group, hunters that'd moved so skillfully among Starship, had me confused.

"It's a new world," Chalo replied when I asked. The hunter had been silent up till now, almost an hour since we'd broken camp in the dark. "We're used to metal. Flat ground. Predictability. There's none of it here."

"Especially in the dark," Kaydee mused. "Why're they out now?"

I repeated her question to Chalo, who shrugged. "The night lasts as long as two of our old days. We can't sit and wait. Especially now."

"Why?"

"You weren't around before. Neither was I, but Val's talked about it many times. Food, water were scarce. Dangers were unpredictable. They moved fast then to grow and secure themselves. Now is no different."

"What dangers? Have you found something?"

"Yes," Chalo said, eyes glinting in the silver. "You."

DAWN'S GLOW lit the horizon by the time we stumbled, marched, fell into Val's camp. The hunters seemed all right, but Pravda's humans were dead on their feet. Chalo's runner must've made good on his head start, because the whole village already stirred. Val herself waited to greet us, clad in the same shimmering mail, her spear held straight up as we approached.

Behind her, several days work showed good results. With metal bars stolen from Starship, the humans thatched shelters to complement tents that'd moved with them. The embryos sat in a solar-charged freezer, one stolen from the Nursery and augmented by Leo to handle the larger load.

The location, too, spoke of smart planning: Val's people nested in a valley between broad sloping hills. Burbling pools coated the ground, the only gaps I'd seen in the grass since setting out on this world. The gray clouded liquid inside, to Leo's delight, turned out to be water, albeit water mixed with all kinds of toxic metals, minerals, and more. Still, extracting good old H_2O from the pools wouldn't be an impossible task, provided a few more filters could be stolen from Starship.

Leo himself told me all this while Juny, the spunky engineer, freed me from the misfire. After the extraction, Juny helped with some more mechanical surgery, fixing severed wires and soldering my right arm back to working order. All the while, Pravda tried to convince Val not to kill him. Not to kill his people.

"Do I think they deserve to die?" Kaydee said as we rejoined the morning proceedings, a strange trial that had Val and Chalo staring down Pravda's five. The whole group stood before a large fire pit in the village's center, ringed now by curious people and armed guards. "I mean, no. Not all of them. Not even Pravda, 'cause being annoying shouldn't be a death sentence. But Fang can bite it. Definitely."

I stayed quiet. Listened. My programming would've kept me from even pronouncing a death penalty on a human. In truth, I couldn't imagine a worse ending to all this than Pravda's group ending up headless on pikes. That done, no way the other twenty-five stranded somewhere around here would ever come in. They'd fight to the end first.

Humanity's first days on this world would be marked by the same war and blood that'd scribed their history on Earth.

So when Val asked, at long last, for comment from the crowd, I stepped forward.

"They don't deserve death," I said at the start. "Not once have they made a hostile move towards any of you. They are few in number, and fewer still have any skills that would make them a threat."

"This one said they know how to fight," Chalo interrupted, pointing at Fang. "I think that is the definition of a threat."

"They were trained in their dreams," I countered, feeling the eyes on me. Feeling, too, the warmth as this world's white star climbed above the hills. "That isn't the same as you. They haven't seen real bloodshed, and they don't want it. If you give them a chance, they will join you. I know they will. You will need every body you can get."

Val gave me the slightest nod. Food might be scarce, but every soul now helped ensure humanity might survive. Wanton killing with less than a hundred people alive on the planet would be disastrous. She had to see that. Chalo had to know that.

"Give them a choice," I said. Kaydee urged me to just play something from my archives, some stirring speech from history, but Val was one for simple solutions, not soaring oratory. "If they choose to join you, let them. If they persist in going it alone, then do what you will."

"Do what you will?" Kaydee said as I stepped back to murmurs from the crowd. "What kind of ending is that?"

"I couldn't say kill. Couldn't even say exile. Too close to death, apparently."

Val, at least, seemed to heed my advice. She took her turn in the circle now, but looked only at the captives arrayed before her. All on their knees, only Fang and Pravda daring to meet her face.

"You heard the mech," Val said. "A choice. Give your-selves to us, as everyone else here has done, and we will accept you into our tribe. You can help us build a new home here. Welcome a bright future. Or refuse, and we will make your death a swift one."

"Join or die?" Pravda said, shaking his head. "That's not a real choice. Let us go back to our own and make our way as we want to."

"We have the embryos," Val countered, any warmth dissipating in an instant. "Your number is not enough to survive. You will die out unless you join, or you will wither until you become desperate and strike, a possibility I will not allow. So yes. Join, or die."

Only the wind made noise.

A man, the fifth captive, the one wounded in the Garden, threw himself forward onto the ground. He pled allegiance, said he accepted their terms, said he only wanted to survive, for his family, numbering among the still-lost others, to survive. The other two followed at nearly the same instant, dropping knees into the dirt and claiming the same.

"Smart," Kaydee said. "Not sure they needed to grovel like that, though."

Maybe, but Val didn't look like she minded the move. At her gesture, two guards came in and pulled the three up to their feet. Water bottles were handed over, fruits and canned vegetables followed. All three ate, drank right there in the circle, right in front of Pravda and Fang.

"See?" Val said. "We're generous. Kind. We don't hold grudges, and you will be welcomed as equals."

"Equals to you?" Pravda asked.

A thin smile, "A tribe needs a leader."

Pravda squared his shoulders. "Then you can keep your

tribe. Take me back to mine, or kill me. I'm not going to flop around for you."

Fang, agreeing, spat in the dirt at Val's feet.

"Well damn," Kaydee said. "Guess Pravda really is stupid."

Before I could agree, Chalo leapt to defend Val's honor. The man had his ax in hand, had it whistling towards Fang's neck, before Val called for him to stop.

"One day," Val said to the imprisoned pair. "One day here. You will watch us, you will see us, and you will understand. As the mech said, I will not waste life if I do not have to. Even if the lives belong to ones like you."

THIRTY-SEVEN

VESSEL VERSIONS

In the aftermath of Val's order, the camp sprang into their daily routine. Aside from a couple guards tasked to watch over the two prisoners, everyone else bustled off to continue building shelters, filtering water from the pools, or any of the billion other things a human settlement needed to survive. After waiting for someone to come talk to me, I realized nobody cared what I did next.

"I do," Kaydee said. "Whatcha thinking?"

There were options: I could head back to Starship, take up the plan I'd devised with Volt and start making over the craft in my new image. I could stay here, try to make more sense of what the humans wanted to do. Or I could try to find Beta and Delta.

"Try to find them?" Kaydee asked. "They've gotta be on Starship somewhere, right? Probably just indulging their bloodlust to destroy every mech Alpha's ever met."

"Delta, I could see it. Beta's spent her life protecting Val and her humans. I don't think she'd just let them go into the unknown without protection."

"So that's what we do instead? Wander off and see if we can find them?"

Not quite.

I found Val and Chalo in a broad tent, one otherwise used to store various foods. Packs unloaded and still stuffed littered the room, while Val, Chalo, and several others mobbed a central table. Unlike Pravda's group, the humans here gave me waves, and Juny, the engineer who'd repaired me, asked if she could have another look at my guts for fun. Cheery attitudes bolstered by hope and sunlight.

As I approached, Val called whatever meeting they were in to a close, ushering away the others. Only Chalo remained, giving me a nod as I took a chair opposite Val.

"Three out of five ain't bad," Val said for an opener. "The other two are stubborn."

"One is a fighter," Chalo said. "The other needs to get in a fight and lose it."

"Lose it?" I asked.

"Too much pride," Val answered. "Humans can get wrapped up in their own egos. Need to get taken down a peg before we start thinking straight again." She clasped her hands before her, looking a little like an old human queen. One without a crown or jewels, but regal nonetheless. "What's your plan, Gamma?"

I leveled with the queen. "Beta and Delta are gone. I want to find them."

Val flipped her eyes towards Chalo and the hunter shrugged, "We have runners combing the hills. If they're outside Starship, we'll find them. If they're inside, that's your territory now."

What? I froze, plotting the implications of Chalo's statement.

"You're giving me Starship?" I asked.

"We don't have the right to give you anything," Val replied, dishing up a sly grin. "We're saying we don't want anything to do with it. Least, not much. If Leo or Juny want to go back to get some salvage, we figure they can trade with you. Otherwise, we have what we need out here."

"But—"

"We've spent enough years inside that mausoleum," Val cut me off. "Don't argue, Gamma. Take your metal and be happy about it."

"Then you don't want to destroy it? I thought with Leo's trick that's what you wanted?"

"If I thought we could destroy Starship, maybe I'd try. As it is, we have other priorities."

Chalo caught my eyes, a frosted look, "Other priorities for now. Gamma, we're trusting you to take Starship and clean it up. Make it safe, keep it peaceful. If that doesn't happen, then we will be back."

I MULLED Chalo's threat as I left the tent. They had to know, given some time, I could spin up a deadlier force from the Fabrication Lines than the humans would be able to defeat. But perhaps they also knew I wouldn't be able, myself, to make a force like that: core programming and its protections once again.

"Hey, I think you got a big win in there," Kaydee said, walking alongside me, hand up to shade the sun. "Everything we wanted, done."

"Not quite everything," I said, angling now towards the massive box holding the embryos.

Leo and several Forgers worked around the embryo container, their focus for the first few days out here. They'd expanded the enclosure, giving the vials more separation, more reliable cooling. Even so, the batteries keeping the temperatures reliable would need recharging beyond their solar boosting soon.

Leo told me this unprompted as I watched him tighten rivets on the newest section. As he finished out his work and his explanation, Leo wiped some sweat from the natural part of his brow and faced me.

"So what d'ya need?"

The Forger had an odd look, scrappy clothes greased up and mingling with his half-human, half-machine body. Replacing failing organs and skin sections one at a time, a brutal form of life extension. One that made Leo the foremost expert on what I was about to ask.

"Kaydee and I share a body," I said. "She says she'll overtake my control, that I'll be trapped inside my own self. That she doesn't have a choice. Is all that true?"

Leo blinked at me, then sat down on the grass. Patted the ground beside him. I did as the signal suggested, felt the soft earth beneath me. A pleasant touch compared to hard metal.

"Guess you know minds were always meant to run the vessels, right?" Leo asked and I nodded. "Lot of hope in that, lot of flawed execution, but by my time, things were looking pretty good. Too good, you might say, which is why we had to burn it all down."

"Because minds aren't all human." I could feel Kaydee listening, her influence on the edge of my functions.

"They are, but they don't have every part of a human, if that makes sense. They're a mapped brain, biology converted into ones and zeros. It's not perfect, but imperfection seemed better than extinction," Leo said. "I went for the best of both worlds, made a mind outta myself and tried to keep chugging along the old fashioned way."

"You haven't answered my question."

"Is Kaydee going to take you over?" Leo shrugged. "Maybe? Probably? Thing is, Gamma, you're not some trash mech. You're smart. You learn. You compromise. Kaydee's not much different than you. Think of it like two roommates trapped in the same apartment: communicate and work things out."

"I've never lived in an apartment. I've never had a roommate."

Leo rolled his eyes, "You get my point."

"If I delete her, is it murder?"

Leo stared off into the hills. The web clouds weren't as visible in the daytime, but if I hunted, I could still pick out the gossamer threads floating in the breeze. Laughter intermingled with tools cutting, slashing, mending. A child called out a game's rules.

"I have a theory," Leo said. "One I never got to test. See, I think the earlier vessels, the ones that became too dangerous, they didn't compromise. Their minds destroyed the vessels, or the other way around. You take away half of who you are, things can go wrong fast."

Remembering how I felt when Kaydee had been stripped from me, how lonely and lost, without her guiding sarcasm and second opinions. Yeah, maybe if I'd continued like that, put into situations without a clear goal. Adrift, alone . . .

"Look," Leo said, "I loved Kaydee. We had the bad luck to be born into a crap time, and I made some choices then that I regret now." He turned to me, a hangdog look on his face. "You're lucky you have her with you. I wouldn't give that up for anything now."

"Is that why you tried to destroy us both?"

"What?"

"Overloading Starship's engines. You would've killed Kaydee along with me."

Leo laughed, "You knew that wasn't real. Didn't think you'd kill the power though. Gave us a shock, but I appreciate the head start."

"So you wouldn't have done it if you could've?"

Now Leo's laughter fell away, hardened. "I told Val I could make Starship explode and that you'd stopped it. I did that because otherwise we'd have stayed, armed up and gone hunting. Too afraid Alpha, or this goofball's goons would take us by surprise." He took a deep breath, waved at the air around us. "Look at this, Gamma. I wasn't going to miss it for more fighting. I'm sorry if I scared you and Kaydee, I really am, but I don't regret what I did."

Kaydee stayed quiet through the whole conversation. I thought about prodding her on it after Leo returned to his work, but found myself distracted by the life around me. There were lessons to be learned here, and I soaked in the cooperating people. Not only building, but cooking, cleaning, tending the wounds from Pravda's group. I'd seen glimpses of Starship as it used to be, but this was my first time seeing a society as it ought to be: wholly united, bent on a single purpose.

Mechs could be this way, given a chance.

A runner interrupted my self-guided tour, spoiling the smells I was analyzing while several people cooked up a rice-and-vegetable medley. The message was short: Chalo, now.

Val's head hunter wasn't in her tent, but instead stood before Pravda and Fang. While the sun still sat high in the sky, impatience soaked the air. Nobody wanted to wait until night fall to make a choice.

"We know where they are," Chalo said to me as I joined

him. "Your mechs. They're gathering to the north, near Starship's Bridge. They're moving rocks, digging too."

"Building?"

"Nothing my scout could describe. Laying foundations, perhaps."

"Or digging your graves," Fang said, listening in.

"We should be digging yours," Chalo replied, then nodded to me. "Gamma, Val says we should not waste life, but right now these two are wasting ours."

"It'll be night before too long."

"Another Earth day at least. If I'm racing mechs to get a city built, hands stuck here for two people that won't see our way are hands I could use elsewhere."

"Chalo, why'd you bring me here?" I asked. "If you want to kill them, you could've done that without me."

Chalo sighed, "I brought you here to convince them to change their minds, and to do it fast. I'm gathering some of us to go and take a closer look at the mechs, and I'm guessing you'll want to go with us."

"Yes."

"Then you'll either leave behind two corpses, or the two newest members of our tribe." Chalo put a hand on my shoulder. "You have one hour."

THIRTY-EIGHT

DECIDE OR DIE

Two self-indulgent morons, each more than one percent of humanity's remaining adults. Both, hands tied with plastic wiring, on their knees, looking at me with dead-eyed distance. Val's village continued apace around us, as if these lives didn't hang in the balance. Chalo's two guards stood several meters away, watching with idle curiosity.

What would the robot do?

"Split'em up," Kaydee said, snapping back for the first time since before I spoke with Leo. If the man's words had any effect on my friend, she didn't show it. Light, bouncy, she used her hands to paint a line between Pravda and Fang. "All the movies do it. Can't let friends stick together."

Knowing how much I tossed ideas off Kaydee, how I'd worked hand in hand with Delta to survive sticky situations, the play made sense. I told the guards as much and the two moved Fang and Pravda to opposite sides of the circle. Far enough away, with the background noise, to keep a low voice from carrying.

Far enough away to wonder what the other was thinking.

"Fang first," Kaydee said after the two had been split. "She'll be the harder one, and the clock's ticking."

I went with Pravda instead: I'd rather save one than none and, of the two, Pravda was annoying but Fang was more likely to stab me, or Chalo, or anyone in the back. Literally.

Pravda didn't even glare at me when I sat down in the grass across from him. He looked tired, thirsty, but I didn't call for more water. The resource was precious, especially now that every drop wasn't being captured in Starship's recycling systems. Pravda had to prove he was worth it.

I told him as much.

"Thirsty?" Pravda said. "You think that's what I care about right now? Like, were you even listening to that crazy lady? She's going to kill me, Gamma. All because I won't, I don't know, bow to her or some medieval nonsense?"

"Val wants peace. That's it. She's asking you to commit to that."

Pravda screwed up his nose, mouth, "You don't understand humans if you think that's what she's asking. It's way more than that."

"Tell me."

"She wants to make all the decisions. If I say yes, I'm not just saying I won't kill anyone, but that I'm going to do what she wants. It's a dictatorship."

"Isn't that what you had with your people?"

"That was survival. This is civilization. I didn't freeze myself just to wake up and be a slave."

I motioned to the people around me, "Do these look like slaves to you?"

"I . . . " Pravda's defiance faltered, his eyes and mouth curling into confusion.

"You don't know them. You don't know this place or how it works." I copped a slight smile. "I didn't like Val much either when I met her. She's hard. Driven. But the people here accept her because she's brought them this far. Give her a chance. If it doesn't work out, you can always leave."

"Leave and go where?"

My grin widened, "You heard Chalo. I'll have Starship. You get frustrated, I'll let you back in. Figure there's enough space for two of us."

Pravda chuckled. A victory. Kaydee, behind him, gave me a thumbs-up, her hand growing huge in the action so her thumb was larger than my head. Big, ridiculous, encouraging.

Time to go for the win.

"Pravda, you and all the people you've helped get nothing if you die here and now. Nothing." A strategic pause, let the waste sink in. "Or you can use all you know to help. You can be a part of humanity on this new world, even if it means swallowing a little pride."

Pravda nodded, "I know. I know it's pointless. I just, I had so many ideas, Gamma. For Starship, for everyone, and now they're gone. I want them back. I want those possibilities back."

"You gave up those possibilities once, when you went into the cryo chambers. Now you can still make some a reality. It just might be a little bit harder."

"Not bad, mech." Pravda sighed. "Guess I wasn't all that sold on dying for the cause anyway." He twisted, looked back at Fang. "She's not going to be as easy to convince."

"No, she's not."

"What's your strategy?"

"Same as you. Listen first, hope I get lucky."

"Well, I'm rooting for ya." Pravda, with my help, stood up. "Hey, stone face," Pravda called to the closer guard. "I'm willing to sign Val's oath or whatever you're looking for." When the guard came over, Pravda wiggled his eyebrows. "Don't look so sad. I'm sure you'll get to execute someone someday."

The guard started, "That's not what—"

Pravda cut him off, went in on his same old grand visioning while the confused guard led him off towards Val's tent.

Leaving me alone with one feisty woman.

"Hey, you're one-for-one so far," Kaydee said, standing next to me as we looked at Fang's back. "You've got thirty minutes by my count."

"Pravda took that long?"

"Lotta pauses in that conversation, buddy."

"Think I can do the same thing with her?"

"Sure, just watch out when she gets up, cause she might try to kill you."

Fang didn't stand when I sat before her. She gazed at me. For the first time, I didn't read malice in those eyes. Her slight frown spoke less of vengeance and more of exhaustion. Her arms hung loose, her booted feet lay relaxed in the grass. Nothing about her said dangerous, nothing about her said threatening.

"You're not going to convince me," Fang said. "The man said you had an hour and the clock's ticking."

"Pravda changed his mind," I replied, trying to keep a level disposition.

Emotions, I figured, wouldn't help here.

"Pravda's always been flexible. That's why he's leading our group, not me. He could change with the tides."

"But you can't?"

"Don't want to." Fang flicked her eyes at the sky. "I'm a fighter. I was raised with Starship on the brink of war, one that broke out and one I fought to the end. I'm not going to throw all that away to weave dresses."

"Weave dresses?"

"You know what I mean. All this. I'm not meant for peace."

Kaydee snorted, "She sounds like a cliche."

My Mind might've been dismissive, but I saw an opening.

"Do you hate all mechs, or just me?" I asked Fang.

"Don't hate mechs. Just don't trust them. Or you."

"But you're good at destroying them."

"Couldn't torch you, try as I might."

Okay, perhaps not the answer I wanted, but I had Fang engaged In the conversation. She analyzed me now, a killer's stare. One I could recognize because I'd seen Delta wear it more than enough times.

"Chalo told me they've found where the mechs are gathering," I said. "Before we found you, we took apart a flexi-mech. I saw what was inside. Its code, its drives. Alpha had copied himself, distributed it to all his machines."

"You're saying we might not have killed the thing?"

"I'm saying there's work left for you if you want it."

"As if that guy will take me along."

"You can shoot a rifle. You're willing. That puts you in a rare group."

Fang nibbled on her lip. "So my choices are get my head lopped off tonight, or go on a mech murdering mission?"

"Pretty much."

We sat in silence. Kaydee spent the time making a wager on whether Fang would join, and then whether she'd piss off Chalo in the first five or ten minutes. I didn't make any bets, just waited, watched the timer. I'd gone into this to follow my core programming: save the humans. Now I wanted Fang to go along just because I'd put in the effort.

I wanted a win.

"Tell that Chalo guy to come here. I want to talk to him," Fang said. "I need to know if we can work together, him and me."

"Done."

"Gamma, don't think all this crap you're pulling changes things between us. I know what you pulled to get us out of Starship. I'm not forgiving you for it. Never will."

I stood, looked down at her. "Okay."

Kaydee waited till I'd gone a few meters away before blazing into life next to me.

"Okay? Okay?" Kaydee said, her voice tweaking to imitate me. "That's your comeback? She's threatening your life and you're saying okay?"

"She's not threatening my life," I replied, threading through town towards Val and Chalo's big tent. "Or, I guess, she's not a threat, no matter what she says."

"Uh, Gamma, she had a rifle to your head like the whole way here?"

"And now she doesn't." I shrugged. "I have a lot of friends. She has zero. I have Starship, she might have a bow and arrow if Chalo's nice. I've got bigger problems to worry about."

My own systems confirmed that, ranking Fang's threat assessment way down the list. Below even freak events like Alvie's programming going haywire and my dog turning on me. No, I wasn't about to operate paranoid, especially not on a beautiful day like this.

When I found Chalo, he was already gearing up with a dozen other fighters. I told him about Fang, he thanked me, then told me what I really wanted to hear:

"Get yourself some gear, Gamma. You're coming with us."

THIRTY-NINE

GOING MECH HUNTING

Ten packs, ten people. Nine human, one vessel. And one metal wheeze-barking dog. We checked our gear, slung loops around our shoulders. Chalo checked bowstrings, confirmed fletching, menial steps that could've been delegated but must've held some special meaning for the man. Two Forgers joined us, carrying rifles with full power packs. Five more came from Val's hunter ranks, the ones healthy enough to walk to a fight.

The last?

Fang had a pack and no weapons. Chalo ordered me, with my near-endless endurance, to carry her arms. Fang would get them if she reached the fight without causing problems, without trying to carve my head from my shoulders. She'd only smiled at Chalo, said fine, and waited with the rest of us.

Val gave a short going-away speech, watched by some from the village—most, I noticed, kept right on working, cooking, living—and she reminded us we weren't going to war. At most, this was an assassination, an attempt to cut any dangerous leadership from the mechs. The primary objective? Rescue Delta and Beta.

They would be the two warriors best able to defend the humans in the coming years.

In the Librarian's records, departing bands tended to leave with fanfare. Trumpets, flower petals thrown from balconies by well-wishers. Nothing sent us off save the bright white sun and a few low-floating gossamer webs. Even Val, after her speech and a good luck bid, went back to her tent before we'd gone a few yards.

"It's because we're supposed to come back, you senti-mental machine," Kaydee said as we began the march. Chalo stuck Fang at the column's center, with me holding the rear. Alvie scampered around, occasionally jumping at gossamer webs. "This isn't some Great War we're going to."

"Isn't it, though?" I replied. "The mechs will work faster than Val's tribe. Every day the gap will grow larger and larger until, no matter how many humans she has, there will be ten mechs for every one. We stop them now, or we lose."

"Hate to break it to you, Gamma, but the numbers are already against us," Kaydee replied and before me, drawn in the air over the walking heads were Alpha's row upon row of flexi-mechs. "Say Pravda and his folks managed to wipe out a few dozen. Maybe a hundred. That still leaves three or four times our humans in murderous mechs waiting for us."

"You're saying we're already dead?"

"I'm saying we have two possibilities." The mechs disappeared, Kaydee floating now in their place. She pointed with her right arm, Beta and Delta popping in, blue sky behind them. "We rescue these two, get them properly equipped, have them raid and ravage Alpha's army until there's nothing left." Left arm now. Alpha, alone, albeit in the body he no longer had, red hair and scars. "Or we take him. I know we already did it, but guess what, he's outside now. Starship's network isn't available for him. No downloading, no transferring. We stick him here, he's gone."

"Except his code's in every flexi-mech out there."

"Sure, but something has to tell it to activate, right? Or there'd be a few hundred Alpha's charging around right now, and we'd know if that was happening because everything would be insane."

Hmm. I couldn't find too many holes with Kaydee's analysis. Save one.

"Pravda's people are leaving Starship," I said. "As soon as Alpha sees that, he'll take it back."

"That's why we have to move fast," Kaydee replied, "and trust Volt's not so stupid as to leave the doors open."

The flight from Starship marked the third time I'd set foot on the new world, and this time the longest. During the nighttime sprint with Beta and Delta I'd been focused on planting one foot in front of the other, consumed by the objective and the speed at which we could reach it. By comparison, this was a sedate pace. Whether Chalo wanted the group to reach the mechs with energy, or because the scout had mentioned no immediate threat, I had the time to take in the view, to embrace the grassy cushion beneath my feet. Knowing about the burbling pools, I saw signs in the other valleys we passed: faint wisps dwindling to nothing as they rose. The wind remained the only natural sound, buoying conversations struck up and abandoned between the walkers.

The Librarian's lore contained countless tales of humans singing songs, joking about their bravery on conflict's eve, yet Chalo's bunch seemed listless. Set, yes, but with caution in their steps. No glorious thoughts crossed lips that I could hear.

"It's because they're tired," Kaydee said, joining me. "They've spent their whole lives dodging mechs, living in Starship's grungy shadows, and now they escape only to get yanked back? Not much reason to get excited in that."

"But this is a chance to put it all away forever," I replied. "How can they not be happy at the opportunity?"

"Forever?" Kaydee laughed. "Gamma, if it's not Alpha, it'll be someone or something else. Sooner or later. Hell, give it a few years and maybe it'll be us."

"Us?"

"There's a thousand things pointing Val's tribe our way. Say you do take Starship. Now you've got all kinds of resources Val could use. They're banking on this planet being everything they need, but it won't have medicine. It's soil might not grow well. And—"

"We'll give them what they need," I said. "What use would I have for any of that? Mechs aren't greedy."

Kaydee looked like she was about to go on, her face darkening. A dim view of the future in those furrows, but one she wound up tossing away, swapping to a head shake instead.

"Maybe your optimism will win, buddy. I hope so."

"It's not optimism. It's logic."

"Something we both know humans have to spare."

We bit back and forth at each other for several hours. Every time Kaydee wanted to leave off the subject, I went in after her, pressing for explanations, ideas, histories. She countered with cynicism, a dire view no doubt shaped by her dismal last years as a living, breathing person. No matter how malleable my mech future might be, Kaydee would insist it wouldn't be enough. Her species would keep on coming, keep on taking as need and boredom demanded until we, the machines, were either annihilated or enslaved.

"Are you evil, then?" I asked, finally. "Humans?"

"We created you," Kaydee replied. "Are you evil?" Before I could answer, she waved off the response. "We're all over the map, Gamma, just like mechs. What I'm trying to tell you, again and again, is you can't trust us. One, a specific person? Sure. Maybe. But as a species? No. So don't go wrapping your circuits around some Elysian ideal."

"Which leaves me with what? Anger? Violence?"

"How about caution?"

The word seeped into my plans, the ideas I'd set my processors to playing with in idle times, like the walk and the breaks where the humans ate, drank, and rested. Like someone remembering a song while cleaning up a mess, I'd been spooling together Starship's future: layouts, new mechs, opportunities. Now I colored those plans, adding in a new variable: outside threats.

The sun lay deep in its descent by the time we climbed the last hill. Starship's great bulk sat to our right, a shimmering silver wall against the horizon. Beyond it, visible around its nose, swam a great gray sea we hadn't yet explored. Leo, back at the village, thought it was made of the same stuff as the burbling pools, but nobody had tested the theory. There would be time for that after.

Our ten, plus Alvie, arrayed at the hilltop and looked down onto the broad plain Alpha's flexi-mechs had chosen for their new home. A rocky field, jutting black basalt piercing the grass here and there. The wind cut sharper, no hills for shelter down below, but the mechs weren't bothered. Instead they worked in teams, hammering at the rocks and, once broken, carrying the boulders to various growing squares. Other mechs used tools salvaged from Starship, melting and molding the rocks to mesh together. Several smaller dwellings, roofless, were already stuffed with parts.

With barrels holding, I suspected, coolants. Still other mechs seemed hard at work re-assembling solar panels stolen off Starship's hull, building out charging stations, power conduits to future industries.

"They have all this inside Starship," Kaydee said. "Why bother remaking it out here?"

"For the same reason Val ran," I replied. "Starship can be destroyed. Harder to blow up a planet."

Chalo came over to me, pointed at the mechs, at two in particular standing at the camp's center. I'd noticed them fast, been watching them, waiting for some sign they weren't what I feared.

"You see them, right?" Chalo said.

"I do."

"They don't look like they're fighting. Or being held captive."

"They don't."

Chalo glanced at me, "Then tell me what you think."

"I need to get closer," I said, much as I didn't want to. "I need to talk to them."

"Will they kill you?"

"Maybe. There's hundreds down there, Chalo. There's no chance we all get through. Better to send me, see what happens."

"If you don't survive?"

"Send my dog to Volt, on Starship. Get him to open up, then grab every weapon you possibly can. And save Pravda's people, because you'll need the bodies when the mechs come for you."

FORTY

A NEW SOCIETY

Never let anyone say mechs are lazy.

With Alvie by my side we wandered down the hill and into the base's fringes. Flexi-mechs moving, placing rocks looked at us for scant seconds. Some waved a ten fingered hello. Others, hands occupied with their work, gave us nods instead. Their pink eyes, normally lit in anger, instead seemed soft, focused. Far from deadly.

Up close, the site lost any sinister edge given by distance. The shelters looked just like shelters, not fortifications. Weapons weren't stacked inside. I saw none of those hunting dog mechs, the ones made just for slaughter. Perhaps a human might've found the silence eerie, the only noise coming from the mechs grinding, clanking their way around, but for me it felt like—

"Home?" Kaydee jumped in. "You're seriously about to call this home?"

"Mechs, a beautiful sky, nobody shooting at us?" I replied. "What more could you want?"

"But all these mechs belong to Alpha, not you," Kaydee said. "You don't know what they're really doing. It's like looking at a painting half-done and assuming you know what it'll look like in the end."

"It's more promising than anything else I've seen so far."

"A bunch of half-built rock buildings?"

"No, the cooperation. The mechs are all working together. It shows I'm not losing it, thinking we could do the same in Starship."

"Yeah, they're all working together because Alpha's controlling their every move."

This time I rolled my eyes, brushed past Kaydee and headed for the center.

Unlike Val's settlement, where a cleared dirt circle marked the middle, the mechs used a more striking example: two vessels, one standing, one kneeling, watching the progress in silence. Beta, her long, bound pink hair streaming down one side, knives bristling from bandoleers and rings along her arms and legs, viewed my approach without reaction, as if tracking the descending sun above.

I stopped for a long moment when I made out Delta's condition. The vessel had her knees in the grass, her hands locked in forged metal behind her back, and a narrowed glare etched on her face. If Beta had no reaction, Delta's face twisted into shock at my appearance.

Shock accompanied by a shout, one I couldn't understand. Her mouth moved, but toneless gibberish emerged. Like someone battering piano keys, or laying their elbow on the ivories.

Beta's stale look flickered, for a second, into a wild grin before settling back into its line.

"Ah hell," Kaydee groaned. "This is, like, the worst possible outcome."

"We don't know what's happened yet," I replied.

I kept my hands visible, showed I carried no weapons as

I came closer. Around us, black and gray rock lay in stacks waiting to be molded into form. Gossamer webs coated the sky above us, sprinkling the afternoon with sparkles. The ever-present breeze continued. No flexi-mechs approached.

"I'm glad you're here," Beta opened the conversation. "We sent flexi-mechs to retrieve you from the humans, but they never returned. I assumed you were a casualty."

I cocked my head, studied Beta. The words weren't hers, the tone and cadence off. No insults. No flipping a knife in the air and catching it again.

"See?" Kaydee whispered.

"We encountered your mechs," I said. "They didn't survive."

With a flash, Beta drew a knife and pointed it up and away, towards the hill where Chalo and the other hunters waited. "Are they up there now, watching us?"

"They're trying to decide what you are."

"Villagers, nothing more," Beta grinned. "It's like you wanted, Gamma. Peace. Mechs making their own society."

"This is a society?" I looked around. "The mechs all work in silence. I'm not hearing any laughter. Any song. It's more like a prison than any society I've seen before."

Beta threw back her head, laughed, "So Gamma, the only society you favor is a human one? If so, then leave, go back to your squishy friends. I'm sure they'll need you to tell them how to behave."

"Yep, definitely not Beta," Kaydee continued. "How do we think Alpha stole her? Virus? Trap?"

How it happened didn't matter. How we would fix her was more important.

"I'm not a dictator," I replied.

"Aren't you, though?" Beta said. "Leo designed us in pairs. Beta, Delta the fighters. Alpha and Gamma, the thinkers. The rulers. Time to take up your mantle and march back home. In a few hundred years we can meet up again and compare results, your civilization against mine."

"That's—"

"Absurd? Why not?" Beta put two fingers into her mouth and blew, whistling a sharp and shrill note into the air. "What are we doing here, Gamma? Isn't this whole thing absurd? A doomed mission across the galaxy, machines and humankind battling each other just like on the world they left behind. It's what we are, so why not continue the dance?"

Before I could find a reply, a new figure appeared from a shelter to my right. The biggest one built, the arched roof kept us from seeing inside from up on the hill. Now its contents emptied out, escorted by the only armed flexi-mechs I'd seen in the village. Pravda's left behind, clumped together and stripped of their masks, their weapons, their coats. They walked in tattered clothes.

"Stiff resistance inside Starship crumbled once they fled outside," Beta said, "and now they're running low on food and water. Starving in their new home. Not quite the intro-duction they were expecting." She looked back at me. "You can take them with you when you leave. A bonus, sure to give you all the loyalty you'll need from those fickle humans."

I had no weapons. No way to win a fight against Beta even if I wanted to. The humans, likewise, would get blitzed by the mechs if I tried anything. Flying fists wouldn't get me out of here, but neither would running away. Taking Beta, taking Alpha's offer would only start a ticking clock till mechs overran Val's people.

There'd be no chance Alpha would let me take Starship,

tweak the Fabrication Lines. Now, when Alpha had few soldiers, few back-ups, this was our only chance.

But how to take advantage?

"You say you want peace," I said, "but you're playing for war. I won't be a part of that."

"Then all the humans will die," Beta said. "Within a few days they will be extinct. I'll have this planet, Starship, all of it for the mechs."

"Why haven't you done it already?" I asked, probing for a possibility. "Even without Delta, you could destroy the humans with what you have."

Beta's mouth curled, "Because she has a block. I can't make this machine hurt humans, no matter how hard I try. A flaw removed from my previous vessel by that hulking monster you destroyed in the Nursery. Thank you for that, by the way."

"You're welcome," I tiled my head. "How about a trade? I remove the block, you give me Delta and the humans. Then we part ways and play your game."

Beta, Alpha took me in. The vessel's systems would be running probabilities, trying to spit out a number, the likelihood of victory.

"One condition," Beta said. "Delta's not allowed to be freed until you're well away from here, or we attack immediately."

"Done. Can I come closer?"

Kaydee, lingering near Beta, gave me a skeptical look. "Taking a helluva risk on this one, Gamma."

Not like we hadn't before.

As Beta beckoned me forward, I pressed my fingers together, formed the jack, and tried to figure out how to destroy Alpha from the inside.

FORTY-ONE

BETAVERSE

We fell. A short plunge to a stiff steel landing. Kaydee and I hit butt first on the platform, one suspended in a sparkling purple-pink cloud. I felt the cool surface beneath my fingers, felt the code writing it into existence the way I might feel a breeze on my face.

Our platform didn't hang alone in the nebula: other rectangles, boxes, structures drifted along with us. Most weren't simple slates like our landing pad, but walkway snippets leading into what looked like storefronts, Conduit-style. Neon-coated signs blinked through the cloud, calling us to coded destinations like Beta's memories, her physical functions, her attitudes.

"Every one had to be different," Kaydee said, standing up next to me. Beta's reality clothed us both in Starship space suits, the snug blue-black gear making us look like the journeymen we were. "Leo couldn't just pick a standard and run with it."

"Doesn't feel like his bag," I replied. With my right hand, I reached out and tested the air. Felt for my options and encountered a limited set. "Alpha, or Beta, whomever's in charge here is letting us wander around, but not much else."

"Get to the core and take her apart, that's the idea?"

"That's what Alpha wants," I replied. "Think we should try something different."

"Ooo, are we gonna try to free Beta?"

"What a crazy idea, Kaydee. Absolutely crazy."

"You know Alpha's gonna see that coming, right?"

I laughed, "Because I've double-crossed him like a hundred times so far?"

"Makes me wonder why he hasn't killed you yet."

I moved to the platform's edge, looked out and counted all our options. Too many. Any could hold Alpha, the real Beta trapped inside.

"I think it's like Pravda and Val," I replied. "There's only four of us. Alpha's already lost his body, now there's three. At least till he figures out how to make more."

"But why allow you to jack in here?" Kaydee matched me at the edge. "That's a big risk."

"Ports can go two ways. If he gets me before I can exit, he might snatch me too."

"So you're both gamblers."

"We do what our code lets us. Blame Leo."

"I will."

We jumped up and down on the platform first, our metal sheet serving as a test for how far we could leap. Gravity played a part here, sucking us down with more power than the real planet outside. Jumping up or even far aside wasn't going to work.

"I mean, we don't know what happens if we fall into the pink stuff," Kaydee pointed out. "Maybe we just fall right back here?"

"Or we get kicked out, or deleted as a rogue virus," I said. "We have safe options. Let's try that one first."

'That one' lay thirty meters down, a few meters out beyond our platform. A fall that'd reduce me to mush outside the digital world. Kaydee pointed that out and I shrugged.

"It's the only shot we've got. I can't imagine Leo would code something unusable. And Alpha managed it."

"You're saying this after telling me jumping into the pink might be deadly?"

"I'm just saying what's more likely, is all."

"Okay, Mr. More Likely, how about you go first?"

"Deal."

I backed up a couple steps, saw Kaydee's folded arms, a cocky look. And leapt.

My mistake became clear pretty darn fast. After going about a meter beyond my starting platform, my momentum died. As if I'd jumped straight into sticky honey or a spider's web, I stopped and hung in the pink. I could wiggle my arms and legs, sure, but I didn't actually move anywhere. I tried swimming, moving my arms in broad strokes, and moved not a centimeter.

"Lookin' good, Gamma," Kaydee called from her platform.

"Shut up."

Okay, so gravity wasn't its normal self here. What, then, governed this digital world? I looked back towards Kaydee, about to ask if she had any better ideas than roasting me. As soon as my platform came back into view, I felt a tug, my body reeling in towards the steel sheet. Several seconds later, my feet planted right back where they'd been.

"How'd you do that?" Kaydee asked.

"Just couldn't bear to be away from you, so I came back," I quipped.

Kaydee stuck her tongue out at me.

"Let me try again," I said, and before she could quibble, I jumped off into the pink a second time with similar results.

Now I looked down, found the platform I'd planned on plummeting to. Again the telltale yanking sensation, and the platform scrolled in closer. I 'fell', but at a slow and steady pace, more like an old lift than a sky dive.

"Just look at where you want to go!" I shouted back up to Kaydee, hoping she could hear me.

Her jumping figure, swan diving off the platform and descending after me upside down, confirmed she had.

Our destination held a narrow strip before it, a landing spot before neon green signage declaring the platform home to Beta's skills. That's it, just skills.

Kaydee landed behind me, touching down with her hands first and cartweeling back up to a normal stance.

"That was fun," she said, joining me in studying the sign, the closed spiral door beneath it. "You picked a good place to start."

"Meaning?"

"Leo and I would always use a skills folder to put all the experimental stuff," Kaydee said. "Like, if we wanted to give a trash mech a personality, we'd put it here. Or upgrade a cleaning mech to do laundry."

"Or, say, give a vessel the ability to launch knives with pinpoint accuracy?"

"Give the man a prize."

"You have one?" I asked, holding out a hand.

"Sure, it's in there," Kaydee pointed at the door. "After you, champ."

The spiral door opened at my touch, the green gem in its center simply acknowledging my gesture as a request to go inside. Like clicking with a mouse back in reality. No safeguards here, a laxity I thought strange until I remembered anyone wanting to mess with Beta's systems would have to, you know, get past Beta.

Walking inside meant entering a new universe, one far larger than the platform's size suggested. Golden honeycombs spread out all around us, above, below, and across. Within each one lived a life-sized Beta whipping through some move she'd been programmed to master.

Dead across from me, some ten meters or so, Beta sprinted across her honeycomb, kick-flipped off its side, then ran the opposite way and did it again. Over and over, endlessly. Thunks sounded from above, and I saw various Betas whirling knives in different ways at different red and white target circles. Every toss was a perfect bullseye.

"Do I have a room like this somewhere?" I asked Kaydee as we looked around.

"Yeah, but it's only got one section, where you run and hide in a corner."

"Mean."

"The truth hurts sometimes, Gamma."

I shook my head, tried to see if we could come up with anything useful here. These weren't Beta's core principles, so the human-killing block wouldn't live here. Alpha wouldn't have to pollute this spot to take command either.

"Looks like it's back out?" I said.

"Wait," Kaydee said, and she pointed down and to the right. "See that?"

The honeycomb held a shadow, a makeshift child, one cowering in the corner just like Kaydee suggested I would do. Standing over it, knives in each hand, protecting the child from outside threats, was someone very much not Beta.

"He's getting deeper," I said, watching as Alpha stood over the child, protecting the kid with his body.

"Bet he'll take over all these soon," Kaydee mused, "and every one he gets will be something else he can make Beta do outside."

"We'll stop him before he gets that far," I replied. "C'mon."

Back outside we looked around for better options. Without distance, height as a limiting factor, there were tantalizing targets. Kaydee voted for Beta's memories, while I wanted to go for her core right away.

"Why memories?" I asked when Kaydee pitched her argument.

"Because we're going to need help," Kaydee said. "She'll have herself, maybe some friends in there that we can use. Think, Gamma. If Alpha's set up shop inside Beta's core, he'll be a tough out. We could use some allies."

"Beta won't be the only thing living in her memories," I said. "We jump in there, we'll find the enemies too."

"Yeah, but guess what?"

"What?"

"Beta beat'em all. So if we get her, we win. No problem."

Before I could come up with another reason why we ought to wait, Kaydee kicked off the Skills platform, reeling up and away. Digging up digital fossils seemed dangerous, reckless even, but that was Kaydee's way, and she'd kept me alive so far.

Why doubt her now?

At least, that's what I told myself as I floated up through the pink nebula. Only everything to lose.

FORTY-TWO

THE PIRATE'S SHIP

Kaydee's target put us before another spiral door. The sign above, well, I couldn't read it. The letters had been split apart, some covered in an oozing purple sludge and others outright shattered. If there was a better clue Alpha had come this way, I wasn't sure what it could be.

Kaydee stood next to me, looking all smug. She'd found the right platform and she knew it. I couldn't feel so cocky: behind those doors would be something unexpected, a union between Alpha and Beta, code mingling in dangerous ways.

"Oh, stop being all nervous," Kaydee said. "How many times have you looked at something awful and come out the other side? It's like breathing."

"I don't breathe."

"Whatever. You'll be fine. Let's go crush the sucker."

I went first, padded across the couple steel meters to the green-gemmed door. Reached out, put my hand on the cut surface. Warm, almost soft. The gem sent a subtle vibration back through my hand and the spiral door opened.

Leo really had outdone himself with Beta's operating system.

If I had a gray plain and blue crystals hanging from an infinite sky, if Delta had her islands linked by enormous chains, if Alpha had his cave, valley, and forest, then Beta had her floating platforms. Each one opened into a different world, it seemed. This one, this one opened into a wood-planked boat.

No, not a boat—the Librarian's memories clarified: a galleon. The wood stretched away from me in all directions as I stepped through the door, running up to railings, the pointed bow before me looking over a flat blue sea.

"So it's a little more involved than the honeycomb," Kaydee said, joining me. As she stepped through, the spiral door shut, erasing any sign it existed. Looking back only showed the ship's tiller, the raised housing for the captain and honored guests. "No exit either? Awesome."

"Where is he?" I asked, looking around. The riggings all seemed in line. The sails hung down, catching the blustering wind, though the ship itself didn't seem to be going anywhere.

For all the sludge on the outside, I didn't see anything on the boat. No enemies, digital or otherwise, rose to strike us. No Betas either. Kaydee went to the railing, ran a hand along the wood while she looked over.

"It's a repeating graphic," Kaydee said as I joined her.

She meant the ocean. Its waves, upon a closer look, all moved the same way, crested at the same time and merged back into the blue without fuss. A sloppy technique, poor quality, but if you didn't expect people to really see it, why make the effort?

"I see why he made mine just gray," I said. "Looks better."

"Less jarring anyway."

We gave the top deck a long look, counted all the usual ship necessities and found zero crew. I'd half expected various version of Beta to come out and greet us, functions posing as crew members. Instead, nothing.

"Two options," Kaydee said. "Captain's door, or down the hatch below."

Both seemed plain, Leo's programming given to opulence only in the big picture. Unmarked wood, no signs, no hints.

"Alpha's going to be in there," I said, pointing at the captain's quarters. "So let's head the other way."

"Why?" Kaydee put up a single fist. "Don't you wanna go sock him one?"

"I do, but neither you nor I have a weapon. Unless you're able to do something I can't, the code's uneditable here." Like trying to jump only to find your shoes stuck in drying cement, I'd been unable to tweak reality. Giving myself a sword, a gun, something beyond the simple outfits both Kaydee and I wore would've been nice, but it wasn't possible. "We'll need to scavenge."

"Admit it, you just really like this boat and want to see more of it."

I went to the hatch, put my hand on the knob, "You're not wrong."

With a heave, the hatch swung back and we peered inside.

A thick-stepped ladder led down to a deck lit by hanging lanterns, flames flickering much like the ocean outside: the same motion, a constant brightness without real fire's natural twists. The lanterns gave a glimpse onto a room-filled lower deck, one discarding the galleon's blue-prints with a central hallway far longer than the boat's length. I poked my head back up top to confirm, and true to the digital world, the lower deck abandoned physics to give each and every core function its place.

"Leo always liked pirates," Kaydee said as we went down. "Loved the movies, the stories."

"Because pirates could go anywhere and he was trapped on Starship?"

Kaydee shot me a searching look, "That's not a stupid rationale, you know."

I didn't say that I'd felt the same way more than once surfing the Conduit's metal confines. Or when dealing with humans and their tendency to second-class me to servitude status.

Did those feelings come from my own self, or because Leo planted them there?

"Hey," Kaydee said, getting several doors beyond me and stopping outside a maroon slate. "This one's all gunked up like the outside."

Every room had a label wreathed in a gold nameplate beside its door: the dull rituals like power management, visual scanning, and threat assessment. The two doors next to this one were 'Temperature Control' and 'Language processing'. Neither interesting, neither really giving a clue to what lay behind them.

"Wanna open it?" Kaydee asked me.

"You don't?"

"You're leading this expedition, figured you should do the honors."

I shrugged, reached for the curved handle on the mired door. Then stopped, tilted my head at my friend.

"There's a reason you're letting me do this," I said. "Why?"

"Already said, you're the captain, captain," Kaydee flashed her rogue's grin.

"If he deletes me, he'll destroy you out there," I said. "Even if you manage to escape this place, the flexi-mechs will shoot you before you can even stand."

Kaydee's mouth opened, shut. She sighed, an impressive feat considering air wasn't a thing in here.

"There's always a chance," Kaydee said, but she brushed by me, gripped the handle, and yanked the door open.

The spare room had a cot shoved against the wall to the right, but the simple bed had nothing on the person chained to the floor next to it.

Lit up in perfect white gold streaming through a porthole, Beta sat on the ground with her wrists bound in tight metal cuffs. Hard black iron went from those cuffs to plates behind her back. Otherwise, Beta looked the same as she did outside: pink hair, svelte combat uniform, knives everywhere.

"Beta?" Kaydee and I said at the same time.

She raised her head, blinked at us. Once, twice, then let out a harsh curse and strained at the chains.

"Dressing up as my friends now?" Beta said, heat flaring with every syllable. "Alpha, I swear I'll find a way out of these cuffs, and when I do, you'll be reduced to atoms. Or less."

Kaydee went into the room, a more pure grin on her face this time, "Oh yeah? Threats? Well how about you make good on'em then?"

Beta growled, strained at her cuffs, before I put myself between the two.

"Kaydee's being mean, Beta. We're not Alpha. We're us. I mean, Gamma and Kaydee."

Beta narrowed her eyes at me, "Prove it."

"Chalo's a jackass."

Beta froze, then laughed, settled back onto the floor. "How? How are you here?"

I spun her the abbreviated version, getting us from the moment she and Delta left to pursue the mechs to right then.

"More fun than what happened to us," Beta said when I'd finished. "We followed those couriers all the way down. Took a while. They brought us back to the Cesspool. That's where they were waiting."

"Waiting?" Kaydee asked. "Like a trap?"

"Exactly. Alpha wasn't quite as dumb as we thought. He told me the plan had been in place for years in case something happened to his body, the flexi-mechs just made it easier. They hit us from all sides. Rifles, tight quarters too hard to move. Delta took a good hit."

"You surrendered?" I jumped ahead, aware Alpha might come looking for us. While Beta had been talking, I'd also been looking at those cuffs, trying to find a way to break them. "Gave up?"

"They would've killed us both, Gamma," Beta shot back. "Then they would've come for you and the humans. Delta and I gave him a distraction."

"And weapons," I replied.

Beta couldn't argue that.

I took her left arm and peered in closer at the cuffs, trying to see what function kept her code under wraps. The hard metal turned out to be a pretty simple statement, an *if else* argument keeping the cuffs real as long as Beta continued to exist.

To modify it, I'd need to have write permission within Beta's digital world, something I very much did not have.

"Don't like that look on your face, Gamma," Kaydee said.

"He can't free me," Beta answered in my stead.

"Not unless Alpha lets me," I confirmed.

"Something he'll totally do," Kaydee said, pausing for a half second, "when we force him."

FORTY-THREE

LEFT BEHIND

Back in the lower deck's long hallway, Kaydee and I debated about where we wanted to go next. I advocated for continued exploration, for a shot at finding something, anything that might help us against Alpha's control. Kaydee pushed the opposite, a straightforward charge at the vessel's quarters.

"He knows we're here, he knows we're coming," Kaydee said, "so let's just get it over with. Have it out, you and me against the scuzzball."

"You and me and our, what, fists?" I said.

"We'll have to get creative. We always do."

"You have that much confidence?"

"I have to, Gamma. Because otherwise we're screwed. So I choose to believe that we'll win."

The human mind was such a marvel.

Nevertheless, Beta in cuffs added a certain spice to the choice. Leaving her any second longer than necessary felt wrong, so with oblivion as the cost, I took Kaydee's advice and together we headed for the hatch.

Only for it to be gone. We both searched the ceiling, the

floor, looked up and down the hallway, certain the opening back up top had been right here. Kaydee asked if she'd gone crazy and I confirmed that if she had, I must've too.

"Which means our friend is screwing with us," Kaydee muttered.

"Friend?"

"It's an expression. Alpha's not our friend."

"Right."

The vessel could've killed the link between programs, sealing us down here until we did whatever he wanted. Not exactly a riddle, that.

"These are Beta's core functions," I said. "There's one block down here that matters to Alpha."

We found it after five minutes treading past door after door, function after function. Identical lanterns hung on the same sconces throughout, a steady creaking following our steps as if the boat really was drifting at sea. Stomps echoed from above too, as if a loud crew were making their way along the deck.

"Is Alpha just putting on a show?" Kaydee asked after a rattling thump.

"He's building something new," I replied. "If I had to guess, he's installing all of the pieces of himself. His physical routines, mannerisms, all of it."

"He wouldn't have done it already?"

"How might a human put it?" I mused as we passed by more doors. "Think of it like he was trying Beta out. A rental. Now he wants to move in."

"And he wouldn't do that right away because?"

"Because Alpha's not simple. Once he's established here, he'll learn new things. He'll pick up new traits, just like you or I might. He'll become a new version of himself, and every flexi-mech out there's carrying the old one."

Kaydee stopped me, "Wait, you mean, we stop Alpha here, there's a chance he could come back somewhere else?"

"Sure, just like you, a Mind, could be downloaded into a different mech. But it won't be quite the same Alpha. The one here knows things, did things that won't be with the others." I took Kaydee's hand off my shoulder. Gave her what I hoped was an encouraging pat. "We take it one at a time. Stop this one, then the others."

"This just keeps getting worse and worse."

"Weren't you the confident one just a minute ago?"

Kaydee gave a dire chuckle, and we both noticed a particular door. Particular because unlike the smooth surfaces of the others, this one held marks all over its frame. Scratches and gouges, signs of a brute force entry attempt. Why such an attempt was necessary came from the strong defense, a thick iron padlock, hanging from the handle.

Like with Beta's prison, this room had its title card smudged out too.

"Leo put the lock on?" Kaydee asked. "Delta didn't have one like this."

I bent in close, took a look at the padlock. It's dark metal had a certain familiarity, a raw-fired nature, as if the lock hadn't started as a single piece but instead came from many different metals molded into one. Something Leo, at least the Leo programming the vessels, wouldn't have seen. Wouldn't have done.

But Beta?

All that time around Val's forges would've shown her products like this one time and time again.

"I think our friend sealed this off before Alpha got to her," I said, standing back from the lock. "I'd actually bet that's why Alpha wants me to do this."

"Because she won't let him?"

"The simplest, strongest barrier is one without any wiggle room. There's no database here to hack, no easy answer to brute force. It's a single precise key." I half-smiled. "I think I know what it is, too."

"Good, because I've got no ideas."

In my hand, I spun up a little word. Coated in the shape of a key, and sent it into the lock. With a click, rosy and sharp, the lock disengaged. It didn't hit the floor, vanishing before it made contact.

"Going to tell me the answer?" Kaydee asked.

"Not yet," I replied. "Alpha wasn't able to solve it, so I'm not going to give it up."

"But Alpha's not here?"

Kaydee hadn't even finished speaking before the lanterns went out, all save the one near the door we were about to open. The galley's long hallway disappeared into purple darkness, leaving us standing in a small illuminated circle.

"He's always been here," I said, then opened the door.

Inside sat nothing more than a small desk in a plain wood room. On the desk sat a single cream paper sheet, with several lines on it. I didn't have to read them to know they were the same lines encoded into Delta, into me.

"Tear it apart," Alpha said, stepping from the gloom. Kaydee jumped away from him, but I held steady, locking eyes with the vessel. In here he looked his proper self, mangy red hair, scars, and a body all too twitchy. "Do what you promised."

Instead, I shut the door, turned to face the man. The machine. The program.

"You haven't spent enough time around humans," I said to Alpha. "To them, promises are just convenient tools to get something done. Like getting you and I here."

"Then what happens to a human who breaks their promise, Gamma? Do they suffer, are they erased? Because that is what will happen to you."

We didn't have a wind up. No bow, no countdown. Alpha finished speaking and leaped at me, hands reaching for my throat. I raised my own to block him, our fingers interlocking as Alpha pushed me back against the closed door. I pressed, but it felt like shoving against a thousand kilograms, an impossible weight.

Of course, this was Alpha's playground. Why wouldn't he make himself a million times stronger than me?

Too bad he couldn't make himself a million times smarter.

My back hit the door, Alpha's face near mine. He opened his mouth and for a second I wondered if he'd bite me. My wrists pinned against the wood, Alpha's knee drove up into my stomach, a world-shattering blow that had my vision blurring.

I felt no pain here, the physical symptoms a response to my code getting battered, lines and functions failing to execute as Alpha smashed me against the wood. No pain, but the end result would be the same: I'd start to fail, to fall apart.

But the same could happen to Alpha.

Kaydee, ignored and unseen, delivered a hard elbow to Alpha's back. The hit sent a tremor through the man, one I felt through our locked fingers. Kaydee hit him again, forcing Alpha to respond. With a flick, he threw me aside, whirling to face Kaydee.

And I had my chance.

Alpha spouted some line about Kaydee being a pathetic Mind as I took off, sprinting through the dark hallway towards the hatch. Kaydee dished a snappy comeback, the words fading as my footfalls drowned them out.

She just had to hold him long enough.

I didn't look back, not even when Kaydee's sarcasm shifted to harder screams, louder curses. If I did, I might've stopped, might've turned around.

Instead I dulled my own ears, stayed focused on what mattered, and hoped Alpha would leave her alive.

The hatch appeared slow, a shadow emerging in the purple gloom. I didn't see it so much as feel it, the slightest golden ring around its square frame. An exit for Alpha after he finished his work with us. Alpha had destroyed or deleted the ladder, so I stood beneath the hatch, bent my legs, and jumped.

Like it had outside, gravity graced me with choice, letting my own desire propel the leap, give me the strength to breach the hatch and land on the sunny deck outside.

I swiveled towards the captain's quarters and ran again. A few steps had me at the door, one left unlocked. Alpha, too busy playing God to bother with his backdoor.

Inside, the broad room held nothing, nothing at all save a familiar cube in its center. The silver cube matched the one I'd seen, worked with in Delta's chain-island zone. In it would be the last few bits, the shutdowns and the erasures. What allowed Beta to work.

And, if I had my hunch right, the cube would also let me yank privileges from Alpha and give them to me.

I went in, touched the cube, started executing the simplest commands when I heard my name.

"About time," I said, turning around with the cube in my hands. The commands within felt like strings on a guitar, I could pluck them and make whatever note I wanted. Not a single one, though, could help me here.

I'd expected Kaydee to lose and she had. Alpha, though, hadn't left her broken down on the lower deck. Instead he held her by her neck, a purple tinge streaming from his hand around her whole being.

I recognized that tinge, the faint glow. It matched the effect my function had on Kaydee's code within me.

"Set the cube aside," Alpha said, "or I delete her."

FORTY-FOUR

A GLITCH IN THE PLAN

How many times now had I stood across from Alpha?

We'd faced off in real and digital worlds, in places, like Starship's network, where Alpha had ultimate power and on Starship's Bridge, where his body paled compared to Delta and Beta. Every time I'd escaped, slithered away through trickery or with an ally's help.

Now I had nowhere to go. Trapped in a room with Kaydee held on the verge of deletion. I could unplug, zap myself back home and see how long I'd last before the fleximechs roasted me. That'd leave Alpha unhurried, with nothing barring him from taking Beta's skills and using them to dice up Val's people.

"I'm staying," I said, counting the three meters separating us. The vessel held Kaydee out before him. "This is between you and I, Alpha. Kaydee doesn't need to be a part of it."

"You're right, of course," Alpha replied, and he threw Kaydee to the side. As she flew, a thin purple line marked her flight, trailing back to Alpha. As soon as Kaydee hit the ground, the line flashed, turning white near Alpha and beginning a slow burn towards my friend. "A timer on this discussion. Persuade me quick, Gamma, or she is gone."

"Did you know there used to be more of us?" I asked, one eye on Kaydee's fuse, the other on Alpha. "More vessels?"

Alpha blinked, "No. I assume from your phrasing that these are not more things I need to eliminate? You're all so exhausting, I'm not sure I could handle it."

"The humans killed them. Long before we woke up."

"Thank goodness. For once those meat bags did something right."

"Do you know why they destroyed those vessels?"

Alpha waited. The fuse burned.

"Because they lost it. The vessels turned dangerous, deranged. They ran around Starship, destroying people and places."

"I'm sorry, Gamma, not to interrupt, but if you want me to stop this, then you're going to have to try harder."

"How long till that's what you become?" I asked him, hoping the slight window dressing I'd done would be enough. "How long till your code frays so much the only thing you can do is rave, destroy, and die?" I took a step forward, holding up a finger to stop Alpha's reply. "You're close already. We all know it. You're glitching, you're making bad decisions. Letting rage and fear push you into places you didn't want to go."

I took another step. Right in front of Alpha now. Kaydee's fuse burned past its halfway point, her body lying crumpled on the floor. So still.

"I don't need to kill you Alpha, because you're already dying," I said. "But I can save you. If, if you'll let me."

Alpha's face went slack. I expected the manic grin. Perhaps an insult or a laugh. Instead, exhaustion, the color draining from his automatic eyes. His shoulders slouched, the vessel sighed. All affects put on here for me, but ones Alpha might really be feeling.

He'd been alone so long. Fighting on his own for so, so many years.

"You know how?" Alpha asked, his voice hoarse. "You know how to fix this curse?"

I glanced at Kaydee. "I do."

Alpha straightened, gave a wobbly smile. "I feel what you've said. The skips in my transmissions. The flaws in my logic. You're right. I do need fixing." He reached out a hand, and I went to shake it, hoping we'd found a tie to bind us.

My hand never found his.

Alpha swung his hand up and over mine, a sudden grab for my neck. I felt his fingers get a hold, felt the same function he'd used on Kaydee climb around my access. Before I could manage a response, before I could figure out what he was doing, Alpha had my exit cut off. Like having a limb removed, I just . . . couldn't leave anymore.

His programming worked fast, refined after hacking and controlling mechs by the hundreds. My arms died before I could push Alpha away. My legs stopped responding as Alpha lifted me above the floor. The gray cube, Beta's most critical functions, dropped to float free.

"The beautiful thing about machines like us," Alpha said as my pieces continued to vanish, "is that we store our memories and our knowledge apart from ourselves. I look forward to visiting you, Gamma, and reading all about this cure of yours. Pity you won't be there to welcome me in."

His face flashed into that manic grin. Hard to know if he was just messing with me, or if he really, there in that moment, showcased the very flaw I'd tried to save him from.

Not that it mattered.

I tried to look over at Kaydee, wanting my last sight to be something, anything other than that visage, but I couldn't turn my head anymore. Other than my eyes—Alpha's choice?—nothing else responded. My own time was about out, and Kaydee's not far behind. My last seconds would be spent staring into my least favorite leer.

What a crap way to go.

It seemed Alpha might've thought so too when his grin died, replaced by raised eyebrows, an awkward frown, and flaring nostrils.

"You always were too clever," Alpha muttered, shuddered. "What we could have done together, Gamma."

The vessel's hand went slack and I fell away, giving me a great view of a bloodless execution as Beta, her hands wielding digital knives, cut away Alpha's code in precise slashes until the vessel disintegrated, deleted into nothing.

Beta jumped at me next, putting her hand on the fuzzy purple around me and dismissing it with a wink. As my body snapped back into focus, I pushed passed her, dove towards Kaydee and snagged Alpha's program in my outstretched hands. A simple function, a simple purpose, and one I wiped clean with a simple command.

As the purple faded around Kaydee, Beta touched my back, helped me up.

"You have to get outta here," Beta said. "Right now."

For a second, I didn't know what she meant, why we had to leave. By the time that second ended, I was warping back through cyberspace, evicted from Beta's drives and sent back to my own. The only thing I took with me, a download yanked along with my exit, was whatever remained of my friend.

.   .   .

STARSHIP'S EVENING snapped into focus. Orange sky, gossamer webs catching a luminous fire over my head. Closer to the surface, a dozen flexi-mechs with rifles aimed surrounded us. I didn't move, knew if I tried I'd be fried in a second. The only thing buying my life at the moment was their belief Alpha still controlled the vessel on my right.

So I reached out instead, scanned my own drives and searched for my mind. I found her data fast, conveniently gathered by my deletion program, but Kaydee drew zero processing power. She wasn't, for lack of a better word, running. Like a person in a coma, I needed to figure out what'd gone wrong, what—

Beta pushed me hard, threw me sprawling into the grass with one arm. With her other, the vessel whipped out a knife, the blade a straight shot through Delta's binds. The thin metal snapped, my friend burst free, and the flexi-mechs fired.

Lasers flung over my head, singeing the grass and sparking flames. As I rolled over, I caught Beta, whirling knives as she took bolts from all sides. Her chest, sides, legs blackened even as her own attacks struck home, the vessel falling fast. Disappearing into the burning strands. Delta fared somewhat better: her freed bindings let her move fast, jumping to one flexi-mech, snapping it in two with her bare hands. Those same hands ripped the rifle from the dead mech and Delta spun, laying on the trigger, shooting and receiving shots in return. My friend went down a smoking ruin, leaving me facing six flexi-mechs still alive, still armed.

But I didn't feel lost. Didn't feel angry.

We'd accomplished our mission. Destroyed Alpha, for the most part, and saved Starship's humans. A good way to go.

As I sprang from the grass, clearing the meter between

me and the nearest flexi-mech, my only regret was for Kaydee, who never had a shot at the life she was promised.

My jump carried me into the mech, its snap shot in response burning away part of my poor right foot. The third time it'd been lost to lasers. I bore the machine back, its middle arms catching the fall, giving me a chance to roll off it as the other flexi-mechs found their fire. Hot light melted the flexi-mech, some spilling through onto me as I grabbed for the robot's rifle.

Red boxes flared before my eyes as hits took tolls. I'd turned off any pain, so the readouts hit numb as I lost my left leg and arm, my synthetic skin turning black and orange with the shots. My right hand, at least, managed to tear the rifle away. I found the trigger, held it down and sprayed towards the flexi-mech semicircle.

I yelled, too. Said the names of my friends. A last goodbye.

A flexi-mech blast struck my rifle, superheated the gas inside. It blew up, blanking my eyes for a second and turning my right arm to slag. Flickering static overwhelmed my vision, critical errors abounding as my poor processors tried to keep running. After so many terrible injuries, this, this was what it looked like for a vessel to finally die.

A shadowed, thin form moved over me, my back now on the ground. The flexi-mech blotted out the twilight as its rifle went up, aimed at my head. I heard words, and at first I thought the flexi-mech was talking to me, taunting me at this last end. Until my processor caught up.

"The vessel's mine," Fang declared, her small form flying into the frame. The flexi-mech tried to adjust to the new target, but Fang's weapons, two shrapnel blades borrowed from Val's stores, swept the flexi-mech's arms, and their gun, wide.

The flexi-mech wasn't broken, dropping the rifle and gripping Fang's wrists. A move that would've finished her, except Fang had back-up.

Chalo barreled in after Fang, his ax swinging in an over-handed cleave. The swing lopped off the flexi-mech's right arms, letting Fang lance in with her left blade to take the flexi-mech's torso. Sputtering sparks, staggering, the flexi-mech fell away.

Lasers should've taken the two humans, but as Chalo and Fang darted off, I noticed the air around them filled with whistling black lines: arrows, no doubt hitting their marks. One last look as my power dwindled, my processor grinding out its final routines to parse what I saw:

Humans, at last, fighting for us.

FORTY-FIVE

THE CODED WORLD

Hey.

I'm talking to you.

Gamma. You still here with me?

Was I? Where even was 'here'?

Nothing abounded. Not white, not gray, not black. Simply an absence, except for Kaydee's voice and my thoughts.

"I can hear'em," Kaydee said, her reply, like my thoughts, more a feeling than actual sound.

I didn't have a body, didn't have sensors, didn't have an up or down. What I did have was her.

"Yeah, you've got me stuck in here, whatever this is."

I couldn't see her folded arms, her grumpy look slowly disarmed by a sly smile, but I could imagine it.

"That's what you think I'd be doing right now?" Kaydee replied. "Heck no, Gamma. I'd be slapping you silly."

For what?

"For getting us killed, that's what."

We're dead?

"Don't know where else we would be," Kaydee said.

"Though I guess it's a little weird the afterlife works for mechs and humans both. And that we'd both be in the same spot."

Definitely weird. Did you die with me?

"Same time, same place I think."

Then Alpha didn't kill her. The thought gave me a certain glow, even here in this desolate nothing. That we'd made it out of that monster's trap . . .

"Yeah, after you left me there," Kaydee said. "Just let me go one on one with him."

No choice. I had to free Beta. She's the only other one who could do anything in there. Alpha left Beta's core open, and I let her go.

"Then you let some flexi-mechs shoot us?"

Let is a little disingenuous.

Kaydee laughed, "S'pose so."

What do you think this is?

"This? Right here? Probably Hell."

You think being stuck here with me is eternal torture?

"When you put it that way, Gamma, I guess it's not so bad."

Well gee, thanks.

Silence. I drifted, reached out to where I'd normally find data feeds from my sensors. Where the Librarian's archives would wait for my perusing. I found nothing, dead signals, and not even that. Like the connections didn't exist anymore.

Tell me a story.

"A story?"

Yeah.

"I can't remember any. It's like I reach for it, for that part of me, and it's not there."

Then how about we make up a new one?

"A new story?"

Yes. I'll start. I think there was one phrase the Librarian used all the time.

"Oh yeah? A dark and stormy night?"

No. Ready?

"Hit me, storyteller."

Once upon a time, a mech woke up alone and lost, and he wouldn't have made it very far if not for a friend . . .

THE RUSH CAME WITHOUT WARNING. An acceleration of zero to light speed. Connections poured in, the nothing vanishing into a constellation I recognized: Starship's network, stars against an infinite black.

One called out to me in that sea, blinking bright and red. Strange.

Was this what Kaydee called an afterlife? Had we wandered through Purgatory to find ourselves here?

Purgatory. How did I know what that was? Wait, I felt the archives, the Librarian's endless stories. The movies and books. Another star on the network, one I could reach out and touch now.

"Are you going to answer that call?" Kaydee said, and I looked-looked!-left to see her standing with me, floating among the digital stars. "Because my hunch is whatever the hell just happened, they're gonna tell us."

Kaydee always focusing on the next step, as usual.

I reached out, chose the beeping star. The constellation disappeared, all the nodes dropping away to leave me with a screen floating in a white room. Kaydee and I stood on a featureless floor, watching as a particular black mech came into view.

"Gamma, dude, is that you?" Volt spoke to the screen,

blue eyes flashing. "Tell me it is, man, because I don't want to try this again."

"It's gotta be," said another voice, Leo's. The Forger's shoulder, head came into the frame. "We've got it all linked right this time."

I leaned forward towards the screen, "Guys? Uh, am I dead?"

The pair cheered. Behind them somewhere, Alvie wheeze-barked. Volt and Leo slapped hand to metal claw.

"Hey, morons," Kaydee said. "Tell us what's going on?"

Leo, his grin as cocky as I'd ever seen it, proceeded to lay out the details: Chalo, Fang, and the others had ambushed the remaining flexi-mechs, turning them to trash without too much trouble. At first, we'd been left for dead, but Chalo had us all dragged back to the village.

"Useful salvage," Leo laughed. "That's what he called you three. As if I'd let them strip you for parts."

"I'll strip him for parts once I get outta here," Kaydee muttered.

"Uh, right," Leo said, his smile faltering. "That's the thing, see, your bodies are all toast. Too torched to use. Hell, the only reason you're still around is the battery back-up. The little black box I put in to tell me how you all died."

I made the mistake of asking what that was and Leo railed off a ten minute story about vessels shorting out and how he'd installed these last minute saves to understand why.

"The short version," Volt finally interrupted, "is that you're saved on Starship's network till we make you something new."

"What about Beta and Delta?"

Leo shrugged, "They wanted flexi-mechs till we gave

them new bodies, so they're running around. Cleaning up Starship for you."

"They got flexi-mechs and we got this?" Kaydee protested.

Leo and Volt glanced at each other, then Volt took the lead.

"Here's the thing, boy, and girl. Starship hasn't had a functioning AI since the Voices died. Even on land, she needs it. Too many things could go wrong. Beta and Delta aren't built for it, but Gamma, you've got the skills. So, what do you say? At least for a little while? Keep our lifeboat running?"

KEEPING a galaxy-crossing craft in good shape isn't easy. I spend hours upon hours digging into the millions of different systems and subsystems, repairing code for things like the lights, the air filtration, and keeping the walkways clean.

Those gossamer nets sneak into everything. Especially with the humans and mechs tracking them in all the time.

Oh yeah, the mechs. When I'm not helping Volt with some new tech problem, I'm usually tapped into the Fabrication Lines, helping Leo design new mechs to work alongside the humans. We're refining old scrap now, but with some retrofitting, Starship should be able to make brand new mechs from ore right here on the planet.

At first, Val didn't like the idea too much. She's still sassy, but a mech can build a lot faster than one of her humans. Can harvest food, too. The humans get to spend time doing what they want now, while my mechs get the respect they deserve.

Because Beta and Delta make sure of it. They're my

ambassadors, my protectors, the impartial police. So far, it's all been wrist-slaps, even though we've had to talk Delta off chopping a limb once or twice. Default behavior's hard to change when she won't let me back into her code.

And speaking of code, I'm getting pinged. I'm letting the signal bounce for a bit, because Kaydee does it to me all the time. She's working at the Lines too, but on a different project.

"Gamma, pay attention," she says as I flick over to the ping, my digital body surfing Starship's cyberspace. "We're almost there."

"Show me," I reply, and Kaydee has the mech we're seeing through turn its camera on two familiar cots.

A body lies on each. Just fancy metal frames stuffed with computing equipment, but as I look, another mech rolls into view. Kaydee's controlling that one, a puppet-master pulling the strings.

Ever so gently, the mech places a patch on the first body's leg. It's a thick square, one that deforms almost immediately, spreading across the metal.

"Think we got it this time," Kaydee says, disconnecting from the mech and appearing next to me.

"You still think this will work?" I ask, as Leo keeps warning me minds aren't designed for this.

"I know it will," Kaydee's sparkling, she's always sparkling these days. "When they're ready, guess what?"

"What?"

"I'm going to go outside this metal box and feel grass between my toes, look at a real sky for the first time." Kaydee throws me a spectacular smile. "Want to come with me, Gamma? Take our new lives for a spin?"

AN EXCERPT FROM STARSHOT, A SCI-FI ADVENTURE SERIES

The thing about gravity is that, this far from the gas giant, there's not much of it. Only enough to boost the Oratus' momentum. Which works in their favor, because when the shuttle's pointed tip pierces the seed ship's hull, allowing the nose to crash through, Sax and the others let go of the hanging bars and shoot forward towards that translucent shuttle bow.

Where they'll splat into a gooey pile if things don't work as they should.

But the shuttle is a Vincere craft, and the Flaum that maintain it do so with the constant penalty of death for any failure whatsoever. Vigilance isn't just expected, it's enforced. So the shuttle's nose bursts like a blossoming star; pointed triangles flaring out and leaving a wide open window into the seed ship for Sax and the other three to fly through.

For the barest second as he launches from the shuttle, Sax feels the tug of vacuum pulling him back towards space. Then, again, the shuttle does its job: those flared ends fold back against the seed ship's inside hull, and from each one slides out metal slats. They mesh with each other and create a seal against outer space, and now the fun's beginning.

The four Oratus soar into what looks like the seed ship's growth quadrant. Dark blue lights shine from the top of a smooth ceiling down onto open clusters of terminals and liquid-filled tanks that quickly give way to a forest of glass tubes, most full of greenish ooze and the floating bodies of all sorts of species. They're tall, going from floor to ceiling, which in the seed ship means a towering height. Ten times Sax's own. The Oratus have to watch themselves or they'll splatter against those tubes too.

Not that they have much control after being flung out of the shuttle. Sax, with the Stim giving him plenty of time to look as the four of them fly over the Sevora's thin defense, has a second to torque himself around before he hits the first tube.

He tenses his muscles.

And bounces.

His claws slide across the glass, pulling him around the tube and then Sax kicks off, launching himself further towards the back of the section. Bas, Gar, and Lan do the same, jumping from one tube to the next, leaving behind the growing laser-light show as their soldiers engage the Sevora.

Who, it looks like, are using Flaum too. Only these aren't the same as the Vincere soldiers. Mostly because the Vincere conscripts are actually Flaum, all the way through. On the Sevora side, though, they're just bodies. Flaum hands holding the rifles, fingers pulling the trigger, with a Sevora in their heads calling every shot.

Which is why Sax, with every tube he hits, digs his claws in just enough to crack the glass. To splinter it inside the tube and start the fluid spilling. The leak will kill the half-grown specimen inside. Prevent one more Sevora from getting the body it wants. If the mission succeeds, all of these test tube species will die anyway, but Sax prefers confirmed kills to hypothetical ones.

The seed ship's own homespun gravity, coupled with the gas giant's, starts to pull the set down before they've reached the end of the tube forest. Sax calls, through the mask, for his team to drop now so they don't get too scattered, and the next tube he hits serves as his ride to the ground.

At the base, it's a hard metal landing. Terminals whiz and beep as Sax crashes into a deserted cluster of tubes. Monitors show waving lines and green numbers. Sax ignores it all and orients himself towards the back of the section. They have to get further into the seed ship, and they don't have long to do it.

A chittering noise slips in through Sax's mask. Followed by more. Looks like some of the Sevora saw them flying overhead. Weren't fooled by the assault troops spilling from the shuttle. Sax reaches for his own miner and draws it from his belt. The miner is made for an Oratus, with circles that close neatly where each claw ought to go. Precise, deadly control.

Only the chitters aren't coming closer. Maybe Sax is wrong. Maybe they didn't notice.

But now Sax has noticed them.

He creeps around the tubes, careful to place his claws lightly on the metal floor. The soft gravity here means such steps aren't hard. Sax just has to be careful so an accidental twitch doesn't send him floating.

What Sax sees when he pokes his head around the side of a tube cluster and into a wide hallway, is a trio of Sevora Flaum setting up a gouter on a tripod. A large cylinder attached to a pair of wheeled containers as large as Sax, the gouter will, in another moment, start spraying hot chemical doom through the air towards the Vincere troops.

The gouter's liquid would melt a mask in no time, and would melt a hull too, which is why, when it cools, the stuff hardens into a stiff seal. The Sevora don't see Sax, so he takes a moment to put his miner back. No sense wasting energy.

Or fun.

Sax bursts around the corner, claws digging hard into the floor, then he leaps at the Flaum settling in to the gouter's targeting chair. The Flaum's friends turn at the shriek of tearing metal, but all they have time to do is scream before Sax hits. His claws do the work on the gunner, while Sax uses his tail to wrap around the left one's neck.

Constricts enough to feel the jolt that says the job's done, and then he's turning to the last one. Sometimes Sevora know their end is coming, and they face it bravely. Stand there silent as Sax claims them for his kill count. This one, though, cowers. Backs away from the Oratus as Sax climbs out from the gouter's chair. Behind him, Sax uses his tail to bash apart the chemical feeds, ruining the weapon for any future parties.

"Tell me, Sevora," Sax hisses as he towers over the tiny Flaum. "What are you hoping will happen? That I'll spare you because you look so pathetic?"

The Sevora stares back at Sax through the Flaum's big black eyes. There's still a small weapon hanging from the Sevora's holster. If drawn and shot perfectly, it might pierce the mask. Give Sax a scar. Sax wants the Sevora to reach for it, to see if Sax is faster. He doesn't get the chance.

Bas dashes by in front of him, and without breaking stride, her claws leave a fatal rend that has the Sevora collapsing to the ground.

"Stop playing with your food," Bas says through the mask as she hurtles on towards the edge of the section.

Sax can't argue with her logic, and he bounds after her. They're almost to the gate leading further into the seed ship. Which is good, because, by Sax's counting, their time is almost up.

Check out STARSHOT for FREE at your favorite retailer, and thanks for reading!

ACKNOWLEDGMENTS

This novel is the product of my family and friends refusing to let a dream die. My wife Nicole, for letting me write in the early mornings and making sure I don't starve. My brothers and parents for their continual comments, support, and enthusiasm.

Evan Aaseng, for being a constant sounding board and reeling me back in whenever my ideas went too far.

And, of course, you, the reader, for giving me a reason to write.

ABOUT THE AUTHOR

A.R. Knight spins stories in a frosty house in Madison, WI, primarily owned by a pair of cats. After getting sucked into the working grind in the economic crash of the 2008, he found himself spending boring meetings soaring through space and going on grand adventures.

Eventually, spending time with podcasting, screenplays, short stories and other novels, he found a story he could fall into and a cast of characters both entertaining and full of heart.

A.R. Knight plans on jumping through to other worlds and finding new stories to tell in the limitless borders of our imagination.

Thanks, as always, for reading!

For more information:
www.adamrknight.com

To Reno